Acknowledgements

There are so many people I want to thank. Let me start with my son, Nathan Froburg. He has been encouraging me for as long as he could read, and pushing me to write and go for my dreams of being a published author. He bought me copies of The Literary Agents Guide, and never let me stop writing–even if sometimes he came off as a nag. So this first one is for him. He also gets all the credit for my book cover design. Even though he doesn't understand my love of the 80s, he embraced the challenge and made me a cover I love so much.

Next I need to thank my husband Shane, for reading everything I have written over the last twenty years. He is not a reader so it means a lot that he always dives right into my work. He gives honest feedback as well as comfort when some of the subjects got a little bit heavy.

I want to thank my best friend in the whole world, and fellow Gen Xer, Stacy Fisher, for also reading everything I have ever sent her and for giving me honest and detailed feedback. I can't imagine what the last forty years would have been like without you Stacy–"Holy Bible!"

A special thanks to my dear friend Katelynn who volunteered to be my impartial reader and who gave me all the feedback as well as all the support, in real time updates. I loved when your texts would pop up out of the blue and you would express whatever I was making you feel at that time. I am blessed you have you in my life!

Dawna Ann Adams, aka my sister mommy, aka Nurse Ratchet, aka the best sister a girl could ask for as well as my Editor in Chief. Thank you for literally everything.

And finally, to all my kids, their spouses and their kids. Steven, Brandon, Jonathan, Michaela, Trevor, Nathan, Chase, Jessica, Joseph, Arayah, and Jenna. My reasons why!

I am dedicating this book to my big Brother, Mark Ralph Faulkner. 1958 to 2024. I wish you were here to see me publish this book. I think you would be very proud of me, because you were always the proudest, most supportive brother and I loved being your "baby sis." Oh how I wish I could hear you say "Hey Sis", just one more time!

Credits

Author - Erica Lavalley
Editor - Dawna Adams
Assistant Editor - Nathan Froburg
Front and Back Cover Art - Nathan Froburg

Praise For Gen Sex

"5 stars! This book brought me right back to the 80s. The details and descriptions were so well written and I felt like I was right there with her cheering her on. It made me so sad reading about all of her traumas, but with all the lows came great highs." - Stacy Fisher

"Great read, in the age of innocence hers was lost, a story of perseverance despite adversity, you will quickly become a cheerleader for Martina to overcome her early trauma and tribulations! A book you will not be able to put down. When it is over you will need more. Give it all the stars!" - Dawna Adams

"This book is a fantastic read. Emotional, tragic, and heartbreaking moments for the main character keep you turning the pages and hoping that she finds her happiness one day. Reading this story will make you feel every single emotion you have. Completely engaging and well written." - Katelyn Volpigno

Chapter 1
1985
"How Will I Know?" - Whitney Houston

Gary was my first. He shouldn't have been but he was. That's because he was twenty-six and I was only twelve. Today we would call him a pedophile. I guess we would have back in '85 too, but my twelve year old self didn't know about that and he sure wasn't going to call it what it was.

We met in the mall. You don't get much more Eighties than that right there. We moved to Daytona Beach Florida when I was a preteen. I was both a little boy crazy and longing for attention. Plus I hated being at home. What eighties kid didn't? Our whole lives happened outside with friends. But in Daytona, I didn't have any friends.

And that's how it happened. I met him at the record store he worked at in the mall and four weeks later I was bleeding on his yellow sheets in his bachelor pad, feeling humiliated as he looked at the spot and said "Oh I guess I didn't pop that cherry last night after all."

But let me backup and explain. I wasn't looking for sex. I didn't even really know much about sex.

We had been in Florida for about six months. My mom had made more friends than I had. We finished the school year in New Hampshire early. My parents had settled in a small country town called Crescent City, Florida which my mom hated. So she made sure that before the beginning of 6th grade, we were in Daytona. Her ideal destination. The beach. My parents had landed a job running a motel directly on the beach and we lived in the manager's three bedroom apartment on the ground level.

It seems likely that I would have met Gary there. I mean right on the beach in a happening place like Daytona in the eighties. But nope. That came later. When we first arrived I was so mad at being moved around so much, I learned how to take the city bus and spent the late summer days at the mall.

I was young but I had started puberty early and I was already at a pretty full blossom. In the days where boob jobs and Dolly Parton were all the rage, I already had more breasts than most and I learned very quickly that they turned heads. It was a means to an end. I needed attention. I wasn't getting any home. I missed all my friends in New Hampshire and I wanted nothing to do with hanging out with my younger brothers.

I really can't remember how I met Gary but I know I met him at Camelot Music in the

Volusia Mall. I took a bus, onto what the locals call the mainland, almost every day. I walked the mall and even did my own back to school shopping there. But I started hanging out in the record store when I noticed an older guy with dark hair and blue eyes checking me out. It was flattering.

One day, when I was looking around he approached me and introduced himself. He was the assistant manager and his buddy— whose name escapes me—was the store manager and his roommate. I was impressed. I was twelve. It didn't take much.

At that time I could easily lie about my age. I was already all curves and tanned skin. My hair was dirty blonde but my mom didn't say no when I asked if I could bleach it platinum. She got me my first bottle of *Sun-in* too. I loved to lay out by the hotel pool covered in *Hawaiian Tropic Sun Oil* every morning, before catching the bus to the mall.

I had curves but there was muscle too. Everything was young and toned and where it should be. I had perky breasts and big beautiful nipples. But I didn't see myself that way. I never saw beauty. I wish my older self could go back and tell my younger self just how beautiful and worthy of real love I was.

I also wish I could have told myself not to be in such a hurry to grow up. Still, for how much older I may have appeared to some, there was no way I looked legal in his eyes. I was twelve and as an adult looking back, I can tell when someone looks older than they are and when someone really is the age they say.

The day I met Gary, I was looking at tapes in the *Hair Band Section*. I loved **Cinderella**, and I had my hand on that cassette when he approached me. Looking back, he had to have done this before. He was too good at it. But naive me only saw a good looking guy who was flirting with me. He said all the right things and flashed me his sexy smile at all the right times. Before I knew it I was hooked. In my head, I had a boyfriend.

I went to the mall as often as I could and he made sure I knew his schedule so I could come in on his work days. Every time I was there, we flirted and he paid me so many compliments. Before long my head was so far in the clouds, I would have done anything he asked. And ultimately I did.

He often asked me if I could think of another place we could hang out but I didn't have one. I was twelve. Where else were we going to be able to hang out? My bedroom, with my parents in the next room? Not unless he wanted my dad to castrate him. I would suggest his place, but he always said it would be hard with his roommate around.

But finally I was able to offer an idea. My moms friend Sherry, needed a babysitter for her two and four year olds. My mom offered my services and since it would be a late night, Sherry said I could just spend the night. She assured me the kids would be in bed when she left and they always slept through the night. When I told Gary, I thought he might explode with excitement. Though he tried to play it cool, he was happy to spend time with me away from the mall and I was excited about the prospect of my first real date.

I gave him the address to Sherry's and he said he would come over around 9pm. Sherry had promised me the kids would be in bed before she left and it seemed like the easiest ten bucks I would ever earn.

I think the reason the age difference never seemed odd to me was that my parents had a twenty year age difference. Sure they got married when they were both legal adults but in my mind, it was a non issue. And Gary knew how old I was, or at least he knew I wasn't yet sixteen, because I couldn't drive. The fact that he was okay with a big age gap made me think it was okay too.

In fact, in my child's mind, I was all grown up. I was excited and it was exhilarating. But I was in no way prepared for what would happen that night.

He was late. He said he would be there at nine but it was after eleven when he finally showed up. My big hair had been done for hours–thank God for *Aquanet*. I had almost fully convinced myself I was being stood up by the time he knocked on the door. In fact, I had started dozing, beating myself up self consciously. I was sure he had changed his mind because he just wasn't that into me.

When I opened the door all that self doubt went away. He looked great and smelled even better. His shirt was unbuttoned down to his nipples exposing his tanned chest, the dark chest hair peeking out at me. I let him in, and the first thing he did when the door was closed was kiss me. Our first kiss. *My* first kiss. It was weird. I don't know what I expected, but I sure didn't expect him to stick his tongue in my mouth. When he was done, I nervously invited him in and we sat on the couch.

Again, I don't know what I expected, but it sure wasn't two minutes of small talk followed by full on making out. Not only had I never done anything sexual like this, I was torn between how fast it was all happening and the curiosity and excitement that I was feeling.

Looking back, the best way to describe it was that he was in a hurry but also had no intention of leaving. At one point he suggested we move the couch cushions to the floor and get more comfortable. I remember feeling both turned on and out of control. I knew things shouldn't be happening this fast, but my curiosity and need for attention overshadowed any doubts I might have had.

Gary moved me onto the floor and my shirt was off an instant later. His hot mouth was on my nipple and my head was spinning. Before I could even process all that was happening, his shorts were off followed by mine, tossed haphazardly beside us. My panties came off next. It was all such a blur. When he slipped a finger inside me I felt both excited and violated. It didn't feel good but it wasn't awful. Like everything leading to this point it was mostly abrupt. He kissed my neck, putting his tongue in my ear, urging me to relax.

He could feel me tensing as he moved the finger in and out of me. He shushed me, whispering sweet things in my ear, his other hand squeezing my breast.

And then I felt it. Something hard and hot pressed up against my belly. I don't even remember what I called it back then. Any reference to a man's penis back then would have embarrassed me. I was a kid. But this was the moment I knew I was about to have sex–whatever that meant–with him. He started to push into me, stifling my pain by putting his mouth over mine and swallowing my cry.

He pushed a couple times. Not gently but as soon as he started he stopped. He heard the car first and rolled off me. He told me to pretend to be asleep so that's what I did. He threw the afghan over us and by the time Sherry and her date walked in, we were fake sleeping, side by side on the floor. She stopped for what felt like a long time as if she wanted to say something about the man on her floor with her babysitter, but in the end, she just walked past, into her room and closed the door.

Gary rolled over and looked at me.

" Wow, that was close," He whispered quietly. "I'm gonna leave in a few minutes. Don't want her to see me still here in the morning."

I was numb. I didn't know what to say, so I just nodded.

"Don't worry, we can finish." he said slyly. Even though finishing was the last thing on my mind. "Come to my place tomorrow when I get out of work. I'll leave you my address. Take the bus, ok?"

I nodded slowly. I wasn't sure if what just happened was everything that was supposed to happen and I certainly wasn't sure I wanted it to happen again. But before he left, he found a piece of paper and wrote his address and what time I should come the next day. And then he was gone.

That night, I lay awake all night. At some point I put my clothes back on. I was so torn. On the one hand I felt very desirable. This hot guy liked me a lot. He was all over me. And it felt good. On the other hand, I felt so far in over my head. One second I had a boyfriend–not that he ever acknowledged that– and the next second I was having sex with a man. Looking back on it now, I know it was wrong. But back then, all I knew was, I felt so grown up. When I thought about his kisses and the butterflies, I convinced myself it had been fun and eventually I couldn't wait to see him again.

The next morning was so awkward with Sherry. She never asked about Gary and she never even addressed the elephant in the room. Looking back I wish she had. But instead she paid me and drove me home right after breakfast.

I had a few hours before I had to catch the bus to Gary's house. The thought excited me. I couldn't wait. My parents were working, my brothers were in the pool. I took a shower and picked out my cutest sundress. I have always loved dresses but back then I didn't realize how cute I looked in them. Cute in an underage sort of way.   Now I see it.

Back then I also thought I was way more mature than I was. Maybe it was because I was often left on my own. I watched my brothers a lot. Even back when I was in New Hampshire. When I was in the third grade, I enjoyed going to church very much. I walked there by myself every Sunday morning and again on Wednesday night–often in the dark for seven o'clock mass. My parents encouraged independence. They never worried I would make it there or home safely. Personally, I would never let my own children do anything like that. Still, I don't think my way is better. I was a product of the time and my children are a product of their times.

Another thing we were allowed to do in New Hampshire, was to walk up a busy road to *Dairy Queen* for the '*full meal deals*' for lunch while our parents worked. In the summer we got season passes to *Benson's Animal Farm* and we could walk the mile and a half with our friends and spend every summer day, walking around that zoo, by ourselves. Then we would walk home afterward. Our parents encouraged it. We played out until the street lights came on. Sometimes in the summer they even extended that. My parents went to dances at the VFW every Friday and Saturday night. We were the poster children for latch key kids and I loved my indepence. But when we moved to Florida, I lost all those friends and I was now alone and independent in a new city, by a very popular beach. It was a combo that would lead to disaster.

And one of those happened that afternoon. I took the bus to Gary's. It never occurred to me that if he was my boyfriend, he could have picked me up. I just did what he asked.

I arrived just before five. His roommate answered the door. He didn't look surprised to see me. This was weird because he had always been so adamant that we couldn't go to his place.

He motioned for me to come in then said, "Gary's in his room. First door on the right"

Let's be clear. The mom in me, who is reliving this and writing it down, is screaming at my naive younger self! How could I be so smart in school and so dumb in ways of the world? But I concede, I was twelve and Gary was a man. Gary's roommate was a man. They had lived double the life I had. They knew better. They knew exactly what they were doing. But I do take some of this blame. I went to that room willingly. I wanted to be a grown up.

Gary was laying on his bed and he had the music blaring. He smiled when he saw me and motioned for me to come sit on the bed. He was so good looking. I mean the kind of eighties sexy that I laugh at now. But during that time, I was very attracted to him.

I made my way to the bed and just like the night before he wasted no time. Now I see it for what it was. He didn't want me to have enough time to think about it or back out. But at that moment it was exciting. We started kissing and he told me he missed me. My heart soared.

Very quickly I realized he was already undressed under his dijon mustard colored sheets–something that has never left my memory, is the color of those damn sheets. He pulled me close, and my dress was on the floor in an instant. He moved on top of me and pulled my panties down. This time, I knew what he expected and I kissed him back timidly. He nudged my legs apart and I reluctantly gave him access. I knew it would hurt, but I wasn't prepared for how much.

He thrust inside me and I cried out in pain. It felt as though I had been ripped in two. A tear escaped my eye. It didn't slow him down. He moved in and out of me, much deeper this time and much harder. I was on fire–a burning pain that, just as it began to get easier– he grunted and stopped, collapsing beside me.

"Damn you are tight." He said breathlessly. I just lay there numb, exposed and unsure what to do next. "That was fun."

"Yeah." I said even though none of that had been fun. The excitement and fantasizing leading up to it had been way more fun than the actual act. This just felt cold and raw. I wanted to cover up with the sheet and hide but he sat up instead.

"You should probably get going huh? You don't want to miss the last evening bus."

Immediately I felt sick. This was it? Ten minutes and he wanted me to leave? I nodded numbly and rolled over to get my clothes. That's when he saw the blood on his sheets. That is when he said those words that have haunted me ever since.

"*Oh I guess I didn't pop that cherry last night after all.*"

I instantly go back to the feeling of being used. *Whitney* was singing in the background, belting out, "*How will I know, if he really loves me.*" I will never forget that moment. I pulled on my clothes and he walked me to the door, giving a thumbs up to his roommate as he made some comment like "that was fast."

He kissed me on the cheek and said "See ya later." As I walked away in a daze.

Now that bus ride was a pretty low moment in my life, but it was nothing compared to what I was about to face at home.

I wanted to head right to my room and cry, shower and cry some more. I felt so disgusting, so dirty. How had I just let that happen? What was I thinking? But the minute I walked in the door, I felt even worse.

My mother charged at me. "Where have you been?" She screeched.

I wasn't prepared. She never asked me that question. I just stared at her blankly.

"Out with your new boyfriend??" She spat out. My face turned so red. How did she know? Did he tell her? "What were you thinking? You little slut!" She screamed.

At this point my mother had me by the hair and was pulling me into the living room. My mother could fly off in fits of rage, but this was like nothing I had ever seen before. She looked pure evil and I was scared. Did she know what I had just done? How? I was speechless but the tears were pouring down my cheeks. I went from utterly humiliated to scared right back to humiliated. Even if I had wanted to tell someone what just happened, it certainly wouldn't be my mother now.

"So I let you babysit for one of my friends and you embarrass me by having a boy sleepover?" Sherry. That was who told her. Was it possible her yelling was getting louder? And where was my dad? He wouldn't let her hurt me. My brother's door was shut. I hoped they were hiding, I couldn't face anyone else. I still hadn't said a word but I was crying, hard. I needed someone to hug me and tell me everything was going to be okay, but as she shoved me in the living room by my hair, I knew that wasn't going to happen.

"So did you fuck him?" Her eyes flashed in pure disgust. I tried to answer. I nodded a little.

"You don't understand," I tried.

"You fucked him!?!" It was more of a statement and her rage increased as she said, "Well there goes a white dress on your wedding day!"

Her words stung more than what I had just done. Today, they still hurt but I can't help but think now, how backwards her thinking was. A man had sex with a twelve year old little girl and somehow that was my fault in her eyes. Somehow, that ruined *me*.

I stood there crying. Sobbing.

"Stop feeling sorry for yourself! You're just sad you got caught!"

And then she had my hair again and in one swift movement, she slammed my head into the cement walls of our basement apartment.

"YOU ARE RUINED! Get out of my face right now! I can't even look at you!" She screamed and stormed off, and I took my disgraced, shaking, twelve year old self to my room. I closed the door in shame. My head was pounding and I felt so ashamed. I didn't even undress, I just climbed into my bed and cried myself to sleep.

Chapter 2
1986
"We Built This City"- Starship

In my best *Sophia Petrillo* voice, "Picture it, Spring Break, Daytona Beach, Florida 1986." If you're a Gen Xer you have no doubt watched at least some MTV coverage of Spring Break, Live from Daytona. In 1986, two things brought the most money to Daytona Beach in the Springtime; **NASCAR** and Spring Breakers.

My first experience with a Daytona Spring Break was when I was thirteen. I was surrounded by miles of beach you could both lay on and drive on. There were hot college guys (and girls) everywhere, soaking up the sun, splashing in the water and drinking. So much drinking.

I was jacked up on both hormones and self pity. It was the perfect storm of more Sexual Trauma and Sexual Education, as I now see it. But at the time, I just wanted to feel something.

I was in middle school. I had just turned thirteen and it was less than a year after my experience with Gary. Gary, who I never talked to again. I tried. I went to the mall a bunch more times. I stopped in and waited for him to come over and talk to me like before. He pretended like I wasn't even there. Like he didn't know me. Like I hadn't been in his bed days before. Even his scumbag roommate pretended not to know me when he and Gary swapped shifts and days off, to try and deter me further. After that, I took my humiliation and never went into that record store again. Occasionally over the next year, I would walk by and look in, out of sheer morbid curiosity. At first I would catch a glimpse of him chatting with other young girls. But eventually, he was almost never there and finally I lost interest.

My mom never talked of that day again either. Not even to check to make sure I hadn't gone and gotten myself pregnant. She probably just held her breath until she was sure I was in the clear, and then celebrated that I hadn't disgraced myself more. She had made it clear what she thought of what I had done, and there was nothing more to say. I was 'ruined' in her eyes and I had begun to believe it too.

I did learn, much later in life, but before he passed in 2001, that my Dad never knew any of what happened first with Gary and then my mother. In fact, he naively thought his little girl was a virgin until I met the man who would become my first husband. When I finally did tell him he was already divorced from my mom. I had two kids and he was visiting me in Georgia. I could see his anger as he squeezed the arm rests on the chair he was sitting in. He expressed to me his sorrow that he never knew what I experienced, at such a young age and that justice had never been served on the man who raped his daughter as well as my heartless mother. It was just one more regret my dad voiced he had for "us kids."

He couldn't change things but he did hold me tight all those years later and apologized for his part in what happened. Because of that I was finally able to close that Chapter in 1993 and move on with my life. It was a healing moment. But it wouldn't come until later.

At thirteen I could only focus on my mothers words, the feeling of being raped and thrown away by a grown man, coupled with my constant loneliness. I had made a couple friends in school, but none that were ever like my friends in New Hampshire. And none that ever would be. But I searched for it. Longed for it. A connection. A feeling of love. A feeling of being wanted. And boy did I find what I thought that was, during my first Spring Break in Daytona.

In 1986 college kids flocked to the beach to the point of overflowing. Driving was halted on the beach during those big weeks, I think. That's what my memory recalls anyway. The beaches were packed with guys in short shorts and girls in string bikinis. The *kids* aka young adults, packed every hotel on A1A, Ocean Boulevard from Ormond Beach all the way to the bridge in Daytona. The closer you got to *The Band Shell*, the crazier things got. This was because that location was MTV ground zero. The spot where all fun took place. And I made sure that I was there as often as I could be, after school and every day during our own Spring Break from school.

Sometimes I went home for dinner, pretended to head to bed and when my parents settled in for the night, I would open my window, sneak out and join the party til the wee hours of the morning. My first Spring Break from school in Daytona is how I met Brad.

I took my 'ruined' self and headed to the beach every day. But this day was the day *Starship* was playing live from *the Band Shell*. I was wearing my cutest yellow bikini– thinking I was way too fat to be wearing it– so I covered it up with a black lace coverup. I wish my adult self could go back in time and see just how inappropriately sexy and *not* fat I was back then. My blonde hair was teased high and pulled back in my favorite banana clip. I didn't need much makeup but I had on my bright pink lip gloss.

The day *Starship* sang on the beach, I was there all day. I weaved my way through crowds until I was backed in with a thousand of the hottest guys I had ever seen. They all smelled like beer, and cologne and they were all wild. I fit right in. I danced and partied my way through the crown until I had weaseled my way right up to the stage and no one was the wiser.

The sun beat down on us. *Hawaiian Tropic* oil slicked bodies all pressed together in the sand, as *Martha Quinn* came out and introduced *Starship*. They began by belting out 'We Built This City'. I could feel eyes on me. I pretended not to notice. I danced and sang along with the crowd. Before the song ended, the eyes I had been feeling became a body pressed to my backside, dancing in rhythm with me.

He kept it up until the song was over and then he spun me around as the next song started. By the time they got to Sara, he was all hands and I was letting it happen. We danced slowly to the beat of the music. His breath, sweet with alcohol, was so close to my face. Finally when he leaned in to kiss me, I let him. He was a good kisser. Even a little sloppy, it's something that stood out to me.

When the concert was over he asked where I was staying. I told him the truth. *The Aruba Inn.* That was the name of the beach front motel my parents managed. He smiled.

"I'm at the *Desert Inn*." He slurred a bit.

Ironically his hotel was next door to mine. I could look out my bedroom window, and see the side balconies of *The Desert Inn*. It was a bit more run down than the Aruba. It was known for boasting $100 rooms during peak season that didn't face the ocean. Oceanfront was only slightly more, And they allowed four to five college kids in each room, which significantly lowered the cost. *The Aruba* would have never allowed that.

Oh they still got the rowdy college kids, they just got the ones with rich parents who wanted their daughters safe. So they paid for two girls or two guys per room, and most of them could afford the rooms that had balconies overlooking both the pool and the ocean.

"We're neighbors," I told him. Although I didn't say anything about living there or that my parents ran the place.

"Wow awesome," he said. "Wanna hang out?"

So I did. I went back with him to his hotel, where his friends were all set up on towels in the sand, behind the hotel. We hung out all day. We splashed in the waves. We went up on his deck and jumped in his pool. We drank. I didn't even like beer,--still don't to this day–but I wanted to seem cool. At one point during the day, someone came back with *Bartles and James* wine coolers and I switched to that.

We didn't really eat. There were Doritos and Cheese Puffs, snacks like that, but mostly we just drank. We dozed in the sun and when I woke up, the sun was lower in the sky and I was burnt on my backside.

Brad–he had told me his name at some point right before he introduced me to his friends–started to stir next to me. We both looked at each other and he smiled. He seemed so sweet and aside from a few random, sexy kisses throughout the day, he hadn't tried much else. He was, for the time being, a perfect gentleman.

"I think my buddies went up to shower", he said, putting a hand on my thigh and looking around.

"Yeah I should probably go shower too." I said. I knew my parents wouldn't even know I had been gone all day, unless I didn't get home in time to cook dinner. They worked long hours during these big weeks. My brothers and I took care of a lot of meals and tonight was my turn.

"Wanna meet up later?" He asked.

"Sure. Where?" I asked shyly.

"Out here on the beach. Around nine?"

"Sure," I said, knowing the only way that could happen was if I snuck out my window. But I was willing. This was the most attention, the most conversation, and the most fun I had with anyone in a long time.

I cooked dinner, burgers on bread, as fast as I could. That was my go to meal because I could make it fast. Then I showered and spent way too much time getting ready. I teased my permed blonde hair up high again. I made sure my eyeliner was nice and dark. Nothing a lighter on a jet black eye pencil couldn't fix. If there was liquid eyeliner back then, I didn't own any. I covered my lids with my *Maybelline Blue* eyeshadow and thickened my lashes with my *Great Lash* also *by Maybelline.* Once I was in my room for the night, no one ever bothered me, so I could take all the time I needed.

Before heading out I slipped on my asymmetric, hot pink, yellow and blue mini dress and fanciest lace panties and bra. I had bought the set on one of my many trips to the mall. Carefully I removed my screen and climbed out of the oversized hotel windows and shut it quietly behind me. My parents room was right next to mine, and sneaking out meant I needed to be extra quiet and get past their room before opening the gate to get out. My brother's room didn't have a gate–lucky ducks! Still with the AC unit running, and all the loud partying up and down the strip, there really was little chance my parents would hear me anyway.

I met Brad out on the beach and it appeared that he hadn't stopped drinking. He could barely stand up and for a minute, I don't think he even remembered who I was. He was sitting with all his friends on the beach, and they were all in the same condition. Some Of the guys had equally drunk girls with them and some didn't. It was dark and the sound of various music could be heard all around us.

The Clash, Bon Jovi, Madonna all mashed together from all directions.

I didn't know what to do at first but once he realized who I was he took my hand and pulled me next to him, planting a sloppy kiss on me.

"Hey Marryn." I didn't correct him.

"Hey." I said. I was definitely sobered up, but someone handed me a wine cooler and in my nervousness, I chugged it quickly. "I need to catch up." I said to no one in particular. He smiled. Another girl handed me a second wine cooler. This one I sipped. Someone passed a joint around but I passed. Surprisingly, so did Brad.

There was laughing and joking. Mostly I just took it all in. Brad held my hand but I don't think he had the mental capacity to do much more. I was ok with that. I was enjoying listening to everyone. Being a part of a group even for a little while.

It was well after midnight when someone suggested we get some sleep. Half of the group had already passed out, a few had started puking, and Brad was barely coherent. Still he offered to walk me back to my hotel.

"Sorry I was mellow tonight." He slurred as he stumbled in the sand. It felt more like I was walking *him* back to *his* hotel. But he never let my hand go and when we got to my pool deck he turned towards me.

"I wanted to ask you back to my room, but I am so fucking wasted tonight." He said,

"That's ok. I get it." I wasn't sure I was ready to be alone in his room anyway so there were no complaints from me. However, at that moment he got a second wind. He kissed me so deep, I thought I might pass out. My head started to swim. It felt good. Too good. I didn't want him to stop, but eventually he did.

"Damn you're hot." He said. I blushed, thankful that his drunk mind still thought I was pretty. "Tomorrow night. I wanna take you to my room. Tomorrow night okay?" His eyelids were half closed, his speech was slurred as he said tomorrow twice. I silently hoped he would forget the offer in the morning. I wasn't ready to do what I did with Gary again.

I smiled and let him kiss me again.

"Ok off to bed with you." I said before he changed his mind and asked me up right then.

"You first." He said. So I said goodnight and headed towards the hotel. I would have to go back in through my window but I couldn't let him see that so I went in the back door by the pool until he left. Once I was sure he was back at his hotel I went back outside and made my way through the gate and into my room.

The next day I was up by midmorning. I was dressed in my bathing suit and went to lay out on the beach. I was hoping when Brad woke up, he would come find me. It was afternoon before I heard him and his friends making their way onto the beach. They had a cooler with them and they looked much better than they had the night before.

Brad didn't see me until much later on. In fact the beach was packed and I had almost given up hope he was going to approach me. And part of me was okay with that. I was having fun with him and he was so cute, but I wasn't ready to sleep with him.

But he found me on the beach eventually and he plopped down in the sand beside me. He rubbed my thigh and smiled.

"Hey you." He said.

"Hey" I said back.

"Where ya been?"

"Here. I didn't know you guys were here." I lied.

"Well, come join us." He said getting up and waiting while I grabbed my towel and beach bag. When we reached his friends, I noticed some had totally different girls with them than the day before. Some were alone playing volleyball on the beach.

For the rest of the day we played in the water, drank, and swam in his hotel pool. I loved it when Brad would pull me close and kiss me. It felt so great to be someone's focus.

As day turned to evening, I got nervous. I didn't have to cook and I had told my parents I would be going to a concert on the beach with friends, so I didn't even have to check in at all. Brad was well on his way to being drunk again, but the evening was young. When his friends mentioned grabbing some dinner, I thought maybe I could go get something to eat too. But Brad said he wasn't hungry and told them to go without him. It was just starting to get dark and there was a concert scheduled at the *Ocean Center* for that evening so the beach was quieter than normal, but still busier than on a normal day.

When the guys left it happened. He asked me if I wanted to go up to his room. My mind screamed no, but my voice said yes. I've never been good at telling anyone no, but in my preteens it was the worst. I am a people pleaser to a fault. Besides, I didn't want the night to be over. I was having a great time with him. He was sweet even when he was almost black out drunk.

And that's how I ended up in his room. It's funny how things stick out in your mind. The blue doors, the gold numbers on the doors. His room was a mess. Four college kids crammed into a small room with two double beds. Tacky gold and blue bedspreads, clothes everywhere. On lamps, mirrors, covering every square inch of the floor. We had to walk on mounds of clothes, just to get to the first bed. He led me to the inside of the bed and we sat down.

I don't remember a whole lot of conversation. I know he was all over me pretty quickly and between the butterflies and the bats in my stomach, a lot of how things started was a blur. He touched me everywhere but he didn't try to take my bathing suit off. We were all over the bed and the kissing was really nice. One minute I was on him and then we switched.

When he was on top of me I could feel him hard against my stomach. He took my hand and put it on him, through the shorts. Timidly I stroked him through his bathing suit, which I quickly learned elicited moans from him. He liked it even if I had no idea what I was doing.

And that is when he whispered in my ear.

"Wanna give me head?" He asked. I had no idea what that even meant, really. I mean obviously I had seen *The World According to Garp*. I knew what a blow job was. But I had no idea how to give one. Still this seemed like a better option than having sex. When I didn't answer him right away, he pulled away and looked at me.

"What's wrong? You don't have to." he said. He looked disappointed,

"I just….." How could I tell him I didnt know how? Had never done that before. Turns out I didn't need to say anything, he just knew.

"Ohhh!" He said, smirking. "First time? I can teach you." He said. He didn't seem shocked, and so I felt better. Maybe I wasn't the only 'college girl' who had never given head. He took his bathing suit off and sand went with it. He laughed brushing sand off his erection with the bed sheet. He was bigger than Gary and I couldn't look away. If I thought he was going to wash the beach sand off I was mistaken. He held his penis in his hand and instructed me to put my mouth on it. He told me to start by moving up and down.

At first my mouth was so dry. Nerves will do that to you. Plus he tasted like the ocean and there were grains of sand in my mouth. But that turned out to help because the feel of the sand made me start to salivate. Pretty soon, I was moving up and down at a good rhythm and I knew I was doing a good job because everytime I took him all the way in my mouth, he moaned so loudly and squeezed my hair in his hand.

It didn't last long and when he got close I knew it was coming because he could barely hold still, his breathing was ragged and he had my hair balled up in his fist. When he came, I didn't know what to do. He told me not to stop so I didn't. I just let it spill out of my mouth down my hand. Finally, he pulled me up to his chest and I lay on it, not looking at him. He was holding me and that's how *he* fell asleep.

After a while I needed to move. I wanted to wash my mouth out and feeling used once again, I wanted to be alone. I could already feel the tears threatening to spill over. He was passed out so I easily got out of his grip and quietly snuck from the room. It was dark but there were kids everywhere. The balconies were a huge draw and all around me, kids were yelling to each other from them. I was able to disappear into the crowd and head home.

I came in and my brothers were watching TV. Dinner had been eaten. I don't know where my parents were. I mentioned showering and heading to bed, not that the boys were listening to me. I went into my room, showered, then brushed my teeth, twice. Used the mouth wash twice, before climbing into bed and finally letting the tears fall.

I didn't know why I was crying. I mean, I had gone to the room willingly. But I guess it just hurts to feel so used yet again. I really liked Brad and I got the feeling he liked me too. But what had happened had gone from feeling nice to feeling gross and finally to feeling lonely all over again. I remember crying myself to sleep and sleeping straight through to the following afternoon.

When I finally went outside, I didn't go to the beach. I didn't want to see Brad today. So instead I set up on our pool deck. I had my walkman and I blasted music on it, drowning out all the noise and activity around me. When I woke up late in the afternoon, I jumped in the pool to cool off and was about to apply more oil, when I saw Brad walking up the stairs to our pool deck. I quickly busied myself with the oil to pretend I didn't see him coming.

When he was standing over me, I had no choice but to look up.

"Oh hey," I said, making eye contact then looking away shyly.

"Hey. You avoiding me?"

"No. I-"

"I'm sorry about yesterday. You knocked me out." He winked. "It was that good."

My stomach did a little flip and I couldn't help but smile.

"Wanna come hang out with us?" So of course I did. It was better than being alone plus he said sorry. So I gathered up all my stuff and followed him like a puppy dog down to the beach.

We hung out again all evening. I had one more night off from cooking so I had no reason to rush home. It was my spring break too and I planned on enjoying it. By the end of the night Brad and all his friends were black out drunk, again. I noticed that a bunch of the girls they were partying with were different from the ones they had been with earlier in the week. I also noticed that they were all taking turns leaving the beach with the girl of the day, and when they came back another couple would head out. I learned that Brad had come with seven other guys and they had two rooms at the *Desert Inn*.

It was almost midnight when Brad walked me back up to the pool area at my hotel. I felt weird about being up there with him. I doubted that my dad was still making his rounds but if he was, I am sure he would not be happy to see me holding hands with some random college kid. I led him to the darkest corner of the deck to say goodnight.

He asked me where the rest of my friends were and I fumbled with my answer. If he noticed–he was pretty drunk–he didnt say anything.

"I'm actually staying with my aunt and uncle. They manage this hotel." I lied.

"Damn. So going back to *your* room is out huh?"

I smiled and shook my head. I was so glad I had chosen that lie. If I said they were off doing something else or that I came alone–doubtful–he would have asked to go to my room. I silently praised myself with a good cover.

"Wanna wait til Bobby's done? We can go back and hang out in my room." I wanted to say no. But I didn't see how I could. At this point it was just expected. Brad and his friends were here to hook up with girls–as many as they could–as often as they could. I actually felt a little flattered that Brad was still seeking me out.

"Sure. Let me go change and I can meet you up at your room in like a half hour?" I said.

He agreed and I went home. I came into the apartment and my parents were already in bed. The place was quiet. I know I had mentioned doing another concert on the beach but I thought at least someone would be up to make sure I made it home safe. I snuck into my room, took a fast shower and put on my lime green shorts and white tank top. My curly hair was still wet so I loaded it with gel and scrunched it up. I applied fresh lip gloss and a thick layer of eyeliner. Somehow I passed for at least eighteen, or Brad just didn't care.

I didn't want to take the chance that someone would hear me leave again, so I left out my bedroom window. When I reached his room the door was half open and I could hear loud talking and laughing from inside. I knocked timidly and no one heard me. I was about to knock again when someone whipped the door open. Brad's drunk friend Matt stood staring as if he was trying to remember my name. Giving up he turned and yelled into the room.

"Brad your *girlfriends* here." He made the word an insult. Like it gave him a bad taste in his mouth. Howling and laughter from the others followed.

"Ok guys! Very funny! Now out! It's my turn in the room." He yelled over the noise. "Come in Martina."

It was the first time he got my name right.

He seemed annoyed by their comments. I chalked it up to the booze. It amazed me how much these guys could drink. I was buzzed after three wine coolers. They had been drinking non stop since he woke up. His friends cleared out and we were alone. I was still standing awkwardly by the door.

"Get over here!" He said smiling. I walked over to him and he grabbed me pulling me onto his lap. He gave me butterflies every time. We kissed like that for a while and I could tell he wanted to take it further. His hands were on my back and with one smooth move, he rolled on onto my back in his bed. He kissed my neck and moved down taking a nipple in his mouth through my shirt. When I moaned he looked into my eyes.

"I want you." He said. "So bad. But I fucking drank too much."

I had no idea what that had to do with anything but I just nodded. He took that as disappointment. And maybe I was a little because I liked all the kissing.

"Don't be mad, ok?" He slurred.

"I'm not." I wasn't.

"Come hang out with me tomorrow? I promise to keep my drinking under control." He looked like a little kid.

"Okay." I said.

"I like being with you. You're sweet." He said. I didn't know what to say back.

"I like being with you too." I said shyly and I meant it.

We sat there a few more minutes and finally he said,

"Well since nothings gonna happen we should give up the room." He said but didn't move. "Unless you wanna," He paused and I knew what was coming. "Ya know, um, wanna give me head again?"

He smiled at me and I knew there was no way I could say no. So I did it again. It took me a minute to get him really hard but once I did, he was done as quickly as it started. And again, I couldn't help feeling used. Except he really liked it, so that made me like it a little more. I liked him and I was making him happy. He wasn't shy about telling me I did it well.

The next day I hung out with him and his friends with a whole new set of girls, all day. I was flattered that I hadn't been replaced yet. However, the more he drank the more sure I was he wouldn't try having sex with me. It did strike me as odd that he could let me suck his dick, but was too drunk for anything else. But none of that really made a whole lot of sense to my obviously childish mind. Besides, I didn't really want to have sex with him anyway. I just liked the kissing and the feeling wanted by someone.

Around four, I told him I needed to have dinner with my aunt and uncle. The week was coming to an end so he didn't even question it. He did say I should come see him around 11 that night. He promised to be sobered up when I got to the room.

So that night once my parents were in bed, I headed out. When I got to the room, it was dark. I knocked. No one answered. I waited and waited. I thought about looking for him on the beach but then I worried maybe I would miss him if I left. I didn't know what to do so I just sat there, waiting. I look back now and see how pathetic, immature and insecure it was.

It was after two when he stumbled up the steps with Bobby and Matt. They were joking and laughing. When they saw me, Brad's face fell and the other two groaned. I stood up ignoring them and walked towards Brad.

"Hey." I said. "Did you forget about me?" I asked, embarrassed because I already knew the answer.

"Oh yeah….sorry I totally did." He said, clearly just as drunk as every other night so far.

"What the hell man?" Bobby said as he opened the hotel door. "She your fucking girlfriend now?"

"Shut up!" Brad said, my cheeks flaming red.

"Seriously dude, she's been with you like every day. When's the wedding?" This from Matt. "What's wrong with you? Play the field, that's why we're here."

They were in the room now but I was still standing outside and Brad was sort of blocking me from them in the doorway. He looked uncomfortable from the jabs but clearly had no intention of speaking up to his drunk friends.

"Maybe we should meet up tomorrow?" He said quietly to me. His back to his friends. Before I could answer they yelled again!

"Get rid of her!" Matt growled

"Move on! You had your fun!" This from Bobby.

"Next!" Matt yelled loudly. Both guys started laughing and Brad cracked a smile too. Looking back he was probably stifling a laugh but I didn't want to believe that. I was humiliated and really just wanted to run off but I would not give them the satisfaction.

"Er, (I am sure he couldn't think of my name so he stopped himself with the two letters he was pretty sure of) I'm sorry they're drunk we're just gonna go to bed and I'll see you tomorrow."

"Yeah, that's fine," I said. I had no intention of seeing him again. But I have always been too nice for my own good.

He was already closing the door. And that was the last time I talked to him.

I walked back towards my hotel but headed to the beach instead. The moon was full and I just wanted to listen to the waves crash. I sat alone on the beach with tears streaming down my face. Not because he meant anything to me. I barely knew him. But maybe he did, a little bit. Because I really thought he did like me and was having a good time with me. I was embarrassed that his friends made fun of me. It really did make me feel like a clingy puppy following him around like I did. Doing whatever he wanted, when he wanted it. At that moment, I told myself no matter what, I would not seek him out the next day. And I didn't.

The next day I stayed up on my pool deck. I saw him with his friends a few times during the day. Drinking and in the water but they all looked much more tired than at the start of the week. Once, around lunchtime I saw him heading to our pool so I got up quick and hid inside the building. I watched him out a window as he looked around the deck for a minute and then left. I like to think he was looking for me and was disappointed when he didn't find me. In reality, he was probably only disappointed because one more hummer would have been nice.

That evening, I saw him one more time heading back up my deck again and instead of hiding, I approached a group of college kids dancing to the DJ on deck. I started dancing with their group and made it look like I belonged. One of the cute guys must have thought I was fun, because he grabbed my waist and started grinding me to the music. It was the perfect cover, again. When Brad saw us he turned and left the deck, I finished the song, smiled at the guy then called it a night.

It was the last day. Most would check out in the morning and head back home. It's funny, I don't even know where he was from. If he ever told me, I don't remember but part of me thinks maybe Indiana. I don't even know if that is true or something I imagine he might have told me. I think about that week sometimes. The week I met my first Spring Break boyfriend. Some girls have summer flings but not me. I had week-long flings, and sometimes, even though I didn't mean for it to happen, they lasted more than a week.

Chapter 3
1986
"The Glory of Love"- Peter Cetera

Like every teen girl, I had my celebrity crushes. Mine ranged from *Tom Kiefer* of *Cinderella* to *Jason Bateman* and even *Chicago Bears* quarterback *Jim McMahon*. But my biggest crush in 1986 was *Ralph Macchio* by a mile. He had a place on all my walls and in my heart. So in the weeks that followed my time with Brad, Ralph Macchio and my VHS copy of *Karate Kid one*, kept me company. I couldn't wait for Part 2 to be released in theaters and I begged my parents to let me go on opening night. As long as I took my brothers, they would pay.

The movie came out in June and though I kept busy with the end of the school year, the time until the movie came out seemed to drag. I spent time on the beach, listened to concerts– including *Cinderella* and *Huey Lewis*– at *The Ocean Center*. I met old guys who preyed on young girls at these concerts and I learned how to avoid them.

The first instance was when I was at the *Cinderella* concert. Some guy, who easily looked forty, approached me in the pit. It happened a lot because I was always by myself. I got better at avoiding them but sometimes, like this particular night, he thought I was easy prey. He danced up to me during

"*Nobody's Fool*", and started grinding into me. Before I could even move away, he pulled me close and kissed me, practically sticking his tongue down my throat. He tasted sour like liquor and he was extra strong as I tried to pull away. When that didn't work, I kneed him in the nuts and broke free.

As lousy as the experience was, at a concert I never should have been at alone in the first place, I still went often to *The Ocean Center* and that is where I met my first love. His name was Eric and he was *only* three years older than me. At least I was legal to him. I met him at a *Huey Lewis* concert and he was so sweet. And kinda dorky. He was only a little taller than I was. He had blonde hair, much lighter than mine and green eyes. He had crooked teeth and a lopsided smile but it all suited him.

We hit it off pretty quickly, talking before and during the show. I learned that he lived in Daytona too, on the Mainland. He would be a Junior in the fall and I was honest with him that I had just finished 7th grade. When the band finished he offered me a ride home. I declined, explaining that it was a short walk home. Still, he seemed unwilling to just say goodbye. So instead he asked me for my phone number.

I gave it to him but truthfully, as we parted ways that night I doubted I would hear from him again. Nice guys didn't find me. At least not according to my track record.

But the next day he did call. He asked me out to a movie and I accepted. When he suggested *Karate Kid part 2*, I almost said no. I mean I was supposed to take my brothers. So I accepted and then got to work on figuring out a way my mom would let me go on the date and take my brothers as well. In the end, opening night was a Friday and Eric had to work. So I took my brothers on Friday. Eric and I went to see it on Saturday. I never told him I had already seen it because I didn't want to hurt his feelings. Besides, it was nice to watch *Ralph* two nights in a row.

The night of our date Eric was a perfect gentleman. He held the door, he bought me popcorn and a drink. He held my hand while *Daniel and Komiko* fell in love. In fact, *The Glory of Love* has always reminded me of that first date.

When the movie was over he asked if I wanted to go drive on the beach for a bit. So we did. But he was again a perfect gentleman. We watched the waves, we talked and got to know each other. He had a sister in college and lived with both his parents. He had plans to go to college and be an engineer like his dad.

I told him about me. How I was one of ten kids, and that most of my siblings were already grown. How my dads first wife died and then he married my mom. I too had big dreams of going to college. I wanted to be a lawyer and

I loved the idea of going far away. I always thought I would go to school in Wyoming or Wisconsin. I have no idea why those states but back then, that was the dream.

When Eric brought me home, after trying nothing with me in the car, I started to wonder if he even liked me. He walked me to the door of our motel apartment and when he leaned in for a kiss, it was a simple kiss, on the cheek.

"I had a nice time." I said.

"I did too. I would love to take you out again."

This news actually shocked me.

"I would like that too."

So we made plans for midweek. It was summer so he was working a lot but he had Wednesdays off. I mentioned wishing I could get a job locally and he said IHOP was always hiring summer waitstaff. He said I should apply and put him down for a reference. So I did. And with that, I had my first job and my first boyfriend.

Eric and I talked on the phone a lot and he took me out to dinners, and we went for long walks on the beach. We went to shows at the Ocean Center and I saw him at work. Because of my age I could only work 4 hour shifts but I made good money, mostly in tips and it was fun. Our first real kiss happened on the one month anniversary of us meeting. It always bothered me that he never did more than kiss my cheek, but that was only because I assumed if a guy liked you, he would force himself on you. Eric wasn't like that. He was shy. And at some point during that first month, I learned he was a virgin. He waited for me to say the same and I could tell he was disappointed when I didn't.

The night he kissed me, we had a picnic on the beach. We watched the sunset. When it was almost dark he leaned over and gave me the softest kiss. It was the first time it felt really right to be kissed and I kissed him back just as gently.

We spent the rest of the evening on that blanket in the sand, kissing and talking. He said the sweetest things, called me pretty and told me he was so happy we met. Before the end of the night I was head over heels for him. Puppy love is what they would call it now, but at that moment it was a big deal to me. I was falling for him hard but more than that, he was falling for me too. Someone wanted to spend time with me. I hadn't had anything like that since my neighborhood friends in New Hampshire and it felt great.

Before he dropped me off that night, he asked if I wanted to see *Genesis* that weekend. Of course I said yes and we planned it. It was also at that concert that things started to change for us. The concert was fantastic. I can see Phil on that stage singing *Land of Confusion* clear as day, even now. And Eric was with me, stealing glances my way and holding my hand. We were getting closer and I could feel he wanted more. I don't know what it was about that night, but something changed and I felt it. He was so different all night. So I wasn't surprised when he drove me home, he was extra quiet on the ride.

He didn't get out of the car to open my door like he always did, so I turned and looked at him, half expecting that he was about to break up with me.

"What's going on?" I asked.

"Nothing," he lied. It was obvious and I made a face. "Fine. Something."

He smiled. I saw no reason to smile when breaking someone's heart.

"What? Just say it." The silence and his nervousness made me just want to hear the bad news so I could go home and cry.

"It's just….I am falling for you. And I like kissing you. And holding you. But…." He was struggling but it didn't sound like a break up speech. "But I want more."

"More?"

"Sex, okay? I want to do more with you." He looked like he was going to puke as he spit the words out..

"Oh!" I was just relieved that he wasn't breaking up with me. "Have I ever given you the idea I didn't want that?"

"No. No. But it's not like we can do it on the beach. And I don't really wanna do it in my car."

I wasn't sure I wanted to do it at all. I was happy with the way things were progressing slowly but the difference was, he was a sixteen year old young man and I was a thirteen year old girl with no good sexual experiences. Still, I wasn't willing to lose him over it either.

"Well maybe I can sneak you into my room." I joked. "Or maybe sometime when your parents aren't home?"

"Yeah I guess that could work." He sounded doubtful.

"You know you can talk to me about this stuff right?" I said. "You don't have to be nervous."

"It's just, you've done this before."

I hated the way it sounded when he said that. Like I wasn't ashamed enough. I don't think he meant it that way but that's how it felt.

"I'm not an expert. Technically I only did it once and it was nothing to brag about," I laughed awkwardly.

He smiled. That seemed to be the reassurance he needed.

"Thanks for tonight." He said.

This time I got bold and leaned in to kiss him. He smiled that lopsided grin again and I melted.

We didn't talk about doing it again. A couple weeks went by, we went on dates, and spent time on the beach. He went up my shirt a few times, and once, when it was a moonless night on the beach, I slipped my hand in his bathing suit and gave him a hand job. It wasn't what he meant when we had that talk, but all the little things seemed to be making him happy. Maybe that and the fact that he knew I was open to the idea.

As the summer came to a close, I was really happy that we had made it three months without having sex. I started my last year of Junior High and he started his Junior Year. We talked on the phone, and saw each other every weekend and sometimes he could sneak away and see me on a school night. His parents were strict that he maintain straight A's, so sometimes it was hard but we did what we could.

My summer job was over, and because I was so young, they wouldn't let me work during the school year. But I had gotten a taste of making money so I asked my parents to give me a job cleaning rooms on Sunday Mornings. It was a big check-out day for the motel so I could make good money, and it helped the regular maids get time off too.

One night, mid-fall, Eric told me he had something special planned for us. He told me I should dress up. He picked me up wearing khaki shorts and a nice short sleeve button down dress shirt. I had on one of my prettiest sun dresses. It was some crazy neon colors but I remember I loved that dress and wore it until it was practically falling apart.

When he picked me up he held a bundle of fresh flowers in his hands. I was pleasantly surprised to learn he was taking me to dinner at the *Top of Daytona*. This was a restaurant at the very top floor of the tallest building in Daytona. It overlooked the beach and the city with fancy food and beautiful aesthetics I had never been, but I had heard many people talk about it around the motel.

That night, we had an amazing dinner. It was very romantic for a girl like me and I just remember being so happy all evening. After dinner he said he had another surprise. We left the restaurant driving up the strip short way, before pulling into a random motel. It was called The *Treasure Island Inn*. I looked at him confused.

"Trust me." He said. "And wait here,"

I watched as he went into the front desk and in a couple minutes, came back with a key. He pulled around the building and into a spot.

"No pressure." He said, sensing my change in comfort. "I just want to be alone with you for a while."

I followed him into the room. It was nothing fancy but I remember the room number. 208. I never forgot because it was the room that Eric and I first had sex in. It happened that night. Even with his no pressure assurance, I was sure as soon as we went inside, it was going to happen. I wouldn't say it was perfect. I mean, we were both so inexperienced. But it was nice.

He was gentle with me. We took our time. We explored each other and when he couldn't wait anymore, he pushed gently inside me. He was smart, he used protection. He was kind and wanted to know if it was ok for me, if it was too fast, if I was disappointed. It made me fall for him even harder. He told me he loved me first and I easily told him I loved him back. We made love twice that night and even dozed in each other's arms. This was nothing like what I experienced in the past. I didn't want the night to end.

From that night on, we still went on a few *real* dates,(mostly when I had my period) but more often we would rent a room. Sometimes it was at *The Treasure Island* and sometimes it was somewhere else on the strip. It happened pretty much every weekend. We would get take out and then spend the night naked in each other's arms. We were addicted to each other and we couldn't get enough. New relationships are like that.

It still amazes me how easy it was for us to check into any hotel we wanted.. Rooms in Daytona were a dime a dozen, and in our case we could rent pretty much any room that fall and winter, for no more than $25 a night. Sometimes we would get a two night deal for forty bucks. We were kids and they didn't care. They rented it to us like it was nothing. Sometimes I would go in, and sometimes he did.

This was before the internet so we just walked in and asked for a room. No one ever said no to us. They took our money and even though we could never stay the whole night, that became our routine date.

We explored our sexuality as much as we could at our ages. We always practiced safe sex, because as Eric said often, his parents would kill him if he ruined his chances at college. And they had already told him more than once they considered me a distraction. They made it clear that if his grades slipped they would put an end to us. He was careful to spend his Sundays studying and we didn't even talk on the phone as much during the week anymore. He told me often he didn't want to lose me, and I didn't want to lose him either. He was my first love and I was his.

As time went on, the awkwardness got less. I learned how to give a really good–according to him–blow job. And he learned how to go down on me, which was a very new experience for me. It was also the only time I ever had an orgasm with him. We had long talks about our futures. We talked about how hard his parents were on him and how mine really never knew where I was. Still we both maintained straight As. We wanted college and we wanted a future. Sometimes when we would have a fight, usually over something stupid and insignificant, he would tell me it was a good thing I was going to law school because I was the best arguer he knew.

It's funny to think back now, how I thought he would be my forever. When you have your first love, no matter how old you are, you think you're grown. And I had grown up way faster than I should have. But didn't most of us *Gen Xers*? I know without a doubt that I was more worldly at thirteen and a half than any of my kids were at that age. But then again, maybe they were just as good as their mother about hiding it.

There was no internet and no cell phones, but we knew about sex. We knew about drugs and alcohol and all the things we now blame on social media. It was part of growing up in the eighties. The Sexual Revolution ended in the decade we were born and the eighties started while we were coming of age. We were right there for all of it. Plus, everyone I knew back then, was expected to finish school, go to college or into the military, get married and have a houseful of kids. As one of ten kids I personally couldn't wait to start my own family.

And as Christmas of my eighth grade year neared, I was already thinking of all those things. And my future had Eric in it. Without a doubt he and I would be forever. But as we all know now, when we were kids, we didn't know shit!

Chapter 4
Late 1986-1987
"The Christmas Song; Chestnuts Roasting on an Open Fire"- Nat King Cole

Christmas in the 70s and 80s was like no other. For me, and my own childhood, Christmastime was the only time I was really happy at home. That is because, of all the terrible things my mother said and did in my lifetime, Christmas was her time to shine. She loved it. And I got my love of it from her. To this day, she and I are among the few adults who still believe in Santa and the magic of Christmas.

At Christmastime she was a different person. She was happy, and joyful. She was slow to anger. The house was festive and so was her personality. We had wonderful, magical Christmas mornings for as long as I lived at home. She went all out. She always got us what we wanted, but also more than that, we got the mother we wished we could have all year.

In fact, the only thing my mother ever did to annoy me during Christmas, was to sing *Chestnuts Roasting on an Open Fire* obnoxiously in my face every time it came on. For some reason, I hated that song as a kid and she knew it. So every time it came on she would blast it, and sing extra loud and get my brothers to join in. She tried it when I was an adult too, but I had outgrown my hatred of the song and as it turns out, I actually like it now.

Decorations in the eighties, for me, cannot be rivaled by any other later decade. The popcorn plastic Santa's, the blow mold yard decor, the garland and tinsel (which my mother insisted we put on one strand at a time). The paper cut outs for the walls and the thick electric candles with the orange plastic flame for the windows. The canned snow, which came in most handy for the Christmases we spent in Florida. But my favorite part of the season was and always has been the music. Give me Christmas music from the fifties through the eighties over the new stuff any day. All of it was perfection in my book.

We were lucky growing up, that my parents made plenty of money so the tree was always full and each year we got season passes to *Disney, Seaworld and Cypress Gardens* so we could visit free anytime a relative or friend visited. We always got lots of clothes and toys and the latest new item of the season. I was into computers and I was lucky enough to receive over the years, the *Commodore 64 and later the 128*. I wasn't spoiled but like I said, Christmastime was different.

This particular year was no different. My parents decorated our motel apartment just like always. They went all out to give the illusion of a winter wonderland. Our first year in Florida, we hadn't made it to Christmas Day in the heat, when my mom and dad packed us up and drove us north to spend Christmas in New Hampshire with family. They were as homesick for a white Christmas as us kids.

But by our second year, it was clear there was no way they could leave the hotel again. They had met the owner of the *Desert Inn,* (a man named Dennis was all I knew at the time) and they were in talks with him to take over the management of one of his other newly purchased properties, *The Voyager Beach Motel.* It was more in the heart of the beach and a much bigger place. They would oversee the running of a 252 room oceanfront hotel. It would be way more money of course. Way more work too. However we would be able to buy a house and not have to live on property. So while those negotiations were going on, it was clear there would be no surprise trip up north. And I was ok with that. I couldn't bear to think about leaving Eric at Christmastime.

In early December, while we were spending time in one of our favorite hotel rooms, Eric asked me to be his date to the high school Winter Semi. He had gotten permission for me to go–which was all that was needed for someone from another school, to come as your date. I was so excited to be asked, I remembered thanking him by climbing on top of him and making love to him for like the fourth time that night.

We were truly two horny teenagers at this point and all we ever wanted to do was get a room and have sex. Eric hadn't told me that all the time we spent together like that, was causing his grades to suffer a bit. But apparently they had been and his parents had really been on him about it. He didn't confide it to me until it was really too late. But in December of 1986, we were so happy together as we prepared to go to our first semi formal dance together.

I remember my dress vividly because it's one of the few pictures I still have of Eric and I. And when I look at it, I think, wow was he goofy looking. But in a cute way. We made a cute couple but we weren't more than babies.

My dress was a minty green silk, with crystal sequins all over the bodice. If that didn't scream eighties enough, there was more gaudy to come. The dress was cut just below knee length and was tucked in on one side, stitched with more sparkles, which made the asymmetrical design leave me showing more knee on one side than the other. It had sparkling gray flowers on it that could have passed for snowflakes, but it was a stretch. I felt so grown up in that dress and there was no way that I looked just shy of fourteen.

Eric wore pressed, gray dress pants and a button up dress shirt almost the same shade as my dress. He had gray suspenders which today remind me of something *One Direction* would have worn. But as my dad said the night of the dance, we looked 'sharp'. And as we left he gave me a kiss on my head and told me I was his favorite Christmas Girl. He always called me that and it meant so much because he was one of the few people who truly understood just how much I loved Christmas. At later, lower points in my life, when Christmas started to lose its sparkle, my dad calling me his Christmas Girl was always just what I needed to pick me back up and dust me off! And because of him I will never lose my Christmas sparkle.

The dance was pretty close to Christmas so Eric and I decided to exchange gifts at the dance. I gave him the *Pink Floyd* album he wanted and a gold bracelet, which today makes me think of the bracelet Joey gave Chandler on *Friends*. The one from the *Liberace House of Crap*. But back then, he loved it and wore it every day from then on. He gave me pretty diamond studs and a matching necklace. I had never received anything from a boyfriend, so this set was extra special to me, and would become the reason I ended up in a knock down, drag out fight. But that's a story for later on.

I was excited to see what a school dance was like because Eric had convinced me to go to highschool with him at *Mainland*, rather than my home school, *Seabreeze*. I would have to take Air Force **ROTC** to go to school with him and even though the military wasn't in my future, it would look good on my college transcripts. My parents had agreed to it provided I had my own way to school since I couldn't take the school bus being out of district. It was all planned out that Eric was going to drive me, so that was no problem. The night of the dance was my first chance to see what high school would really be like. And who I would be going to school with.

That night at the dance I met Eric's friends. It was amazing that he had so many, considering all the time we spent together, but he did. They were all really smart and nerdy but just as sweet as he was. I found myself wishing we hung out with them at times, but that would mean giving up the time we spent having sex and we both just weren't willing to do that. Not yet anyway. I loved the closeness and the intimacy of it. I think he just liked all the sex.

We had a wonderful dinner at a table with his friends and their dates. All of them were in high school. We danced to every slow song and a few of the fast ones. He held me under the Christmas lights and told me over and over how happy he was. He told me he loved me and I believed him. It was magical, it was my favorite time of the year, and I was in love. But by late January things would start to fall apart and I was in no way prepared.

The start of 1987 meant our report cards came home, two weeks before my birthday. Mine was great as usual. Not that my mom noticed. It was expected of me and I would only hear from her if it wasn't. So I made sure it was always good. I was really good at school and it came easy to me. I genuinely liked school. Eric on the other hand was taking very hard honors classes and he spent more time *in* me, than he did studying or doing homework. His ambition for school was non-existent and when he needed me to push him and say 'no stay home tonight and study for that big calculus test', I didn't. If he wanted to spend time with me instead, I didn't try to change his mind. It was a recipe for teenage disaster.

The week after the report cards came out, Eric stood me up on a Friday and then Saturday. I tried calling him of course and his mom said he was grounded and couldn't talk. I couldn't see him at school because we went to different schools, I couldn't talk to him on the phone, I was allowed zero contact with him. I was crushed. I cried so much the next two weeks and I was so lonely. He and I hadn't been apart this long since we met.

Finally, on the third Friday since the dreaded report cards came out, (and one week before my birthday) he called me. He said he was finally no longer grounded and he needed to see me. He asked to take me out the following night. He would pick me up. Of course I said yes.

I was so excited to see him and just as I thought he would, he took us to the *Treasure Island Inn.* We got our special room. The one we had the first time we were together. I thought it was so romantic of him to pick that room after us being apart for what seemed like an eternity.

We wasted no time catching up. Kissing him after all those weeks and feeling his arms around me felt amazing. It was almost like the first time all over again and I began to think that maybe the time away had been good for us.

When we had made love twice, Eric pulled me onto his chest and held me for a long time. It was perfect to be back in his arms again. I never wanted to move.

But then, as quickly as it all started, he pulled away, got up and started to get dressed. I sat up, confused. It was still early, but maybe he was going to pick up take out. He did this sometimes. I wrapped the sheet around me and smiled.

"Hungry?" I asked.

But he didn't answer right away and his back was to me as he fastened his belt. When he turned around he had tears in his eyes. He shook his head.

"What's going on?" I asked. God, I was so naive.

"I can't see you anymore." He choked out.

I was struck dumb. Confusion was evident on my face, I am sure.

"What are you talking about?" I said. He had to be joking. But those were real tears.

"We have to break up. I can't see you anymore." He said again, almost like he had rehearsed it.

"What? Why?" I know my voice sounded shrill and I kept thinking this had to be a joke. We had just had sex minutes before and now he was breaking up with me?

"My grades. My parents. Everything. We spend too much time together." He was rambling.

"Eric, you just fucked me!" I screamed. The tears sprang to my eyes even as I willed myself not to cry. I wiped them away angrily.

"Stop yelling." He said. "I wanted to be with you one more time. I wanted you to have good memories of us."

I was pissed. Used, once again.

"No! You wanted to get laid one more time! Or you would have told me before you fucked me!" I was hysterical. I knew I was and I didnt care. He had just used me, one last time. I felt like he had never loved me. How could he just walk away from me without a fight?

"Please stop yelling." He was crying harder now too, but I didn't care. They seemed like crocodile tears. If he loved me, he would have fought harder to be able to be with me. When he said, "I'm sorry." I scoffed at him.

"I can't believe this is happening!" I couldn't stop my tears at all now. "I am already enrolled to go to highschool with you! I changed schools for YOU!" I sobbed between sentences. But he didnt take me in his arms, he didn't tell me we would work it out. He didn't comfort me at all. He just said "I'm sorry." once more before walking out of the hotel.

I had no choice but to get dressed and follow him.

He drove me home in silence. When he pulled up at our motel, I got out of the car and slammed the door as hard as I could. I never looked back at him. I didn't say a word, not even goodbye. I went to my room and I felt like I stayed there for two months, crying. I went to school. I worked. I let my parents have a stupid cake to mark my 14th birthday but as soon as I blew out the candles, I went back to my room. Most of the time I was in my room crying. My brothers tried to cheer me up but I mostly ignored them. I did try to call him a few times after we broke up and I had calmed down some. My young, broken heart still wanted him. I missed him so much. But his parents always said he wasn't home or couldn't come to the phone when I called. Once, he answered and told me himself, I needed to stop calling. He was moving on and I should too. I was crushed all over again when he finally got tired of telling me it was over and he hung up on me.

It was my first real love, my first heartbreak and it was not something I handled well. In fact I know I handled it awful but I was thirteen when we broke up and barely fourteen the day he hung up on me. I was a child. And I was not equipped to deal with any of what was happening in my life. And worst of all I was all alone all over again.

Chapter 5
1987
"Always" - Atlantic Starr

After Eric broke up with me, I was lost. I know I was depressed but I also had this horrible habit of trying to find comfort from men. It was the only time I felt like I was worth anything but also something that made me feel used. It was a confusing time and I was not mature enough to handle the situations I was putting myself in. I needed more guidance but I couldn't talk to my mom. Talking to her was impossible. I hadnt been able to tell her I had been raped. I couldn't share with her my heartbreak over Eric.

I remember when I got my period. I was barely twelve and I was more sick over having to tell my mom than the actual PMS I was experiencing. When I finally mustered up the courage to tell her, I choked on the words. In turn she became more uncomfortable than me. I remember she said something like "oh you started your period. Pads are under the counter," then walked out of the bathroom, closing the door between us.

The next day, she made it even worse by having me called down to the school nurse. It was from this stranger I learned about periods, tampons, pregnancy and all the stuff my mother should have told me. I was mortified to be discussing all of this with a complete stranger. Even the most basic of life's needs and knowledge I couldn't get from her. But everytime she did something like this, I swore to myself that someday I would be the complete opposite of her. It was a vow I made and followed down the road of life.

I know I am not the first teen that was unable to talk with my mom about anything personal. But since the move to Florida, I didn't have friends to confide in either. Just school friends but I barely knew them. I couldn't just call my old best friend. Calling New Hampshire was a long distance call and a sure way to get my ass kicked if I racked up a big phone bill. I did write her letters, and I tried to share what I could. But it was usually two weeks between my letter and her replies so that wasn't much help either. She did visit once as well. But that was not the same as having someone to talk to daily. It was a lonely existence. So instead, I found comfort and friendship in men. People who popped in and out of my life as fast as they came in. It was wrong, I see that now. But at the time it's what I knew.

So as soon as Spring Break started in 1987, I went right back to my old ways. My parents were still managing the Aruba Inn, but they had started house hunting and learning the ropes at the Voyager. They were busier than ever. So my freedom was easy to come by.

The first official week of Spring Break I was still in school. But I would hit the beach right after I got home. I also snuck out nightly to attend room parties and concerts. I partied and danced half the night, slept a few hours and then headed to school. I loved the attention of all the guys and now that I had my own money, (I was picking up as many shifts as I could now to keep my mind occupied) I could buy my own cute outfits, most of which left little to the imagination. Anything to numb the pain Eric had caused.

At the start of the second week of Spring Break, a new group of guys and gals moved into their hotel rooms. I was cleaning a room when I caught the eye of a particularly handsome dark-haired, dark-eyed young man. He was checking in next to the room I was cleaning. Since he had obviously seen me cleaning, I didn't even try to say hello. I was certain he had not come on vacation to get together with the hotel maid. Still he was nice to look at. And when he spoke to his friends, the accent told me he was most likely from New York. It was a thick accent I had heard many times being a yankee myself. My guess was Long Island.

That night when I woke from a nightmare about Eric and some new gorgeous girlfriend, I snuck out of my room to clear my mind. I planned to take a long swim and then hopefully

I could sleep some before school. The pool deck was packed. It was night one for most of the college kids and most of them were well on their way to getting shitfaced. This night was extra warm and I wasted no time diving right in the pool. I loved to swim. I still do. But that night I was swimming to forget. I had done four or five laps, dodging all the bodies splashing and playing in the lit up pool, when someone grabbed my foot. I spun around to tell them to knock it off. Just as I did, my eyes locked with him. My Italian New Yorker.

"Hey! They let the employees swim after hours?" He asked. I was right, he had seen me cleaning. More impressively, he remembered me.

"My parents run this hotel. I live here." I said before I thought the answer out. This was something I never told the Spring Breakers. I wanted them to think I was 'one of them.' But he had caught me off guard and the truth spilled out.

He looked at me surprised.

"Oh that must be cool." He said.

"Yeah, it's ok. It's nice to live on the beach."

"I'm sure it is." he said. He swam up closer and we were both holding on to the edge of the pool in the deep end. We had to talk kind of loud because there was music playing on the deck.

"Except when I have to get up for school after staying out half the night, or listening to everyone party all night." I said, another slip of the tongue.

"Oh you're in school? Are you a Senior?" He asked, already sure of his answer.

If you say so, I thought.

"Yeah." Now the lies were back.

"Cool, are you excited to graduate?"

"I guess so. Still have a couple months." Little did he know, I meant Middle School Graduation.

"You going to college?" He sure was full of questions.

"Yeah, in Wisconsin." That was more like it. The lies came easily once they started. If he knew the truth he would have already swam away.

"I go to *NYU*. I'm a Freshman. We're close in age then huh?"

Nope. Not really. But I would never see him again after this week, so it was not a big deal if he didn't know the truth.

"I'm Danny." He said. He smiled. He had a gorgeous smile. He was what I would call dreamy. Dark skin, muscular, soft eyes.

We talked for about a half hour until I started to shiver from being in the pool treading in one place for so long. A stiff sea breeze had rolled in, and the temperature had definitely dropped.

"You look cold." He said kindly.

"Yeah. I should probably go in. Besides, I need to get up in a few hours." I added that so he wouldn't be tempted to ask me back to his room. I was all set with getting used after talking to him for less than an hour. To my surprise he didn't ask anything like that. Instead he asked if I would be around tomorrow after school.

We made plans for dinner on the beach for the next night and I headed in. I was pleasantly surprised he didn't make a single move on me. In my experience, even in just what I observed during all the weeks of Spring Break, that was not the norm.

The next day I met him on the beach in the late afternoon. He had a blanket set up, near his friends, but far enough away for a little privacy. He had picked up some Chinese food and he had a small cooler of beer, sprite and a bottle of wine. When I approached he jumped up, welcoming me to the blanket. At some point he offered me some wine, but I took a sprite instead. He took the time to introduce me to each of his rowdy friends. They were a lot of fun to talk to and no one questioned that I was at least 17 years old.

We played volleyball on the beach, we swam and we drank and I picked at the Chinese food he had brought. I had never been big on eating in front of guys, but since Eric and I broke up, it was even worse. The entire night was one giant group date. The guys had all met girls around the beach and paired up. It was different than hanging out with Brad and his friends, but it was also the same. The hooking up had begun but Danny had yet to even hold my hand.

But after dinner he asked if I wanted to take a walk. It was getting dark and the walk sounded perfect. As we walked, he talked about his family, his dorm, and how he was going to school to be an accountant. He loved music and working on cars. He was indeed from Long Island and he bragged about the Polish-Italian deli his father owned. He was so proud of his family and of his life in New York. He was going to take over the family books and investments as soon as he graduated.

I told him my dream of becoming a lawyer. How I loved to argue and how I loved a good debate. I told him how much I loved school and that I was a straight A student. He told me I should shoot for Harvard instead of middle of nowhere Wisconsin. We talked about my family a little but I changed the subject and talked more about school and the few friends I made since moving to Florida. My closest friend was just a girl I had the most classes with. Her name was Peggy. I called her *Pegret*. It was a fun nickname. Half Peggy. Half Margaret. She was a cute redhead who always made me laugh. But we didn't really hang out after school. She worked a lot of hours to help support her family, so our time was limited to class and lunchtime. We walked for a long time up the beach before we finally decided to turn around and walk back to the hotel.

That night he walked me into the hall and told me he had a great time. I told him I did too. I was about to head in for the night when he took my hands and kissed me, gently. Just one nice, soft kiss on the lips. I felt nothing.

"You're beautiful," he whispered. I was speechless. "You know that don't you?" And he almost made me believe it. Almost. But years of my mother saying I was fat, and critiquing everything I ate that wasn't salad, had me feeling like a cow as a size 12.

"If you say so." I smiled back. He shook his head at me.

"Can we hang out tomorrow?"

It was Tuesday so I had to work after school. It was just a couple hours in the laundry room so we agreed to meet for dinner again. I told him about *Cinderella* being at the *Ocean Center.* He liked them as much as I did, so we made plans to go see them after dinner. I found myself excited about a real date. Maybe the attraction would come.

That night I didn't cry myself to sleep over Eric and I didn't dream about him either. I still missed him like crazy. I couldn't turn my feelings off that easily. My heart still ached for him. But Danny would be a nice distraction for the week he was here. I focused on that.

After work, I told my parents I made plans to see *Cinderella* with friends. They knew how much I loved them, so they didn't bat an eye. They had no idea I either snuck in, or bought scalped tickets to all these shows. They just thought it was cool that I was able to see so many shows. Like the beaches and the concerts could make up for moving me away from my friends and my family. They didn't realize how much I hated everything about the move and they would laugh when I would say things like, *as soon as I turn 18 I'm going back to New Hampshire.*

More than my friends, who were a huge part of my life, my family was there. My Nana was there. I used to be able to spend every weekend with her. We would watch the *Celtics,* her drinking *Tab,* while I cooked for her and learned to knit. The move ended those weekends abruptly. My older sisters and brothers were in New Hampshire too. Even though they were a lot older than me, and married with kids, they were my safe space. If I needed to get away, I would go stay with one of them.

Right before we moved, we were living in a two family home. My older sister lived below us with her husband and my niece. Whenever my mother was on a rampage, beating my ass for one of her stupid reasons, my sister would beg her husband to let her come upstairs and save me.

When the punishment was over, I would find solace down in their apartment. I would lay on her couch and look at her beautiful velvet pictures. She had some of Pegasus and others of Unicorns. I used to pretend they could take me away. Now I had none of that. Now I just had two younger brothers who just didn't get their moody teenage sister. It was an adjustment, I never really got used to it.

Danny took me to dinner at *Bennigans* that night, which took us almost two and a half hours because they were so packed. Spring Breakers didn't cook. Going out to eat was something you didn't even try, if you were a local, during the busy season. Honestly as a kid we never really went out to eat ever. We cooked at home. All of us took turns. Restaurants were for very special occasions and even then it was rare. Pot lucks were more popular back in the eighties. So going out when I did with Eric and now with Danny, was a big deal.

During dinner, and waiting for a table, we really got to know each other even better. Well, I got to know him. He got to know the me I made up as I went along. A few times, I almost slipped when talking about family. Like saying my brother was two years younger than me which meant he was fifteen when he was actually only twelve. Danny would never meet him so it was fine. But I needed to be more careful.

We had a great time at the concert. *Cinderella* was wild. They rocked out and Danny impressed me by scoring us tickets almost on the stage. Seeing *Tom Keifer* up close was a dream come true. As much as I hated living in Florida, I had to admit I loved all the concerts I was lucky enough to see. It was an eighties music lovers paradise.

After the show Danny walked me home. At the door he said he had a great time and I told him I did too. It was then that he made his first real move. Another kiss. And it was then I knew I didn't feel anything for him. Except maybe friendship.

His kiss was sloppy with too much tongue and way too wet. He was sincere and sweet but I felt no spark. He clearly did, based on the smile he gave me when it ended. He was so cute and so sweet, but I was still so in love with Eric. I missed him so much it hurt. But Danny was a nice guy and I could never hurt his feelings. He was leaving in less than a week and we would never see each other again. So when he asked me to hang out again, I said yes. He was a nice guy and the closest I had come to a friend in a long time.

We hung out every day of his Spring Break vacation. He never tried anything more than kissing and I let it happen, knowing it was just a fling for both of us. On his last night in Daytona, he asked me if I would come to the beach and stay with him all night. He knew I snuck out of my room at night so he knew it wouldn't be a problem as long as I was back before my parents got up for work. His last night, being a Friday, I didn't have school the next day anyway so I agreed.

People spent the night on the beach all the time and mostly no one bothered you. I knew there was no way he would try and have sex with me, out there with everyone, so I felt safe in saying yes. It would be a nice way to send him off. He truly was a sweet guy, I just wasn't over Eric. And that wasn't his fault. It was dead before it even started. And the lousy kissing sealed the deal. Except as the week went on, his kisses did get better,

That night we seemed to talk all night. Danny was a wonderful listener and conversationalist. I had told him about Eric and he told me about his last girlfriend, Polly. I told him about Gary, sort of.   I left out some of the humiliating parts so it seemed like a really bad hook up. Plus he didn't know I was only twelve when it happened. We talked and he held me all night. The beauty of it all was that he was a perfect gentleman. He liked me even though I am sure he knew I was not interested in having sex with him. I wouldn't say I was cold to him, it was more like a vibe I gave off, or lack of vibe maybe.

At one point during the night, I almost confessed the whole truth to him. I was so close to telling him my real age, it was on the tip of my tongue. But in the end I chickened out. It didn't matter. By next week he would be back in New York and he would have forgotten I existed.

We said goodbye on the beach that morning in the wee hours and he kissed me one more time. As it happened it was a perfect kiss and I remember thinking it was the perfect way to say goodbye. Maybe I had taught him how to be a better kisser in the way that he taught me girls and guys could be just friends. He held me tight before letting me go. He told me he would really miss me. I thought I saw tears in his eyes, but they were gone as quick as I thought I imagined them. I had to admit I would miss our long talks and all the laughs. He was not only cute, he was really funny.

When I finally walked away, I was convinced I would never see him again. So I never even turned back around to see him one more time.

A week later, when my own Spring Break started I was already checking out the newest cuties to arrive on the beach. Maybe one of them could help me forget about Eric. But when I got home from a particularly feisty wet t-shirt contest that MTV was taping, disappointed that I hadn't met anyone new, I got a big surprise. On my desk was a letter, addressed to me, from Long Island. Danny. And from that day on, I had a pen pal.

He wrote to me every week and I wrote him back. He had used his receipt from the hotel to get my address and said he hoped the letter would find me. He wasn't ready to let me go. He even told me he had fallen for me and couldn't stop thinking about me. I would answer every one of his letters telling him all about the end of my fake Senior year, and some real things too. If I was honest, I missed him too. I loved having someone to talk to. Even if it was through mail. His letters came fast, I would get two or three a week and I matched every one with a return letter of my own. He wrote to me about everything going on in his life. I told him everything going on in mine and a bunch of fake stuff that wasn't. I always loved creative writing. I found myself looking forward to his letters and I always wasted no time in writing him back.

And having a pen pal would have been fantastic, if it had stayed that way. But that is not what life had in store for me. And once again I was unprepared for what came next.

Chapter 6
1987
"Never Say Goodbye"- Bon Jovi

As the school year ended, so did my chance to switch back to my neighborhood high school. In truth, I wanted to go to *Mainland.* If there was ever a chance that Eric and I would get back together, we would have to be at the same school. So I prepared myself for a long ride on the city bus to and from school every day. By then, we would be in our new house on Ormond Beach. My parents had picked it out and the moving had already begun. By May 1st we would be in our new home and my parents would only be running *the Voyager.* Our days at *the Aruba* would be over. I could no longer say Eric would be my ride. So I studied the bus maps and made sure when the time came, I would be able to get to and from school.

But that would come later. Right now I had the whole summer ahead of me. Three more weeks and school would be out. I had a plan to work all summer at the new hotel and save money. My mom said I could train on the front desk and when school started I would have a whole new, more mature wardrobe.

It was coming up on a year since Eric and I had met and started dating. As the date approached I became more depressed. Was he thinking about that too? Did he miss me at all? Was there a chance he would see me and want me back? These questions plagued me every day. It seemed as though it was all I thought about.

Then one day in late April, I came home to a surprise on the desk in my room. It wasn't a letter from Danny. Instead, it was a big, beautiful dozen roses, in the deepest red I had ever seen. It had a small card addressed to me. I ripped it open wondering who it was from. I was, of course secretly hoping they were from Eric, but instead I got an even bigger surprise.

Let Me Be Your Senior Prom Date??
May 9th Right?
I Miss you!
Love, Danny

I don't think I could have been any more surprised at that moment. What is that line in *A Christmas Vacation* that *Clark* says upon seeing Cousin Eddie show up for the holiday? *"I don't think I could be more surprised if I woke up tomorrow with my head sewn to the carpet."* Something like that. Yes, that is exactly how I felt at that moment. The fact that Danny still thought I was graduating next month was a problem I figured would just go away. Now, not only was it not going away, it had somehow become more complicated. He had taken it a step further and knew when the *Mainland* Prom was. After seeing the card, I called Peggy whose older brother's best friend (who Peggy had the biggest crush on) was a Senior at *Mainland*. After a few phone calls, it was confirmed that the 9th was indeed the date of the prom.

I didn't even know how I was going to answer his question. I sure couldn't mail him back an answer. By the time it arrived my imaginary prom could have already taken place. But it was obvious he expected an answer. I had his phone number but I had never used it. Long distance calls were not cheap, so when he sent it in one of his letters, I really never thought I would use it. Still, to be nice, I sent him mine too.

I was still wondering how to deal with my problem after dinner that night. My parents asked who the flowers were from. I just said, 'a friend' and I left it at that. At least for the time being. The thing about my mom was, if I told her they were from a guy, she would be happy. She was happy I'd dated Eric because all she wanted for me was to find a man, (she didn't think I had it in me) get married and settle down. That was the mark of a successful woman, in her eyes. Sure she was a career woman, but only because she wanted more money than my dad made anymore. Ever since he advanced in age, and started to have more heart issues, all of a sudden he wanted more than he could provide. But he was an older man. Almost sixty by the time we moved to Florida. And I know he was tired.

After dinner, the phone rang and my littlest brother answered it. He loved to torture me so of course he put the phone down and called out, "Its a boy, for yoouuuu!"

Everyone looked at me. I hadn't had a boy call since Eric and I broke up. My mom actually looked hopeful. I guess since I was already a ruined woman, any boy calling was a good thing.

I took the call in my room and waited for Kenny to hang up the other line. I flopped on my bed which was the only thing besides my desk, not already packed up.

"Hello?" I shouldn't have been surprised. It was Danny.

"Hey! Did you get something from me today?" He asked.

"Danny! Yes! Thank you. They are beautiful."

"I'm glad. Soooo......." He was really calling for an answer. What was I going to do now?

"Well I am shocked. How did you even find out when my prom is?"

"Not important. Can I be your date?"

I should have kept the lies going by saying I already had a date. But he would likely have seen through that because in our letters, we both discussed how we weren't dating anyone. Instead I told a different lie, which I thought would be better.

"I would love that. But proms are expensive. And you're in New York. I'm in Florida. The whole thing including travel would cost you a small fortune. I think I'm just going to skip prom."

"Hey! You let me worry about cost and travel. I wouldn't offer if I wasn't sure I could afford it. And skipping your prom is lame. Go pick out a dress. You have a date."

"Danny, I…"

"There is no use arguing with me. My flight is booked. I am coming in on Friday and flying home on Monday. I just need to find a place to stay that will be near your family's new house. Can you suggest a few places?"

I didn't know what to say. This was a huge mess. There was no way he was going to take no for an answer. I should have just told him the truth right then. But I really loved his friendship and the last thing I wanted to do was hurt him. He was coming to Florida for my senior prom and I was not even close to being a senior.

By the time we hung up, I promised to have some numbers of places he could stay. He told me he would call me in two days for that info and If I had found a dress he wanted to know what color it was, so he could order his tux. He was so organized and sweet. But now I had to clean up the mess my lies had caused.

As an adult looking back, I want to shake my childish self. The depth of my deception was so ridiculous. But in the long run, it did teach me a valuable life lesson. Nothing, absolutely NOTHING good comes from lying. But it wouldn't be something I learned until my fake prom weekend.

I immediately called Peggy. If I was going to this prom, I was going to need tickets. Luckily in the eighties, prom tickets were fairly easy to come by. They didn't have strict rules. You could bring whoever, because you were graduating and you would soon be an adult. Peggy promised to ask her brother to get me two tickets. But she was so excited about the prospect of me going to a prom, she instead asked her brother's friend if he had a date. As luck would have it, he didn't. So Peggy graciously offered to be his date. She was crushing on him so hard, but I think he liked her too. It was almost like he couldn't ask her out because it was his friend's sister. But once she suggested it, he was all for it. And with that one problem was solved.

The next day, I made sure I was up extra early. I wanted to catch my mom having coffee before work. I didn't know how I was going to pull this next lie off, but I had to try. So when she was at the table, drinking her coffee, I pounced.

"Guess what?" I said.

"What?" She looked unimpressed.

"I got invited to prom!"

This raised her attention. Her ugly duckling had caught someone's eye.

"You did? By who?"

"Just someone I met here a few months ago. But there is a catch."

"What's that?"

"He thinks it's *my* prom. He thinks I am a senior."

"And why would he think that?"

"Because when we met, he thought I was a senior and I didn't tell him he was wrong."

Now most parents at this point would have told their child that what I did was wrong. But in my mothers warped way of thinking, I was used goods and she could capitalize on my lies. After all, in her eyes now that I lost my virginity, I would be lucky to even get a man. I never understood her way of thinking as a parent myself, but back then I used it to my advantage.

"So who is he?"

"He's from New York. He stayed here. He's a freshman at NYU. His parents own a

Polish-Italian Deli on Long Island" Now I had her full attention. She immediately heard, *rich New Yorker.* She might even be able to pawn me off yet.

"Then how are you going to his prom?"

"He is going to *mine*! He wants to come here and take me to the prom he thinks is coming up for me"

"Wow. How did you impress this one? Did you sleep with him too?" She always had to insult me. And it was always some backhanded comment that stung.

"No actually." I looked down ashamed even though I had no reason to be, at least not for reasons she thought I did. "We're really just friends. But I think he likes me more than I like him. And so I was hoping that while he was here, you just might not tell him I am not a Senior in high school."

"At some point the truth is going to come out."

"I understand that. And I will tell him. I just can't do it right now."

"Well, I guess if he sticks around after you tell him the truth, you might just land yourself a good guy, so fine. I'll play pretend for the weekend. When is this happening?"

I gave her the details. I cannot believe, looking back at how crazy all of this was, that she was so easy to convince. She was crazy.

I mean, she still is. We don't all end up with normal parents. She should have told me no. She should have given me guidance. What is ironic is today she says she has no recollection of any of this. Convenient for her, even if it wasn't for the rest of us.

The last two pieces of my puzzle was to find him a place to stay for the weekend, near our new house and buy a prom dress. I found a few small motels near the house, because we were moving to a side street within walking distance to the beach. That part was easy. Then, Peggy and I got together and went shopping for prom dresses. She was more excited than I was. Her crush on Jack was off the charts and she gushed, thanking me for making all this happen so she could finally get a date with him, and at his senior prom no less.

Since we didn't drive, the plan was to all go in Jack's van. It was a crap brown chevy with maroon velour seats. We would be driving to prom in pure 80s style. Peggy made sure Jack knew that he was supposed to pretend we were both seniors whenever Danny was around. Looking back, this was an elaborate plan considering I wasn't even into Danny at the time.

Prom dress shopping turned out to be a blast. Exactly what I imagined it would be like if I got to do it in New Hampshire with my best friends. I ended up buying both our dresses. I knew Peggy couldn't really afford it and every penny she made went to help her family. Besides, she was doing me a big favor and I was making good money for a teenager. It felt really good to help her out the same way she was helping me out with the whole charade.

By the weekend of prom, we were all moved into our new house on Ormond Beach. Danny checked in that Friday, right up the street at the *Coral Sands Beach Motel.* My mother said we could invite him for dinner. She wanted to meet him and somehow she had convinced my dad and brothers not to let anything slip.

When Danny was settled into the hotel, he called the house so I could walk up the street and meet him. Upon seeing me, he scooped me into the biggest hug, spinning me around. (Someone should have told my mom if I was as fat as she always claimed I was, he wouldn't have been able to do that.) When he set me back on my feet he kissed me. It was soft and gentle but it conveyed just how much he had missed me. I had to admit it felt nice. I had missed him too. His hugs always felt great.

Together we walked back to my house holding hands and I prepared for him to meet my family. My dad was working. It seemed like he was always working and it showed in his face. He never looked old to me until we moved to Florida. He had been diagnosed with

Congestive Heart Failure, he was always struggling to breathe. He should have been slowing down, not ramping up. I never realized just how hard life in Florida was for him, until my parents divorced and he moved back to New Hampshire. I always assumed he wanted the move south as much as my mom did. That was not the case.

By the time we got to the house, I was both scared and excited. We had a nice dinner where my mother fawned all over him with compliments and questions. She asked him about school and his parents' deli. She asked about the Brownstone they lived in and what his plans were for the future. My brothers and I barely got a word in. But Danny was gracious. He did his best to include everyone. I will never forget how much my brother embarrassed me that night at dinner.

We were all eating, talking about different things, when my brother piped up and said, "I bet you only like my sister because she has big jugs!" Giggling like the little nine year old he was. Everyone at the table laughed too. Except me. Because that is not what I heard. What I heard was totally different and I snapped at him, appalled.

"I DO NOT DO DRUGS!" I practically yelled, to which everyone started laughing all over again. My brother was rolling on the floor laughing so hard I almost wished he had peed his pants. When I finally realized what he said, I ended up laughing with everyone. To this day, memories of that night can still make us all laugh.

After dinner, Danny stayed and we talked for a long time, even after everyone was in bed. We sat outside on the patio catching up on things that letters couldn't convey. He sat with me on the rocker swing, holding me close and occasionally kissing the top of my head.

I felt so comfortable in his arms. In fact, I was starting to have real feelings for him. More than just friendship. It was so unexpected, I didn't know how to react. But I liked it. So before he headed back to his hotel for the night, I got bold. I turned to him and this time, I initiated the kiss. He seemed pleasantly surprised.

"Thank you for coming. Thank you for doing all of this, for me." And I meant it. As crazy as the whole situation was, it really did mean so much to me that he was willing to come all the way from New York, for a weekend just for me. He cared for me, and I cared for him too. Maybe more than I had before. Things were getting more complicated instead of easier.

"You're worth it. You know that right? You make me so happy when I am with you."

Again I felt like I should tell him the truth. I knew I needed to before he started saying he was in love with me. That wouldn't be fair to him. But I was in so deep by now and honestly I was scared. I needed someone to tell me how to fix this but there was no one.

So the weekend went on. Saturday morning Danny had breakfast with us. Then he went to pick up his tux and a corsage. I went to my hair appointment with Peggy. I got my hair freshly permed and styled. The stylist teased my curls up and tucked some babies' breath in a small bobby pin behind one ear. She also did my make up, very subtle except for my eyes. Those she made pop with black liner and blue tint lashes to show off my blue eyes. Peggy had her red hair swept up to one side and her makeup was painted on thick with deep emerald eyeshadow to match her emerald gown.

My gown was the palest peach color and it was covered in white lace from head to toe. It was strapless and my already full chest spilled delicately out the top. Both Peggy and I wore elbow length white gloves which made us both feel so sophisticated. We each had pumps dyed to match our dresses, which Peggy didn't think we needed. I know she felt guilty that I was paying, but I insisted. I wanted it to be special for us both.

When Peggy and Jack got to my house, Danny was already there, talking with my parents. I hadn't come out of my room. I was so nervous for him to see me. Especially with my parents around. One never knew what might come out of my mothers mouth.

Peggy knocked on my bedroom door and we both gushed when we saw each other. We both looked and felt like princesses.

"Why haven't you come out? Danny's here. You look incredible!!" Peggy admonished me.

"I was waiting for you. I am so nervous."

"Well let's go! Everyone is waiting!"

So together we went out into the living room. Everyone oohed and ahhed. My dad told me I looked beautiful and he seemed like even if he disapproved, something about Danny put him at ease.

Danny approached and handed me the most beautiful peaches and cream wrist corsage which he carefully slid on my wrist, kissing the top of my hand. The florist had also included a peach boutonniere. which I tried to pin on him. But after two tries, my mom moved me out of the way and did it herself. As if I couldn't even do that right.

He looked so handsome in his white tux with a peach cummerbund and bow tie. Even the white shoes. He looked like he was made for that tux, and in those exact colors. Jack had worn a white tux too with the same emerald green of Peggy's dress accenting the waist and his bow tie. We were two lucky girls with very handsome dates.

Dinner was being served at the prom so we headed out pretty soon after pictures were taken.. Peggy and I sat in the big bucket seats in the back of the van. They were ideal for big gowns. We could spread them out and not get wrinkled. Plus they were really comfortable. Danny and Jack started talking and in no time they seemed like old friends.

The prom was at some big hotel on the mainland. I think it was a *Holiday Inn* or something like it. They had big banquet tables set up in the school colors or Blue and Gold. The theme was 'Never Say Goodbye.' At first, I worried that Danny would wonder why I didn't know anyone, but he never said a word. We sat at a table that Jack picked and Danny was so focused on me, he didn't notice that the only other people I talked to were Peggy and Jack.

Dinner was nice. It was some type of stuffed chicken and potatoes. But the best part of the whole prom was when we danced. We danced to slow songs and fast songs. He held me tight for both. And when the last song of the night, 'Never Say Goodbye', played, he looked deep into my eyes and I knew I was starting to fall for him.

"I hated saying goodbye to you after Spring Break. And I am going to hate it on Monday too." He whispered in my ear. I didn't know what to say back. I just knew I couldn't keep lying to him. It wasn't fair.

After the prom, Jack asked if we wanted to go to the beach. Danny and I were all for it. When we got there, Peggy said they were going to take a walk. She winked and said, "You have the van to yourself for an hour. When we get back it's your turn to walk."

Again I was speechless but Danny was clearly happy for some alone time. He made a spot for us in the way back, on the floor with all the throw pillows and blankets Jack had back there. Obviously Jack used the back of the van for this before.

Danny and I wasted no time. We started making out. We had never really done that, but everything about the night had been perfect up to this point and it seemed like the next step. Only this time, I really felt like I wanted a real relationship with Danny. I didn't think about our real age difference. I didn't think of the complication of all my lies. I just thought about how loved he made me feel in a time in my life when I never felt lovable.

After just a few minutes of lying side by side, he climbed on top of me moving my dress. I could feel his erection through his dress pants. My dress was lifted up over my waist, and he was gently grinding into me. His soft moans both turned me on and made me nervous. I hadn't been with anyone since Eric and all of a sudden, I knew I wasn't ready. But I didn't want to be a tease either. I loved the kissing and the closeness but making love again scared me to death. Still, Danny had come all this way to take me to my prom–even if it was fake–I was certain he wanted more to finally happen. He had been more than patient.

I kissed his neck and made a quick decision that would hopefully stall things. Even for a little bit longer. I played my tongue around his earlobe and spread gentle kisses all down his neck. He tried to go back to kissing my lips but I stopped him by grabbing his erection in my hand and squeezing. And then, without thinking, I undid his tux pants. He seemed hesitant at first but there was no way he was stopping me now. I stroked him gently as I moved down his body and took him in my mouth.

I worked slowly. I teased with my tongue at first, blowing on him and doing my best to drive him wild, before finally taking him all in my mouth. He cried out more than once, gasping for breath. I gave him head with everything I had. In my mind, this was different from sex. I wasn't ready and I had no idea how to say that to him. So instead, I found another way to pleasure him. And I did. He enjoyed every second and I made sure that I took my time. Leaving no time for anything else after was my goal. This was easier than being honest. I really had started falling for Danny but for some reason I couldn't be honest with him about anything.

When he finished, moaning loudly and grabbing my hair, he collapsed on the pillows. I wiped my mouth and came up to lay on his chest. I could hear his heart pounding through his still buttoned shirt. He kissed my head and started to say something like "Your turn." But it was too late. I had taken my sweet time, and now Peggy and Jack were banging on the van.

"Times up lovebirds!" Jack said. We could hear Peggy giggle and we rushed to put ourselves back together. We didn't speak as we climbed out to give them their time alone. Jack high-fived Danny and I smiled and winked at Peggy, as we turned and took off down the beach.

"You didn't have to do that." He said when we had walked in silence for a few minutes.

"I know that. I wanted to. " He looked at me like he didn't fully understand. "You've been so sweet to me. You came all this way for me. I mean, it's totally been a great weekend. And I don't know about you, but I feel like we are becoming more than friends. I think I am falling for you."

"Jesus, I hope so. I have wanted to be more than your friend for a long time. I fell for you way back when we first met. I fell in love with you before I ever went home last time. I just knew you weren't ready. You weren't over your ex. You needed time and space. And I was willing to give that to you. As long as it took." He held me on the beach for almost an hour that night. Just held me. He had told me he loved me. It felt amazing. I was so starved for love. But I didn't say it back. When we finally walked back to the van, I was sad to see the night end.

Looking back, Danny was truly one of the good guys. He was sweet, and caring and he loved with his whole heart. If I should have been honest with anyone, it should have been with him. But I was too young, too selfish, too immature, to know how to handle these adult situations I never should have been in.

The night ended with us thanking Jake for the ride. Danny kissed me goodnight on my front steps before hopping back in the van for a ride back to his hotel.

The next morning I was on cloud nine when Danny arrived mid morning to see me. I missed him in the couple hours we were apart and I couldn't wait to spend the last day with him. My brothers were watching cartoons, and my mom was off cleaning something. My dad was back at work. I was so happy to see him. He had given me such a great night. My plan for Sunday was to treat him to a great day on the beach. But we were taking the day slow, after the late night. We sat next to each on the couch, drinking coffee and just chatting about the prom. And that's when it happened. My long overdue punishment.

Maybe it was my guilty conscience or maybe I was just so comfortable, I wasn't thinking. But everything fell apart with one stupid sentence. I don't even remember how it came out actually, but somehow, I said something to the affect of:

"I cant wait til Monday when Peggy and I get to tell all our friends we went to the Senior Prom."

And with that one slip of the tongue Danny knew the truth. It was such a stupid slip. My brothers' heads both turned my way as if to say "what did you just say you idiot?" And the look on Danny's face told me that no amount of back peddling was going to make this nightmare go away. There was absolutely no turning back the hands of time. In one split second I had ruined everything. He looked shocked, then angry, then sad. It happened in a blink. The realization came over his face. But he didn't speak. I am not sure he could at that moment, and I couldn't either. It felt like we stared at each other for an eternity. My brothers stared too. The silence was deafening. In all the scenarios I thought he would find out, this one never crossed my mind. So when he got up and headed for the door, I almost couldn't follow. But finally I made my legs work and I went after him out the door saying, "Danny please wait!"

He was outside and at the end of the driveway before he finally spun on me. His eyes had tears but they also flashed a fire I had never seen.

"How could you?" He spat.

"It just happened so fast. You assumed. I never corrected you. I thought it was a spring break fling."

"And when it became more?? Why didn't you tell me then?"

"I didn't want to hurt you!"

"And yet here we are!" And then he started walking away again. I started to go after him when he spun on me again. "Just tell me one truth, how old are you really?"

I didn't want to tell him. I felt sick. I thought about lying again but in the end I knew he deserved better. He deserved the truth.. So I looked him in the eyes and said, "Fourteen."

Look of sheer disgust he gave me then, will probably haunt me forever. And since it was the last time I would see him, I think that made it hurt even more. Because he turned and walked from me, not looking back again even once. And I didnt follow. I had played a child's game with a grown man and I came out as the villian. And rightfully so. I hurt someone who never had anything but love for me. I never meant for it to go that far, but I learned a hard truth.

There is no place for lies. Especially where hearts are involved. I broke his heart and I knew it.

Later that afternoon, I did go to his hotel to apologize. I owed him a true and heartfelt apology. But he had checked out early. The front desk said they were pretty sure he got an earlier flight. So I did the only thing I could do. I wrote him a letter.

I apologized and I tried to explain everything. I spelled it out. I took full responsibility. I spent pages trying to convey just how badly I screwed up and that I was sorry.   But he never wrote back. In fact, I never heard from him again.

And to pour extra salt in my wounds, my mother wasted no time in telling me what a fool I was. How stupid I was to slip up and let him find out the truth about me. How I blew my chances with a really great guy. How I could never do anything right.

So that's when I decided to stop beating myself up. Sure I was wrong. And yes I hurt someone with my lies and deceit.   But I also acknowledged, after she was done chastising me, that if I had a proper role model, maybe just maybe this whole chapter in my life never would have happened.

Chapter 7
1987
"Make it Real"- The Jets

After Danny disappeared from my life, I became more depressed. I knew what I did was so wrong but not being able to have him accept my apology made it hard for me to forgive myself. On top of that depression, the anniversary of dating Eric came and went. I heard nothing from him. I don't know why I thought I would. Other than the fact that I was just a naive girl. I just couldn't get over the fact that he meant more to me than I did to him.

That summer before high school, I worked. I needed to stay away from men because I clearly didn't know how to handle them. So I took a full time nanny position for a family in our neighborhood during the day. Then I worked the front desk, second shift at *the Voyager,* where I learned even more about life than someone my age should have known.

The owner of the hotel, Dennis, was often in and out of the front desk area, while I worked in the evenings. He would come to the front desk, take $15.00 from the till, and leave a note with his initials. On nights he did this, I never saw him again. As time went on, he got bolder. He would come to the desk with another person. Always a shy looking teenage boy.

Finally, one day I asked my parents about it. They implied that these were boys he was paying to have sex with him. I was shocked. Others knew what he was doing and no one cared? Once I mentioned how young these boys looked. My mother told me to keep quiet. She said the police had contacted her and my dad and they were on to him. She said they would move in on him, when they had enough evidence. I couldn't believe it. It sounded fake. Like something you would see on TV. And sadly, though the police did finally arrest him, it wasn't until many years later. And the charges didn't stick the first time. He bought his way out of those charges and two more sets of charges in the years after that. Finally, in 2011, they were able to make some very serious charges stick and as of now he is finally rotting in Federal Prison. But how many victims did he leave in his wake? How many young boys were ruined because of this man? At fourteen, I learned all about the sick people in this world. It can leave you jaded.

As a nanny, I got to see what it would be like to be a mom. I knew almost immediately I wanted to be a mom someday. I took care of two babies. One was two and the other was 6 months old. Their parents had a cute house with an even cuter in-ground pool. It was smaller than any in-ground pool I had ever seen, but I have always loved to swim. So every day, while the babies took their two hour nap, I would swim.

Their backyard was a tiny oasis, all surrounded by a fence and beautiful trees. There was a hot tub in the corner of the yard which I never understood. Climbing into a hot tub when it was 100 degrees outside was not appealing to me. But what I did love was skinny dipping. Sometimes, I would get brave. Instead of changing into my suit, I would strip down to nothing and dive into the cold water of the pool. Those were my favorite swim days. I probably should have been concerned that at any time, one of the parents could come home, but they never did. Not once in the entire time I babysat. Still, maybe it was the fear of getting caught that gave me the adrenaline rush. During that summer, I needed to feel something. Sadly, the only time I did, was when I took that chance, and swam naked.

During that summer I met a whole lot of interesting people. Rich families who visited yearly and families who were seeing Florida for the first time. I met businessmen and women just passing through for a convention or training. I met young couples checking in for a honeymoon and cheaters who just needed a few hours away from their spouse. And I met young girls just like myself, checking in to have sex with their boyfriends. We had cheap rooms and expensive rooms. We had an olympic sized swimming pool and a nightclub called *Big Peckers Lounge*. It was always packed, year round. Dennis stole the idea from a place in Ocean City, Maryland where he was from. Everyone thought he was so clever. Everyone who didn't really know him, that is. We had a guy named Sam who worked with my dad in maintenance. He looked so much like *Kenny Rogers* that they used him in a promo brochure for the lounge. These are the things I took away from my first summer as a front desk clerk.

At the end of the summer I had enough money in the bank to get a whole new wardrobe, and still have a nice little nest egg. I even bought myself a **Swatch Watch**. It was purple and yellow with a lime green band. I thought I was so cool. I got several pairs of *Jordache* stonewashed jeans, and cute tops in every color. I had pumps and high top *Reebok* sneakers and slouch boots in black and white.

My last week watching the babies before school started, the couple I worked for gave me a going away dinner. They thanked me for taking such good care of the kids, by taking me out for a nice dinner and giving me a card with a one hundred dollar bill in it. They made me feel special, and proud. I was going to miss my job with them and the babies.

The first week of school came fast and it was rough. To begin with, I had to be up by

4:30am after working until 10:00pm the night before. Once I was ready I had to walk to the bus stop at the end of my street. From there I took one bus across the bridge to the mainland, then caught another to the high school for a 7:00am start. My day did not end at 2:00pm like most students. I had to stay until 3:30pm for R.O.T.C training, three days a week. It was all part of me being allowed to go to that school. In the afternoon, I took the buses either back home or to work. Now that the school year started, I was only working three nights at the hotel. Thankfully, I always had time at work to read, so I would just replace that time with homework. To make all that I had to do even worse to go to school there, I never saw Eric even once that first week.

I was at R.O.T.C. drill training the first time I saw him, in the second week of school. He happened to be walking by when one of the upperclassmen (who were also the Officers) was yelling at me about bending my knee during an about face. He screamed something about putting a cast on my leg to keep it straight. I waited all this time to finally see him again, and it just had to happen in the most embarrassing way. He and his friends laughed before walking away. It might have been my imagination, but it did almost seem like he looked sad when our eyes met.

I made it through the first month of school and the only bonus was that I never saw Eric with another girl. That gave me some hope. And despite all it took for me to get there, I really did like the school. My honors classes were hard but I was handling them with ease. My English teacher was my favorite. My Spanish teacher made me laugh. He was an old man, who was himself Spanish and spoke it fluently. We all had to pick Spanish names. I picked *Sara*, mostly because I needed to practice rolling my Rs and I thought the name sounded pretty. ' *SahDdah*'. Who knew I would hear him say it so much. As it turned out, I made a lot of friends in Spanish and we always got caught talking.

"Sara! ¡Callate La Boca!" Became his favorite phrase to use on me. And ironically it's the only thing I remember readily from that class. Back then, a teacher could tell a student to "Shut your mouth!" and no one batted an eyelash. Still, for as mean and cranky as he could be, he was still one of my favorites, because he always had us laughing.

It turns out that the friends I made in Spanish class would make my days at school a little brighter. There were five of us. Adam, Dustin, Joy, Amy and myself. We just hit it off. The guys and Amy were always cracking jokes and who doesn't love a class clown? They made Joy and I laugh every time we were all together. We would laugh until our sides hurt, which in turn always got us yelled at by *Senor Cranky Pants.* The class also took place during lunch, so they became the people I ate with too.

One day at lunch someone asked me why I didn't go to Seabreeze and for the first time, I answered honestly.

"I came here for a guy!"

I was bombarded with questions so I explained while the group joked with me about bad decisions. Even Joy got in on teasing me. At the same time, they were also supportive. They asked if I had seen him or talked to him at all. I told them about the day at drill, when I was being called out by the officers. Adam was in R.O.T.C. too. He was at drill that day.

"I think that officer has a crush on you." He said. "He was razzin' you hard!"

"Doubtful. I think he just likes to pick on girls. Did you hear either of them mess with anyone else?"

"No. That's why I think he likes you." I rolled my eyes.

We debated it some more and they asked me if I had any plans to try and get back together with him. I said I didn't but I sort of did. I just wasn't ready to tell them what the plan was. I didn't want them to think I was crazy or desperate. The plan was something that came to me one night when I couldn't sleep. That night, I turned on the radio and the song *Make it Real was playing by the Jets*. As I listened to the lyrics, an idea came to me.

'*Tonight, it's been a year, we met each other here. Here I am all alone as thoughts of you go on.*'

I kept thinking how once we had sex, he hadn't wanted to stop. So maybe that was the way I could get him back. It had been almost a year since the first time we made love. It was haunting me.

'*I loved you. You didn't feel the same. Though we're apart, you're in my heart. Give me one more chance to make it real.*'

And right then I had my plan. I would rent our special room at *The Treasure Island*. The same room we had sex for the first and last time. I could invite him. Maybe mail him a card since he didn't take my calls. Or I could slip him a note if I could figure out which locker was his. It was crazy but it seemed like the perfect plan.

That day, after R.O.T.C. I asked Adam if he could help me figure out which locker was his. He knew a lot of people so he was my best chance in finding it.

The next day Adam met me when I was getting off the city bus in front of the school. He looked smug.

"Hey there, Guess what I have?" He smiled. He had really nice straight teeth, the kind that almost always come from wearing braces. He had soft brown hair and hazel eyes. I always thought he had a lot of *Jason Bateman's* features and boyish charm. He also had the comedic timing down. I think that's why I was always comfortable around him. At least in the beginning.

"You found out that fast?" I was only semi surprised. He was a Sophomore and had a lot of friends at the school.

"Yes I did. But it's gonna cost ya!" He was being his playful self.

"Ok, what do you want?"

"A date with you." I was speechless. He could have said pretty much anything else but that shocked me. I wasn't even sure he was serious.

"What? Come on. Be serious." I had no idea he liked me. I assumed we were just friends. Classmates.

"I am being serious. I would like to take you out. And since I don't like being turned down, I figure this is a sure thing."

"So let me get this straight. If you tell me where my ex boyfriend's locker is, I have to go out on a date with you. You understand I want to get back with him right?"

He laughed, and looked completely calm.

"Yep. But I think once you go out with me, you will forget all about Eric Whatshisname."

"I see, and how do I know you won't just tell me the wrong locker so Eric never gets the note."

"Well for one thing, I wouldn't be that shitty, But you are more than welcome to hide out and see who takes the note from the locker. But also because I have faith that you will have such a good time with me, you will forget this plan of yours to get him back."

"Pretty sure of yourself huh? Fine, you have a deal. And a date. Although I work all the time."

"Are you free Friday or Saturday night?" He looked very sweet asking and I hated telling him no. It took a couple tries as he offered up different dates, but I finally told him I would take the following Saturday off and we could go out then. The date set he walked me to Eric's locker. As luck would have it, he was there getting books out. I turned around and pretended to be talking to Adam so he wouldn't see me.

"That's him?" He asked, jetting his chin out in Eric's direction.

I nodded. I refused to turn around.

"Shit! I am cuter than him." He said playfully. "Lets just call your plan off, and you can be my girl instead." He was very cute with his playfulness and made me smile.

I laughed. If only it was that easy to turn off feelings. Well I guess it was for some, since Eric had.

"Come on, let's go. The bells gonna ring soon." I said.

We walked away together and I didn't look back. But that day, I spent every free minute at school and work composing the perfect letter that would manage to get Eric to meet me at the hotel in a couple weeks and rekindle all his feelings for me.

It had words from the song, *Make it Real*. Things like "**Hear me crying out your name, you said never never would I leave. Here's a tear from me to you…**"

I put the date and the part about it being a year. I put the hotel and room number. I told him no one had to know about us meeting, and even if it was just one more time, I would be ok with that. I told him I missed him. I poured my entire 14 year old heart out. And the next morning, before I could change my mind, I slipped it in his locker after the morning bell rang, and he was already in class.

Of course hanging out after the bell made me late for English, but my teacher was so sweet, she acted like she didn't notice me sneaking in. Besides, I was one of her best students. I didn't cause problems, did all my work, was polite and got A's on everything.

I hadn't heard from Eric at all before I went on my date with Adam. Our anniversary meet up was still a week away so I hadn't really expected to. Still some part of the romantic in me had hoped he would have read it and been so moved he wouldn't have wanted to wait.

Adam and I went roller skating for our date which I was both excited and nervous about. I had not been on roller skates since New Hampshire. Lucky for me, it all came back to me easily, and we skated the night away. We even did backwards skate to "*Another One Bites the Dust,*" and a few couple skate's to something by *Air Supply,* and "*Every Breath You Take"* by *The Police*, to name a few. He was right, I had a great time with him. I laughed all night at his jokes and him being goofy and showing off.

When he took me home, he walked me up to the door. He took my hands in his. I looked at him hoping he wasn't going to try and kiss me. I wasn't ready, not with everything with Eric still a hope in my mind. But he wasn't like that.

"So I had a great time tonight." He said.

"Me too. Really. And I didn't fall on my ass once."

"Well I wish I could say the same," He laughed. "But I will tell you I would love to both ask you out again, and kiss you goodnight." He held his hand up to me before I could respond with a no. "But I am not going to do that. You do whatever you need to do with Whatshisface. And when you decide that he isn't worth all your effort, then we will go out again." He kissed the palm of my hand and then let it go. "So until then, I'll see you in Spanish." He was about to walk away, but he turned real quick and said one more thing. "Hey if you need a ride to work after **ROTC** this week, I can drive you and save you a couple bus rides."

"Wow, ok thank you! I would appreciate that. And thank you for tonight. See you Monday."

The next week seemed to drag on. Adam acted a little standoffish in class when the others were around. However, he was his normal playful self when he drove me to work on Tuesday, Wednesday and Thursday. He made sure he teased me about how much I was always getting picked on during drills. The two Officers in Charge were always on my case for one thing or another. But he didn't ask if I heard from Eric. Classes seemed to drag all week, and I barely slept. But then it was finally Friday and the next day was THE day.

I went early and rented the room even though I had already made a reservation. My plan wouldn't work if I didn't get the right room. I set the room up with candles everywhere. I picked up drinks and ice. I turned the bed down and sprayed it with my *Exclamation!* Perfume. I had asked him to meet at 7:00pm.

By then, I hadn't eaten all day and I was a nervous wreck. I was showered and I was wearing a pretty pink nightgown I had bought just for that night. At seven, I started waiting. I watched the clock and as each minute passed. I made excuse after excuse as to why he hadn't arrived yet. I couldn't take my eyes off the clock.

By 8:00pm I was fighting back tears. By 10:00pm I had been crying for an hour and a half. I cried and cried. I cried until I think I ran out of tears. I felt so stupid. I couldn't believe that I meant so little to him that he couldn't even come by and say something. Anything. He knew I was waiting on him. Even if all he did was reiterate that we were staying broken up. That would have been easier to take than just completely standing me up.

But that's exactly what he did. And it hurt. It hurt so much. My first big heartbreak just kept going on. I told myself this was my punishment for what I did to Danny. I told myself I wasn't worthy of him and his family knew it. I convinced myself that is why they broke us up.

Still, just because something doesn't go your way, I learned that, like it or not everything happens for a reason. Eric not showing gave me closure I should have already had but didn't. It actually made me hate him, which isn't any better, but I knew I could see him now and it wouldn't hurt anymore. I was free to finally move on for real. And that's exactly what I did.

Chapter 8
1987
"Hit Me With Your Best Shot"- Pat Benetar

The next week at school started differently. I was no longer going to *Mainland* for someone else. Now I was there for me. I even sort of liked **ROTC** We had to start wearing our uniforms on Friday's and I had to admit, I was excited about it. I felt proud when I looked at myself in those Air Force Blues.

Monday in Spanish, Adam passed me a note. When Senor Cranky wasn't looking my way, I read it. He wanted to know how it went on Saturday. To my surprise, I didn't tear up when I wrote back, 'it's over.' I cried the last tear over Eric on Saturday. He wasn't getting anymore. He wrote back, 'Wanna talk about it?' and I shook my head. Before class was over he sent one more note, which I swear almost got us caught. He asked if he could drive me home after school today. I didn't write back, certain Senor was just waiting to bust me. Instead I looked back at him, smiled and nodded yes. He smiled back.

That afternoon, I met him at his car. It was nice to not have to take the bus. It was hot and he put the top down on his red Fiero convertible.

"So you want to talk about it?" He asked as we were leaving school.

"Not really. There isn't much to say. He didn't show up."

"Wow. I'm sorry."

"It's fine. I am so over it."

"No you're not." He said. He put his hand on my leg.

"No I totally am. I cried over him for the last time. It's been almost a year. Time for me to move on." And I meant it. I think this was the first time I felt like I was growing up.

"So does that mean you will be my girl?" He looked over at me. He gave me butterflies.

"You sure you still want me to be?"

"Yes." He said, squeezing my knee. "So give me your work schedule and I'll give you mine. This way I can plan a date, as a real couple."

It turned out that neither of us was free until Sunday. So he asked me if I wanted to go to the beach. I did. So we made plans. He also told me that *his girl* wasn't taking the bus anymore. He would pick me up every morning and any day he could, he would also drive me home. And that's just what happened. Every single day that first week he picked me up every morning, and he drove me home or to work in the afternoon.

On Wednesday, I was of course the target the two officers picked on, again. By then I knew their names were JP and Claude. JP was the Commander and Claude was the Vice Commander. They both razzed me equally. I was either out of step, (I wasn't, but when one of them questioned me, it would mess me up) or my *about face* wasn't tight enough. If they said I needed my leg casted one more time…..

After drill, I was fed up. I went up to confront them. Adam was waiting at a distance.

"Sir." I addressed them properly.

"Yes." JP said.

"I want to know why you're always picking on me. My *about faces* are perfect and I have been marching since I was six. I know for a fact, I was not out of step."

The one named Claude smirked at me.

"Marching since you were six?" He said, as if I were lying.

"Drum and Bugle Corps. I did it for 5 years, before we moved to Florida. I know how to do a perfect *about face*. And when and if I am out of step, I can fix it without you even seeing it."

"Impressive. Well, maybe we were being a bit hard on you." Claude said.

"I know you were. But why?"

"Well I was kinda hoping you might ask for extra help." He winked at me. "Ya know, like private lessons."

He was flirting. When I look back now, I wish I had known that guys found me attractive. When I looked in the mirror, I saw the fat girl my mother always told me I was. But that isn't how guys saw me. Still her damage was deep and even if they told me over and over, I found it very hard to believe. In fact, I just didn't. I thought they wanted one thing and one thing only. Thanks Gary. Thanks Brad. Maybe that is what some of the guys wanted from me, but not all of them. It took me a long time (thirty plus years) and the right person to finally make me start to believe it. And even now, I sometimes still don't.

So here I was, a Freshman in high school. And the attention I was getting made me uncomfortable. I really thought they were pulling my leg and at any minute they would call me a fat cow! And while these two officers were cute, well Claude was. JP wasn't ugly even with his face full of acne and pock marks. In fact, he had a nice body and dark green eyes, but something about his cocky attitude made him even less attractive. He had an air about him that said he thought he was better than everyone else. They both had that, but somehow Claude came off as less arrogant than JP.

"Well thanks but I don't need private lessons. And please lay off the constant picking on me." It made them smile again.

"Fine. I'll try." Claude said. "Hey I've seen you taking the bus. If you ever need a ride, I could drive you."

"Thanks. I have a ride though." I said, looking over at Adam.

Claude nodded at Adam. Adam moved his head just enough to acknowledge him. Mostly because he outranked him.

"Well if you ever need a ride. Just ask." He said again, winking. He knew that at much as Adam wanted to tell him to back off, he wouldn't because of the ranking.

"Ok thanks" I said. And I turned to walk away. Only when I did, I almost walked right into a female officer. She must have just come up behind me because I had no idea she was there. She was a short Spanish girl with the tiniest waist and big brown eyes. She was beautiful and she knew it.

"Excuse me ma'am." I said, acknowledging her rank even if she had been the one to come up behind me. She scowled, but I just kept walking. I heard one of them call her Ana but that's all I could hear as I made my way over to Adam.

"Wow she's full of personality isn't she?" I said.

"I'm more concerned with those two, clearly trying to steal my girl."

"Please, they don't stand a chance." I said.

Our clique in Spanish class embraced the fact that Adam and I were officially dating. We still all hung out together. The only difference was that Adam and I held hands now.

On Sunday, he picked me up early for the beach and we stayed until it was dark. We had the best time. It was fun hanging out with him and he was easy on the eyes in his swim trunks and tanned chest. He was muscular and strong and even though he wasn't too tall, he was still a little taller than me. We played in the water and he was constantly pulling me in close to him, but he hadn't kissed me yet. I was starting to get impatient. Everytime he pulled me close, I expected it to happen and when it didn't I found myself disappointed. What I didn't realize at the time was, he was teasing me. Because when he finally did kiss me, it was incredible. Probably the best kiss I had to date. The sun was setting and we had been playing in the waves when he finally spun me around without warning and pulled me close. He looked me deeply in the eyes and then slowly he kissed me. Soft at first and then more intense. It seemed like it went on for a long time. I didn't want it to end.

However when it did, he didn't let me go. He just pulled me back enough to look into my eyes.

"That was worth the wait." He said.

I smiled. He literally took my breath away. I couldn't even find words at first.

"I agree." I croaked out and I could tell my words made him happy.

That night he didn't kiss me again until he walked me to the door. But after that he gave me the sweetest kiss every time he picked me up or dropped me off. He also gave me a kiss when he saw me in the halls or when we parted for class. He made me feel special.

One day about two weeks after we started dating I saw Eric. But this time he wasn't alone. He had a girl on his arm, and when I saw who it was, I almost laughed. It was none other than Ana, the officer that almost crashed into me a few weeks before. It was a Friday so we were both in uniform, which meant I needed to salute her when I walked by. Talk about a kick in the gut. But I felt nothing when I looked at Eric anymore. So I raised my chin and gave my best salute as we walked by. She saluted back but barely looked my way.

After school I told Adam about it. He said he had heard rumors that they were dating but he hadn't fully believed it was true. He always called Eric a dork and told me I was way too good for him. I liked the compliment even if I didn't believe him.

That weekend Adam and I worked opposite each other so he came and hung out with me at the hotel while I worked on both Saturday and Sunday. It was then that he told me his parents were going away on business—they were both in sales—and he would have the house to himself on Monday. He asked me if I wanted to come over after school. I said yes without even hesitating. Something about Adam just made me feel comfortable. Maybe because for the first time I was with someone close to my own age. He was a sophomore but only eighteen months older than I was.

Monday morning he picked me up at home. As soon as I was in the car, he asked me if I wanted to skip. Now I was a bad girl for a lot of reasons, but I had never skipped school. I didn't even know if it was something I could pull off. Like what if they called my parents. So I asked him how to do it and if he was sure we wouldn't get caught.

"What I do is erase the message from the answering machine before my parents hear it. That's all you would have to do too."

My parents usually didn't get home until 6pm or later so I could most likely pull that off. It was settled. I was going to skip school for the first time and spend the day with Adam. He took me to Burger King for breakfast before heading back to his house. Even though he made it sound easy, I had a knot in my stomach that somehow, someway I was going to get caught. But it wasn't enough to stop me from doing it.

His house was really nice. A dark brown split level with a two car garage. The yard was meticulously landscaped and his dad's Ford Pick-up was in the garage with his moms Toyota Camry. We went in through the garage, walking through the kitchen. It was clean and bright, decorated in creams and beige colors. They stopped in the living room. They had big plaid sofas and dark wood coffee tables. There was a stereo cabinet with tons of albums. Adam put on a record and offered me a seat. It was Elvis. I knew he was a huge fan of Elvis before we were even dating.

We ate breakfast talking about what classes we were missing right then. But as soon as we finished, he asked if I wanted to see his room. I was not nervous at all. He made every situation easy. His room was big and covered with posters on every paneled wall. Everything from ET, to Skid Row and of course Elvis. Even a couple Swimsuit models which succeeded in making me instantly self conscious. As if reading my mind, he pulled me to him as he sat on the bed.

"Ignore them." He said, wrapping his arms around me. "Right now, I only have eyes for you. You are beautiful. And all mine."

Before I could say anything he started kissing me. He kissed me for a few minutes and easily coaxed me down on the bed, my head on his *Florida Gator* pillows. Kissing him always made me giddy. He kissed my neck and ran his hands gently up my arms. Nothing happened quickly. He took his sweet time with me.

He kissed what felt like every inch of me as he undressed me first and then himself. Part of me wanted to hide under his covers but he made it clear he wanted to be able to see everything. And he had every reason to be proud of his body. He was fit, with tight muscles. And his erection was bigger than any I had seen in person and in movies. He definitely knew he looked hot, but he never made me feel like I was anything but beautiful in his eyes.

He took the lead with everything we did, but I didn't shy away like I used to. I stroked him back, and kissed his neck, his chest and his stomach muscles. I even got brave and stroked him until he was losing control and climbed off me. He was only gone long enough to grab a condom from his drawer, open it and slip it on. When he was back over me, he kissed me deeply and I grabbed him and guided him inside me. It's crazy that we never talked about it beforehand. We both just knew what the other one wanted. And unlike every other time, this one honestly felt right.

He wasn't quick and awkward. Instead he was slow and perfect. In the end, I realized he was holding out for me, and while it felt amazing, that was not going to happen. Not only had never had an internal orgasm, I barely knew what that even meant. Whether he made me feel more my age or not, I was still so naive. So I faked it. I knew he was struggling to hold out and I appreciated his care and concern. But he was waiting for something that wasn't going to happen. So I moaned loudly and arched my back like I had seen in the movies, pushing up and letting him bury himself in me to finish.

Adam didn't roll away, instead he collapsed back on the bed taking me with him. He held me for a long time. He whispered in my hair against my ears sweet things as we both dozed in and out of sleep. But before the day was over, we had made love again. This time, I was in control which made it much harder for him to hold out as long. We slept again. I lay in his arms talking for a long time too. It was uncomfortable at first when he asked me if I had been with anyone besides Eric. I just said yes. I didn't want to get into all that when everything was going so perfectly. He said he had been with one other person too (as in also). I didn't correct him. There would be time for that another day.

When the day was almost over, and I knew he needed to take me home if I was going to get to the answering machine before my parents, I started to get dressed. Reluctantly he dressed too. When he dropped me off, he wouldn't let me out of the car until he told me at least twice that he had an unforgettable day. We kissed goodbye and he told me he would see me in the morning.

As it turned out, there was no message on our answering machine. I rarely missed school, so I hoped the school just assumed I was sick. And that's what I told all my teachers the next day. Everything was great until I was walking to English class and someone grabbed my arm before I could walk into the classroom.

I turned around expecting to see Adam playing around. But instead I was face to face with Ana, again.

"Excuse me?" I said pulling my arm away

"Listen! Eric told me about the necklace he gave you. He wants it back."

I looked at her blankly. Was this chick for real right now?

"Yeah, ok." I said sarcastically and turned from her walking into class. Not that I ever wore the necklace or earrings anymore but this girl was crazy if she thought I was going to start giving her the gifts he had given to me. Who even asks for gifts back ten months after you break up? It was a Christmas present.

I was still stewing at her audacity when school ended for the day. I went to **ROTC** but I couldn't wait for it to be over, so I could tell Adam what happened. Just as the drill was ending, Ana came up to the group with Eric on her arm. If it was supposed to bother me, it didn't. In fact, not only did it not bother me, I felt nothing seeing Eric with her draped on his arm. If anything, I felt disgusted that he had his girlfriend asking for a gift he gave me back.

When we were dismissed Ana went to talk to Claude and JP, with Eric and I left our formation to grab my books and meet up with Adam. He came over to me first and when he was close enough, he kissed me on the cheek.

"You ok?" He asked. He looked concerned, even though it probably bothered him more than it did me to see Eric..

"I'm fine." I kissed him back. This time on the lips. ""I am better than fine but oh my God do I have something to tell you!"

He took my hand and we headed towards his car.

"Spill." He said, giving me his full attention.

"So today I was approached by his new girlfriend."

"Ana? What for?"

I told him how she demanded the necklace he gave me back. I told him that I just didn't get it. Why would she want it anyway? Not like I wore it anymore but it was the principal of it. Who does that? He laughed as I was telling him.

"That is crazy." He said. "But if you want her to leave you alone, just give it back."

"I'm not afraid of her. And I am not giving in to her because there is no need to."

"I heard she is scrappy." He said, a little more serious now.

"I'm fine." I told him and I meant it.

That is until three days later.

I was at my locker after Spanish and this time Eric came up to me.

"Hey." It was the first thing he had said to me, since he hung up on me that last time. I turned around looking as unimpressed as I could.

""Whoa! You CAN still speak." I said sarcastically.

"Listen." He said, ignoring my comment. "Ana wants the necklace and earrings I gave you. She isn't going to stop until you give them to her. Just bring them tomorrow and she will leave you alone." He looked like such a wimp to me, in that moment. I had to ask myself what I ever saw in him.

"So I have tried calling you and getting in touch with you for months. I sent you a letter pouring my heart out. And the only thing that gets you to finally acknowledge I was ever your girlfriend, is the fact that your new girlfriend wants a gift you gave me. Cool Eric. Real cool. You're both pathetic." That stung and I saw it on his face. I turned to close my locker and when I turned back he was still there.

"Please, just bring it tomorrow then she will go away."

"Yeah until she finds out about some stuffed animal or other trinket you gave me. Give me a break!" I rolled my eyes and finished with, "Yo go away."

I was about to push past him when Adam walked up beside me.

"You ok?" He asked. He looked at me but then turned on Eric.

"I'm good. I was just leaving and Eric here, was hopefully going away too." And with that, I took Adam's hand and walked away.

Now most people would think that this would be the end of it. I had said all that needed to be said, and I assumed Eric would relay it to his beautiful yet insecure girlfriend. However that was not the end. The next day, I was leaving Math class and without warning,

Ana was in my face yet again. This time she had the craziest look on her face, and her eyes were glaring at me angrily. She blocked me as soon as we were just a few steps from the doorway.

"I'm not going to tell you again. I want the necklace. And the earrings."

Now I was just fed up. This girl had lost her mind. So I looked right at her and as calmly as I could, I said the one line that got me punched, right in the face.

I said–and I will never forget these words, "If Eric only cares enough about you to give you my hand me downs, thats YOUR fucking problem!!" And that's when she hauled off and punched me square in the jaw. So that is the moment I lost my shit on her. I threw my books down and proceeded to kick that so-called, scrappy bitches ass. I punched her again and again. I pounded on her–and she did get a few more good licks in too– until two teachers pulled us apart. At that point, with her face bloody and swollen, I can only imagine she was wishing she had never picked a fight with me.

In the Principal's office we waited for our parents to come to school. I was pretty sure I would be dead when my mom got there. I could already hear them talking about suspension for both of us. My mom was going to kill me.

First Ana's parents arrived and the three went to talk in the principal's office. When they came out, my mother had arrived and was sitting silently beside me. Ana's face was starting to bruise and she was definitely still crying.

Now it was our turn. I remember wishing my Dad had come. The principal called us back and I followed my mom into his office. I listened to the principal relay to her what had happened. He was mostly accurate. She *had* hit first and I *had* beaten Ana up, probably more than was necessary, as he put it. Therefore I was being suspended for a week and I would receive zeros in all my classes for that entire week, as would Ana.

"What do you mean 'more than necessary'?" My mom asked. "You just said this girl attacked my daughter, unprovoked. Who gets to determined what was necessary"

"Well yes, but your daughter said something mean. And hit her many more times." He tried again leaving out *than was necessary*, this time..

"Ok and *that girl* cornered my daughter as she was leaving class. Isn't that what you said? And she punched her."

"Well yes, but let's be honest. Your daughter is, um, much bigger than Ana is. She could have really hurt her."

Well that was the point where my mom lost it. Apparently she could call me big and fat anytime she wanted to, but God help anyone else who dared do it. She let that principal have it. For once in my lifetime, and I promise you this never happened again, my mom actually stuck up for me. These were her exact words. (Yes I memorized them! When your mom picks on you all your life the one time she's on your side you better believe you pay attention and hold onto that moment.)

"Mister, let me tell you something. My son is 60 pounds soaking wet and if you punched him, I promise you he would defend himself and he would win. As for my daughter being bigger, perhaps *Ana* (she said it like a bad word) should have sized her up before *she* decided to throw the first punch. My daughter defended herself against a bully. And since she fought back, she will take her punishment of suspension. But because she had to defend herself, in your halls, she will be allowed to make-up all of her work, while she is out. Are we clear? Or do I need to take this over your head?"

Apparently it was clear, because I got the week off from school, I didn't get in trouble at home and I was able to make up all my work while I was out. Unlike Ana, who had to take zeros for starting the fight.

In that one instance, I really loved my mom. She had never stood up for me before or she certainly hasn't since. But for that one moment in time, I felt like she loved me. She was proud that I had stood up for myself. And it felt great.

Chapter 9
1987
"Don't Dream it's Over"- Crowded House

So I am sure that by now, you are thinking I needed to get it together. And you would be right. But bear in mind I am still only fourteen, and although our ancestors married and had relationships at this young age, times have changed and I was not only searching for love in all the wrong places, I was doing it without any adult supervision. Welcome to the 1980s! I have often reflected on my own life as to the exact way I didn't want to raise my own children. However I have said it before, hindsight is 20/20.

Back then I was so into Adam. And that was ok. Because we were close in age. I think that's why I never thought twice when he called me his girl. I liked the way it sounded. That's why I wish what happened next hadn't happened. Things would have been totally different. But then again, if it hadn't, I wouldn't have the life I have now. And I wouldn't know what I know now. I have certainly learned a lot. One thing is for sure, you've gotta take the bad so you can appreciate the good.

It was November and Adam and I were getting really close. In fact only days before, on Halloween, he took me for a walk on the beach and he said he had something to tell me. I never worried it was something bad. He was always loving and kind to me. I never thought he would hurt me. So as we walked I was relaxed. When we got close to the pier he pulled me close. It was so dark out but the lights from the pier cast soft shadows on our faces.

"I love you." He almost blurted it out. He had never said that before and neither had I. But it felt right. So I smiled and told him I loved him back. We talked about how we loved spending time together and how glad we were to have met each other. It was really sweet. I wonder if he still thinks about that night fondly like I do. I doubt it. I don't think he ever found out the truth.

A few days after Adam told me he loved me, he got sick and was out sick from school. JP and Claude noticed his absence right away, and used it to their advantage. As drill was ending, they said they wanted to see me.

"Hey your boyfriends not here huh? Need a ride?" This was from JP.

"I would have offered but JP drove me today." Claude said.

Ya know that thing I said about hindsight? Well in hindsight I truly wish I had taken the bus that day. But I didn't, rode in the back until we dropped Claude off. He lived closest to the school. When he got out, JP told me to climb up front. So I did. I gave him directions to my house. When we were almost there he pulled over a few houses from mine. Beside us was just an empty lot that had yet to be developed. He cut off the engine and turned towards me.

"Ya know, you're one of the hottest girls in ROTC," He said. I was immediately uncomfortable.

"Thanks. But I have a boyfriend."

"He doesn't need to know." He leaned in so close and I knew he was going to kiss me. As he did he grabbed my crotch and squeezed. Immediately, I squirmed away saying things like stop, and I don't want this. "You know you want me. I have heard about you. Ana's boyfriend told us how easy you are." He kissed me again, only this time, I turned my face so his lips landed on my neck. His other hand was trying to get to my breast from the bottom of my shirt and bra. I pushed against him but he was a big guy. And he was practically all the way on top of me. When the opportunity finally presented itself, I took the upper hand and kneed him as hard as I could in the crotch. When the pain from that distracted him, I poked him in the eye as hard as I could, with my thumb and nail. He moved back just enough, calling me a 'cunt', and grabbing both his groin and eye, long enough for me to open my door and fall out onto the cement. I left my bag behind and ran as fast as I could, the rest of the way home. I didn't look back. I was too scared to see if he was following me.

When I got home, I threw myself on the bed and cried. Not only had what he did made me feel disgusting, his words stung too. I wanted to tell someone but I was too afraid. And even worse I was thinking what he said was true. I wanted to call Adam but I couldn't face him. I was so ashamed. So instead I took a shower and scrubbed. I tried to wash all of him off me. Including the memory. Maybe if I could convince myself it didn't happen, none of it would be true.

The next day, Adam was back. He drove me to school and I was really quiet the whole way. He kept asking what was wrong and I kept saying "nothing."

When we got to school, he started to walk me to class. It was then that he noticed I didn't have my bag. He started to ask me about it, when JP walked up and handed it to me.

"You left this in my car yesterday." He said winking smugly, before walking away. He was definitely trying to piss Adam off and it worked. It was partially my fault. I should have at least told Adam who drove me home. Since I didn't it looked like I was trying to hide it from him.

"He drove you home?" He snapped at me.

"Yeah, Claude was there too."

"Who got dropped off first?"

"Claude did. Why?"

"So you were alone with him and just happened to forget your bag?"

"Yes, I was in a hurry. Why are you giving me attitude?"

Now at this point, I know I should have told him everything. But the way he was acting, I didn't feel like I could.

"Because, I know what kind of guy he is."

"And you know what kind of girl I am." I said. I was hurt so I let him have it before walking away. "You believe whatever you want. I am going to class. I'll see you in Spanish."

That day in Spanish was so awkward. Everyone could tell we were fighting. But no one wanted to take a side just yet. Towards the end of class, Adam slipped me a note. It just said, 'I'm sorry. You're right, I should have trusted you. I love you."

I didn't respond because I was still hurt and feeling really alone all over again. I skipped lunch and went to the nurse without telling anyone. My mom gave me permission to leave when the nurse told her I was feeling nauseous. She didn't come get me of course. I had to take the bus. I went home and when Adam called later that night, I told my brother to say I was asleep.

I felt so lost. The person I should have confided in, and should have been able to confide in, thought the worst of me. And wasn't that the same as what JP thought? As well as an extension of what my mother thought ever since the thing with Gary happened. The problem with rape and sexual assault is that, if even person doesnt believe you, you're automatically a liar. And if you are easy, in the eyes of whoever, then you must have wanted it.

I stayed home the next day too. Facing everyone was too much.

Now I only know what I heard after all was said and done, through the gossip at school. So some of this is hearsay. But when I stayed home the next day, and wouldn't take Adam's calls, that made him even more convinced I was hiding from him because I was guilty of something. Then I heard from Joy that Adam confronted JP. He asked him exactly what happened on that ride home. And JP, needing to keep his stud status, told Adam that I was all over him. I couldn't keep my hands off him. He went on to tell him not to act so surprised. He told Adam he had to know that he wasn't my first, or even my second.

I think the part of all that that hurt the most, was that he took JP's word. Not mine.

Not the girl who had never given him reason not to trust her. He didn't even give me a chance to defend myself. Defend myself against my attacker. Let that sink in. Nope JPs word was law from that point on. No one, not even one of my so-called friends, asked me if it was true. This is why high school sucks for so many.

The next day, when Joy gave me all of this information glittered with all the gossip, Adam had stayed home. Everyone was saying poor Adam. I heard at least ten times how heartbroken he was. I was some kind of pariah. I couldn't stand it! I hadn't done anything wrong. That day after drill, I walked past JP and up to Claude instead.

"Can I speak to you in private?" I asked.

"Sure what's up?" We walked a few feet from JP.

"Listen, I need a ride. But I am not taking a ride from him." I said in disgust, as I pointed a thumb behind me. "And if you so much as lay an unwanted hand on me, I will cut your dick off. Clear? Now, can I have a ride to Adam's house? I need to speak to him."

Claude agreed. He had clearly heard the rumors. He didn't even question the stuff I said about JP. Even with the smug asshole smirking behind me.

We drove to Adam's in silence. With the exception of me giving directions as they were needed. When we pulled up out front, I was a little calmer and asked him to wait in the car. He did. The car didn't have air conditioning, and so because the windows had been open, my hair looked like I stuck my finger in a light socket. I didn't care. I just needed to tell Adam the truth. He needed to hear it.

I knocked and after a few minutes, I rang the bell. I knew he was home. His Fiero was in the driveway, I knocked once more, this time harder than I needed to. I was frustrated. How could I explain if he wouldn't answer the door? And I was only explaining to set the record straight. Because the fact that he trusted JP over me, told me all I needed to know about him.

I was about to give up. I started to walk back to the car, when I heard the garage door open. I was in front of Claude's car but I turned to look. Adam was coming out of the garage and he looked pissed. There was rage all over his face. At first I didn't care, I was going to say what I came to say. Before I could, Adam was in my face.

"How could you?? How could you fuck him?" He practically screamed at me.

"I didn't! And maybe if you could just listen for two seconds–" but I didn't get to finish my sentence. Without thinking, he pushed me hard. I stumbled back a bit but he just kept coming.

"Don't lie to me!" He pushed me again. "Everyone knows you're a slut!"

I never saw Claude get out of the car. I was stumbling backwards and he had managed to crush my heart even further with just one sentence. "You make me sick!" He shouted. Tears were in his eyes. I didn't care. His words stung and I was crying too.

He was still coming at me, and was about to push me yet again, but Claude grabbed him from behind. Everything was such a mess. Claude threw Adam to the ground and yelled, "Don't touch her again."

I should have been happy for the help. Except all that did was make Adam even madder.

"Why is she fucking you too?" He snapped.

"You're an idiot." He said to Adam. To me he said, "Get in the car."

I did as he said. There was nothing I could say that would erase all the damage JP had done. Adam was an idiot. He didn't want to hear my truth. He wanted to believe the worst. I know now it was his bruised ego and his age. Still, I considered myself lucky to be getting away before I was in too deep, and strapped to someone who could so easily put his hands on a girl he supposedly loved. If only I had known back then, that is exactly the kind of man I was destined to attract over and over again.

Claude drove me home in silence. I think he wanted a *thank you* for saving my ass. I just didn't have it in me. I was dead inside. He dropped me off at home and asked if I wanted a ride to school the next day.

"No, I need a couple days." I told him and he didn't push the issue.

"Ok well if you change your mind, here's my number." He wrote it on a piece of notebook paper. I shoved it in my bag with the intention of never looking at it again. That night, I told my mom I was still not feeling well. She said I had missed enough school and I needed to go. But I was in no shape to see anyone at school. Especially my *friends* in Spanish class. So I pretended to leave for school, no one ever checked. Then, when the house was empty I went back inside and stayed in bed all day. I did this for two days. I knew after the weekend, I would have to go back to school, but I needed the time away.

I wondered what was being said about me. Joy never called to check on me. No one from our group did. I was sure then that everyone had taken Adam's side, and he had likely not shared any of what he did when I went to his house. That was fine with me. I didn't care. Looking back I was severely depressed. I had been sexually assaulted for the second time and had received exactly no help at all.

I almost called Claude on Sunday to ask for a ride on Monday. In the end, I took the bus. I knew he and JP sometimes rode together and even though it was a no-brainer that I didn't want to see him, I couldn't take the chance that they would show up together.

I kept to myself all day. I was so numb. I sat alone at lunch. In English, my teacher asked me to stay after class. When everyone was gone, she asked me if I was ok. I assured her I was fine. She didn't believe me but she didn't push either. At this point, she was pretty pregnant and she rubbed her belly, as she tried to make me smile.

"I was kinda hoping I would have a babysitter for this little one in the future." She said, "So let me know if you need anything. Maybe we can be there for each other."

Oh how I wished I had confided in her that day. If I had, maybe I would have gotten the help I so desperately needed. But I didn't. And two days later she was gone. We had a sub, and the principal came in to tell us all that our teacher would be out for the remainder of the year. Her baby, the one she had only recently asked me to babysit, had been stillborn. I had no idea what that meant at the time. But I did my research the minute I could get to the school library. My heart broke for her. I wanted to reach out to her, but I never did. The principal had asked that we respect the families privacy and proceeded to introduce us to our new permanent English teacher.

That day we had **ROTC** drill. I had managed to avoid everyone the first part of the week. I even asked Senor Cranky Pants, who was being uncharacteristically nice to me, to move my seat and he did. Adam wasn't at drill and rumor had it, he had asked to drop the class. Fine by me.

Claude came up behind me as I was heading to the bus stop.

"Hey! Hold up!" He said. "Let me give you a ride home."

I really wanted to say no. The bus was quiet. I could be alone with my thoughts. The only problem was, I had been that way for days and I needed someone to talk to me. Especially with the news about my English teacher. Plus I had to go to work, and I would be alone on the desk all night. So having someone to talk to for fifteen minutes on the drive over, might be nice.

From that day on, Claude drove me to and from school. I am sure there was talk but I didn't care. We were just friends. We mostly just talked. One day when he was driving me home, I blurted out what happened with JP. I don't even remember what sparked it. All I know is, I saw an opening and I grabbed it. The worst part was that he was not surprised. He said he knew as soon as JP started the rumors, that I had turned him down. He just hadn't realized how bad it was. He also said he couldn't sit back while Adam pushed me around. The irony of that, will come later.

We talked for a really long time, and for the first time since everything happened, I felt better. I was still sad, and felt awful about myself but there was a weight lifted. Just telling someone had helped. The next day, when people whispered behind my back, I held my head high. I had told my truth even if it was only to one person. I could see Adam was hurt, but so was I.

What inevitably happened next was that Claude became my person. My only friend and the only person I could talk to. I was shut off from everyone else. I saw him every morning and every afternoon. He was no longer speaking to JP unless it was necessary for **ROTC** I was still working a lot. But when I wasn't, he would invite me over. I hadn't accepted. He would talk about his home life. He told me he had moved from New York and lived with his parents and elderly great aunt.

The week of Christmas arrived and he asked if I might come over and meet his family and have dessert with them on Christmas Eve. I was very reluctant to accept. I felt like I was always going from one guy friend to the next after they turned into a boyfriend and broke up with me. But I didn't see what harm could come of just meeting his family. He had been so nice to me, and without him, I would have no one to talk to. So the day before, I finally agreed. We were starting Christmas break so there would be ten days with no school drama.

He had warned me that his dad would likely be drunk and just overly friendly. He also said his parents were smokers in case that would bother me. But my parents also smoked. Most people did in the 80s. Still, I don't think I was prepared for just how heavy his parents smoked.

The house was the typical one story brick on the outside. Inside, the walls were darked paneled and the furniture was also dark with huge orange and yellow flowers all over them. But everything was covered with a thick layer of tobacco smoke. The mirrors on the wall were tinged yellow too. The smell hung heavy in the air, and it was as if we walked into a giant smoke cloud.

The other thing that surprised me was that his Mom, Edna, was sitting in the big chair in the house. His Dad, Tommy, was on the couch. In my house, my dad had the recliner which he frequently napped in, especially after a long day at work.

In Claude's house, his mom had *the chair*. I learned she was the only one who worked. She worked in the bakery and deli of a local supermarket and provided for the entire family. His great Aunt LuLu had bought the house when they moved from New York and now she was retired, living on Social Security. Claude's dad did nothing, mostly he said, because he couldn't hold a job. Claude often referred to him as a "waste". And just as Claude warned me, his dad was indeed drunk but still laughing and joking happily even if he was stumbling everywhere. He was obviously ashamed of his father, and proud of his mother. In fact, he unapologetically still called her Mommy. It was a dynamic I had never had. (I still don't) I loved how his mom took on all the responsibility of the family and earned herself *the big chair*. I could see why he admired her after just a couple of hours talking over dessert. She was really nice. We hit it off in an instant.

After dessert he wanted to show me his room. It seemed like a typical guy trap. I also expected his parents to say no to having a girl in his room. I learned very quickly, they didn't tell him no, very often.

His room was small, with lighter paneling and more thick brown shag carpet just like the living room. He had a small table with two folding chairs, which I went to sit at, even though he sat on his bed. We talked for a long time and eventually he asked if I wanted to come sit with him. I did, but only because the folding chair was getting uncomfortable.

And as if history had not repeated itself enough, this is where he gave me our first kiss. That is all that happened that first night. But that night, I became his girlfriend and my whole entire life changed. Just like that.

Chapter 10
1988
"She's a Little Runaway"- Bon Jovi

As I mentioned before, I had rarely skipped school. But everything with Adam turned me into someone who skipped more often than I should. I never let my grades slip, but I felt I was doing really well in school and at not getting caught. The few times Claude wanted to skip I always said yes, because we would just hang out at his house. His parents didn't care. He was set to graduate and head to the Air Force after graduation. Our dating life, just like every other part of my life, moved fast. That's just how we did it in those days.

Our relationship turned sexual very fast and we became inseparable. Looking back, the thing I loved most about hanging out at his house was his mother. Edna and I became really good friends and I found in her, the mom I never had myself. If I wasn't working, or in school, I hung out there. Edna and I talked for hours. We played board games almost every time I was over. After a while it became fun to shop for new games to play, and surprise the other one with it. My favorite, to this day, was called *Taj Mahal*. Oh how I wish I still had that game. It was so fun.

Claude played too. But sometimes he would just leave the two of us and go play his video games. I was fine with that. Edna and I always had so much to talk about. Truth be told, it really was nice to have a mom. I found that in her. But if someone had told me back then, that was the reason I was with Claude, I would have said they were crazy. I didn't see it. I didn't see how badly I gravitated to her as a mother figure.

Others saw it though. There were times when Claude's dad was drying out and he would lash out at Edna. When he did this, his *go to* insult was that I was Edna's lover. He would say we spent so much time together that I must be her lover. Did I mention he was crazy? If she played Nintendo for too long after work, he would also accuse *Mario* of being her lover. We got a lot of laughs at his expense when he would lash out. Honestly he was much nicer to be around when he was totally plastered, but to get that drunk, he had to steal money or jewelry from his Aunt or his wife. He stole from Claude once, and he got so angry that Claude took the entire haul of beer his dad bought, and smashed every single can into the wall of the garage.

Despite the sometimes off kilter family dramatics, I still preferred to be with them. At home my mother only spoke to us long enough to give us lists of chores or yell at us for not doing our chores correctly. Besides, most of the time Eddie was asleep and we didn't see him.

One day when we were talking, Edna mentioned wanting a second job. She was good at bookkeeping and she had done that in New York for a time. As it happened the Voyager's Bookkeeper had quit. To be fair, I think she got tired of trying to hide all of Dennis' spending on the boys he had sex with.

I talked to my mom and she agreed to not only hire Edna, but she could do the job on second shift. This meant she could work at the bakery and come to the hotel in the evening. Not only that, but with her working there, it meant I had a ride to and from work, and a friend to work with. When I turned fifteen, Edna and Claude took me out to dinner to celebrate.

When I got home, my mom seemed annoyed that I wasn't home on my birthday. I assumed she had nothing planned because she hadn't said a word. Even when I asked for the day off, she never mentioned wanting me home.

My dad was in his chair and he smiled.

"Happy Birthday Mrs. Doolie." He said. He always called me that from the time I was a baby. He handed me a card with a box that had a new sweater and jeans in it.

I hugged him tight and thanked him.

"Do you have room for some birthday cake?" My dad asked.

I hadn't had dessert when we went out so I was game.

"Yes please!" I said. My dad called my brothers and I thought my mom was going to get the cake. But true to character, she didn't say a word. Instead she stormed past me, into her room and slammed the door. When my dad came out with my brothers, he rolled his eyes and brought the cake over. Together, they sang Happy Birthday to me and he served up the cake. My mom remained absent. The next morning when I got up for school, my dad was asleep in his chair.

Before leaving for school, it was my job to empty the dishwasher. Tim filled it and Kenny pushed the button to start it–he was my moms baby. That day he must have forgotten because when I went to empty it, all the dishes were still dirty. I was closing the machine back up, when my mom came out for coffee. She opened the dishwasher to get a mug and glared at me.

"Why isn't this already emptied?" She snapped.

"Because it's still dirty. I think Kenny forgot to start it?" I said.

"Bullshit!" She said, you didn't accuse her baby of anything.

"No, look. They're all dirty!" I argued, showing her a dish. That was my first mistake.

"I said empty it!" She yelled. I could see my dad sitting up in his chair, his newspaper shaking, but he never really crossed her. She could be manic and he knew it, so we never wondered why he didn't say much. No one, not even my dad wanted to deal with her wrath.

I wasn't going to argue further. Instead, I started to empty the dirty dishes into the cabinets while she grabbed a coffee mug from the cabinet. No sooner had she poured herself a cup, when she turned on me again.

"What the hell are you doing?" She screeched. "These dishes are dirty!"

"Mom, I just told you that!" I said, probably louder than I should have. But she was out of control. And that was it. She started punching me as hard as she could. She punched my arms, my face, my chest.

"Don't you talk back to me!" She yelled between punches. "You put dirty dishes in with the clean! Now you will take every single dish out of those cabinets and wash them all by hand!   Then dry them and put them all away! BEFORE SCHOOL!" The punches kept coming, in between her pulling stacks of dishes out of the cabinets and slamming them into the sink.

I guess that was the moment my dad finally had enough. Because from behind I saw him fly out of his chair and face her square on. He stared her down, and let her have it. And it was at this moment, I realized my parents' marriage was almost over.

"She tried to tell you the dishes were dirty! I heard her! And you insisted she put them away anyway. Now she will not be doing *any* dishes!" He turned to me and told me to go get ready for school. As he turned back to my mom, she looked as crazy as I had ever seen her. Picture *Cruella DeVille* in the cartoon *101 Dalmatians*! When she spoke again, my dad just stood there, unphased. Still she yelled.

"If you don't like the way I discipline your little princess, YOU deal with her!" That is exactly what I heard her say as I retreated to my room. After that day, my mom didn't speak to my dad for almost two weeks. Secretly, I think that made him happy. She didn't speak to me either and that definitely made *me* happy.

The next couple weeks were actually really nice. She didn't even talk to me at work. She would leave me notes with the things she wanted me to do, on them. My dad slept in his chair. I confided in Edna and Claude about what had happened on my birthday and they couldn't believe a grown woman would behave that way. Welcome to my world.

After the two weeks of hating us was over, she just started talking to both of us again. To this day, I have no idea who did the dishes that she had piled in the sink that morning. But after two weeks or so I came home and all of a sudden she was speaking to me again.

One of the first things she said was that she found me a car to buy when I turned 16. Now I had only just turned 15, but she didn't seem to care. She said it was a good deal and I needed to reimburse her what she paid for it. Then it would sit at my house, and she would drive it to and from work sometimes, until I got my license. My mother loved making deals that would benefit her. I think this was her way of not having to ride with my dad whenever she was mad at him. This was also about the time she started having her affair, though we wouldn't find out about it for a while yet. So somehow I bought and paid for my own mint green box car. I don't even know what kind it was, all I know is it was the lightest mint green, old and boxy. And it cost me $1000 from my savings.

As Claude and I got closer, so did Edna and I. Especially at work. We talked all the time. We ordered dinner at work every time we worked together. Eventually my dad even gave Claude a night job in the maintenance department. That meant we were always together. Claude and I went to school and then worked together. Edna worked her two jobs, one of which was with us. Plus we spent weekends together. It was around that time that Claude told me he loved me. I said it back but looking back, I didn't have a clue about love. I loved not being home. I loved the friend he was to me and I certainly loved his mother. But after so many bad experiences, I clung to the normalcy I had with them. But there were no butterflies. There was no great love story like I expected.

Someone should have told us we spent too much time together. No one ever did. Claude saw his friends and we were both still in **ROTC**, but even when we would skip school, we were together. On the rare occasion we wanted extra privacy, we would go to my house to skip. My parents were at work and even though his parents never cared if I was in his room, sometimes it was nice not to think that his parents knew what we were doing, when we were alone in his room. And they would have been right, because if we weren't having sex in his room, we were out playing games with his mom.

One day we skipped school and we parked at the end of my street until we were sure my parents had left for work. We were just hanging out when Claude suggested we try out my parents' waterbed. We no sooner got undressed and were climbing into the bed, when we heard a car pull up. In a panic we raced to put our clothes back on and hide.

My parents bedroom had once been a garage that the previous owners had turned into a bedroom, so their room was almost right next to the side door leading into the house. From there we could hear someone messing with the door and becoming agitated that it wouldn't open. My parents notoriously left our doors unlocked because we lived in a safe neighborhood, but whenever Claude and I were there on a skip day we always locked the door. I don't know why, maybe I thought it would give me a few extra minutes should someone come home. Up until that point no one ever had.

From the swearing I knew right away it was my mother. She was clearly pissed off that she couldn't get in. I am not sure if she just didn't have the house key on her, but she was not getting in. At one point I heard her mutter, "Fucking Kenny! I've told him a million times not to lock this door!"

I chuckled. Kenny was getting blamed and here I was on the other side of the wall, the real reason she couldn't get in. After a minute she went back to her car, and peeled out of the driveway. I assumed she was going back to get keys, so Claude and I wasted no time. We finished dressing and high tailed it out of there, leaving the door locked. We raced out the door, up the street and left in the opposite direction. We didn't laugh, or even breathe a sigh of relief until we made it safely to his parents house. And we never skipped at my house again. But that was mostly because of what happened next.

It was early spring, I remember not quite spring break. I had an afternoon off so I went to Claude's to hang out after school. We were in his room, about to fool around when my mother called his house. She had never done this before. I had actually forgotten she had his number. When I picked up the line I knew it was going to be bad.

She was speaking at me in a low growl, like one would if they were speaking through gritted teeth. She must have been at work, but did not want anyone to hear her. I asked her to repeat herself because she was impossible to understand the way she was speaking. I heard her office door close and then she let me have it.

"Get your ass home immediately! You are in so much fucking trouble. When I get a hold of you, I am going to kill you." She ground out, still gritting her teeth but louder and with an anger I had never heard before. And I was always the recipient of her anger. This time, I truly believe she was going to kill me. I mean what would be worse than having my head slammed into a wall? I had been beaten by her plenty of times. This time she said she was going to kill me. And I believed it.

I hung up the phone in pure panic. I did not want to go home. I was scared for my life. When I told Claude what she said, he started to laugh it off. But then he saw the sheer look of fear in my eyes. I kept saying I couldn't go home. I was in tears. I was terrified; hysterical. He offered to go with me.

I didn't even know what I had done at this point, but I agreed to let him go with me. She couldn't kill me with a witness. So he drove me home and we had barely walked in the door, when my brother announced that my mother was on the phone. She was checking to see if I was home yet. She wanted to speak to me.

Slowly I took the phone from him and put the receiver up to my ear.

"You are fucking lucky you are home you little bitch!" She screeched. "You wanna skip school? Just fucking wait til I get my hands on you. You wont need to worry about going to school. You will be fucking dead. I am on my way!"

Now when my mother said things, even things like that, based on her track record with me, I believed it. There is no doubt in my mind that if she had gotten ahold of me that night, in the state she was in, I would have been dead. Or at the very least beaten to near death. My dad wasn't home and I had about ten minutes before she would be pulling in. I was in full panic mode. I was hysterically crying and I didn't think about what I did next.

I told Claude we needed to leave. I couldn't stay. I was petrified of what she was going to do to me. I had seen her at her worst, she was violent no doubt, but this sounded scarier. The thing is, he believed it too. He didn't even question me after the second phone call. He loved me and he knew if I said I was dead, I was indeed going to be dead. He told me to grab some clothes, and any items I might need. He helped me throw the items in a bag and we were back out my door in under five minutes.

As we drove, I asked him where we were going. He said his house and immediately I said no way. She would find me there in no time and when she got her hands on me, that would be it.. He wouldn't be able to protect me there. I was a minor and if she wanted me home she could get me home. So we came up with a plan. We would go back to his house so he could pack a bag too. We would take his Aunt's car, and leave his. She never drove anymore and her car would be much better on gas than his boat. We were running away.

I waited in his car while he went inside. Edna was working. His dad was asleep. He packed a bag, took all the cash he had in his room, grabbed some drinks and snacks and left his mom a note. He explained briefly that he needed to get me away from my mom to keep me safe. There were no cell phones, so this was the only way he could let her know without tipping my own mother off.

We swapped cars and started driving. We were heading north, since that was the only way out of Florida and by the time we made it to the Georgia state line, it had been decided. We were driving to my sisters in New Hampshire. They could help me. They knew what she was like and I had no doubt they would help us. We ended up counting the money not long after we left. We didn't have debit cards. You couldn't just stop at an ATM like we can now. What we had on us was $137. And that needed to get us to New Hampshire. That needed to cover gas and food and a place to sleep. I couldn't drive yet and he couldn't do twenty-four hours driving without rest.

Somewhere in the Carolina's we stopped. I am not sure how long we had been driving but he could barely keep his eyes open. We found some sketchy looking motel off the highway that had a sign advertising $26 a night. It was dark and dingy but we were exhausted and it was all we could afford. The room was something I will never forget. It was anything but nice. The bed was made but the comforter had burn holes in it and the room smelled like mildew. I opened a closet door and the floor was made of dirt! There was a banana peel in the dirt and metal hangers bent and dangling. The place was disgusting but we had no choice. We had to stretch the money as far as it would go.

We laid on top of the covers and he held me as I cried myself to sleep. My whole life was changing again and I had no control over it. I shouldn't have skipped school. It was wrong. Most parents would ground their kids or punish them in one of the million other normal ways. Not my mother, my mother meant to beat me— possibly to death. She was that angry. I heard it in her voice. And she was crazy enough to do it too.

It wouldn't be the first irrational thing she did. When I was in first grade and my parents could no longer afford the horses and the big farmhouse, a mysterious barn fire occurred. We lost everything in the barn, including animals. But not the horses. The horses who would later be sold without us being able to say goodbye, would fetch a pretty penny. Many speculated quietly at how my Mom was the only one home when the fire happened and how the settlement helped us get out from under the weight of the crushing debt she created.

And who could forget how, when we first moved to Florida, and my Dad bought land and a brand new double wide in central florida—not the beach like she wanted—how the house mysteriously "blew up" minutes after we all left for work and school. The house was only 60 days old. We lost everything in that beautiful new home. Including my entire Cabbage Patch collection and my mother got her way. A job working directly on the beach in a hotel. Which is when this story started. But that was all hearsay. Still, thinking my mom would kill me. That wasn't a stretch.

After a few hours of sleep, I got up to pee. I swear, I saw a mouse scurry past. I screamed which woke Claude. He sat up in a panic. He obviously needed a minute to orient himself and remember where he was. Once he assured me the mouse was gone we both tried to lay down again. But the squeaking had us both wide awake in no time. The rest we had gotten would have to do. We washed our faces and hands, and headed out.

It took almost thirty six hours to get to New Hampshire with the stops. The first place we went was my sisters. I don't know why I thought they would be surprised to see me. My mom had already called them. I guess where I was going wasn't hard to figure out. She had us call Claude's mom and then she called my dad to tell him we were safe. I don't know what my mother said at the time. But later I learned she had wanted to call the police and Edna had convinced her not to. Claude was 18 and if arrested it would have been for transporting a minor across state lines. That would have meant he wouldn't be able to go in the Air Force. And so a deal was struck.

My belongings, all of them, were already packed in boxes. My mother had put them outside within hours of realizing I was gone. My dad had moved them all to the carport so they would be safe from the weather. He couldn't convince her not to pack up her fifteen year old child's belongings but she didn't touch them when he put them in the carport. Once the deal was struck, my dad helped to move me.

The deal was, if I would come back to Florida so Claude could finish highschool and go in the Air Force, I could move in with Edna and Claude. My mother was easily convinced to get rid of me. I shouldn't have been surprised. If I was going to go to the lengths of running away, she knew she could no longer put her hands on me.

But there was more to her deal. I needed to get a job and pay rent to Claude's parents. My mom needed her employees so she would graciously let me keep my job at the hotel. In fact we all could. She wanted no further parental responsibility for me. I would buy my own food and pay my own bills. I was on my own. It was that or be dead. I think I made the only choice I could. The fact that I was even given a choice like that at fifteen still baffles me today.

Chapter 11
1988
"Running Up that Hill"- Kate Bush

After the deal was made life changed for me. I had to support myself and pitch in on rent and utilities at Claude's house. I tried to stay in school, but after a month I couldn't keep up. Plus I missed more than two weeks of school and work during the time I was in NH, and I couldn't seem to catch up on all my work. So I quit school and started working full time. I was barely fifteen and no one stopped me. In fact, my mother used it to her advantage and scheduled me to work in the restaurant and sometimes with the maids too.

Claude, against his mothers wishes, quit too. He had fallen behind as well. But he still wanted to go in the Air Force, so he promised to go back part time the following year and graduate. He only needed four classes to finish. I, on the other hand, had only just begun high school and my only choice was to take the GED. Goodbye dreams of College. Goodbye dreams of being a lawyer. I was on my own in so many ways. I worked to survive. Thanks mom.

None of this made my father happy. However he was still married to my mother and we all knew what would happen if he crossed her. He was an older man now. In his late fifties, he had started having more heart issues. My mother, not even forty, had grown tired of her old husband. He was out of money and couldn't work as hard as he had when they were first together. The houses and cars he used to own, had all been sold for bigger and better. Instead of living out his later years in comfort for all his earlier hard work, he was doomed to keep on working. Keep on paying for more.

Until he couldn't anymore. That would happen later in the summer. But for now, he just kept on working hard. But his heart, I would learn much later, broke when all my dreams went out the window.

Oh and that car I had paid for? The one my mother said would be mine when I turned 16. Well she had that sold to a guy in the bar for what I had already paid her for it. She made double the profit and I never even got to drive it once. I believe it was sold before I even got back from New Hampshire with Claude.

Another Spring Break was upon us when I came back and there wasn't even time for me to mourn the loss of the rest of my childhood. I was working sixty hours a week. Edna took me to the places I needed to go. Work, the grocery store, even the doctors office. She taught me how to clip coupons and in no time I was a pro at knowing when it was double and even triple coupon days at *Publix* or the *Piggly Wiggly*.

I cooked what I could for Claude and I. I cleaned our two rooms. My parents thought I had my own room there. That is what Edna had told them. When in reality, even though we did have two rooms, one was our living room and one was our bedroom. We also had our own bathroom. I also helped clean the whole house so Enda didn't have to. I hated how it always smelled like cigarettes, so I would scrub and clean every chance I got. I loved the scent of Pine Sol and I purchased a bottle every time I had a coupon.

I didn't know how to cook very many things back then, but frozen meals were easier anyway. We practically lived on *Micro Magic* Burgers and Fries. It was all the rage back then, and they were cheap. Especially if you had a coupon. I still splurged and ate out with Edna and Claude at work, but I was more of a full time working house wife than anything else. The cleaning and extra money coming in, definitely made Edna happy. Plus I think she saw me as the daughter she never had. Even if I was paying to live there.

Besides learning how to coupon, I was also learning to pay bills. I budgeted my money and worked hard. I always said yes to overtime. When I wasn't at the front desk, I was waiting tables in the hotel restaurant. When I had free time, between tables, I always made my way into the kitchen. The cook, a younger guy named Grant, would teach me how to work the line. I enjoyed it but I liked the money in tips better.

Things between Claude and I were fine. There were no issues but there was no excitement either. Looking back, we were an old working couple before we knew each other a full year. We lived together, slept together, worked together. I had no teenage life anymore and I found I missed it. Especially when Summer was in full swing.

I found myself checking in gorgeous guys who were all in town for fun. I waited on them in the hotel restaurant. But I never got outside. I never made it to a beach party. I never got to have any fun of my own. In my off time, I was still playing board games with Edna. Claude retreated more often than not, to his room and his *Super Mario Bros.* I could feel myself slipping into depression but there was no way out of it. Not that I could see.

One night when I went to bed, Claude was still playing. It had been hours since Edna and I finished our latest board game. We had played that, cooked dinner-which he ate in front of the video game–cleaned up from dinner and watched TV. In all that time, Claude never once came out of the bedroom. By the time I was ready for bed, I was furious.

I came into the room, saw his empty dinner dish and immediately knew I was going to start a fight. So instead, I grabbed a pair of pajamas, didn't say a word and left the room again. In our living room, I changed into my pajamas and pulled the afghan down off the back of the old couch. I fluffed a throw pillow and shut off the lights, fuming. I tossed and turned for a long time before I finally drifted off. The worst part was he didn't even notice. Not for a few more hours anyway.

I woke up to him standing over me, the light from the hall streaming across my face. He looked worried.

"Are you ok? Why are you sleeping in here?" He asked as if he didn't have any idea.

"You were playing your game for hours and I wanted to go to bed."

"You could have told me."

"Like you would have noticed." I sat up now, annoyed.

"What do you mean by that?"

"You played that stupid game for almost ten hours."

"So what? You were playing a game with my mom."

"Yeah for an hour. You didn't even come out to eat dinner. And you didn't notice when I came in and got my pajamas. I am sick of having no life."

"You could have said you wanted to do something."

"And you could have spent some time with me."

He looked truly baffled and it was just making me madder. I rolled over so my back was facing him.

"Just go to bed. I will see you when we go to work tomorrow." I said sarcastically and ended the conversation by pulling the blanket up to my eyes.

He stood there for a minute. When he left the room, he slammed the door harder than he should have for the middle of the night. I didn't sleep the rest of the night. I couldn't. I tossed and turned trying to figure out how I ended up in this situation. I knew the events that led up to all of this, but I was mad at myself for letting it get this bad. More than once the thought crossed my mind that maybe I should have just seen if she really would have killed me. Maybe she wouldn't have, or maybe, just maybe being killed would have been better than the way I was living now.

A couple hours later, I dragged myself into the shower and when I was dressed for work, I headed out. I didn't want to wait for Claude, so I left him a note saying I was going in early and taking the bus. Edna was already gone to the bakery. The ride in to work was quiet and just what I needed. By the time I got there, I had calmed down and talked myself into having a good day.

I had time before my waitress shift started but I went to the restaurant anyway. I made myself a coffee and an English muffin and took it outside to sit on the beach. I had not been on the beach for pleasure in a long time. It was nice watching the tide coming in. There were couples waking up together and trash everywhere. A few city workers were still doing the nightly clean up.Still it was beautiful. The sun was up but there was a cool breeze and it put me at peace.

I was mad at Claude, but more than that I was mad at myself. I was not ready to give up my teen years, but it was already too late. My mom had seen to that and she had zero regrets about it. The way I saw it, I had two choices. I could feel sorry for myself or I could go after what I wanted. But I didn't even know what that was. I mean I knew there was more to life than work and sleep. I had experienced fun for a short time. But now that I was with Claude, I felt like that part of my life was over. He never really wanted to go on dates. He wasn't in school right now so all he wanted to do was work and play video games. I liked playing too, but not for hours on end. I needed more. I needed fun, and excitement. I needed to laugh and I needed friends my own age. I just needed to figure out how to make that happen.

After breakfast I went to work. That was something I had no choice in. Still, I went into the day with a positive attitude. When Grant came in, he noticed the change in me.

"I can't tell if you're in a good mood or bad mood. But you look different today." He said.

"Your guess is as good as mine." I laughed. He smirked. "I had a fight with Claude. But I feel better now."

"Did you make up?"

"Nope. Haven't even seen him yet today. I took the bus to work."

I was restocking my station and he was following me around doing the sugars. I don't know why I never realized how cute he was, but today he was very handsome. Tanned and blonde and very muscular. He looked concerned but also intrigued. Looking back, I think I just wanted attention. Any attention would have done.

"Wanna talk about it?" He asked.

"No. Yes. I don't know."

"Spill it." He said.

"I don't know. It's like we're barely a couple. We work all the time, when we get home, he's on his video games. We go to bed and start over the next day. I just feel like there should be more to us than that."

"Yeah you guys never go out with anyone from here either."

"Nope. We don't do anything."

"Well, go out with us." He said sincerely. "We go out almost every night after work."

"Claude would hate that." I said.

"So leave him home. You don't have to do everything together." Until he said that to me, the thought never occurred to me. I mean I lived with them, so to me that is where I needed to be all the time. But did I? I told him I would think about it.

When Claude got to work, he came into the restaurant. I was slammed with tables and really didn't have time to talk. But he stopped in anyway and cornered me out back.

"Why didn't you wait for me? What's going on?"

"I just needed some time to think."

"About what?"

"I don't know. I just feel like you are always on your game and we barely do anything besides work."

"Well that's because you moved out and quit school." He snapped.

I didn't have time to argue. But that comment made me want to rage.

"Yeah. You dropped out too."

"Only for now."

"Yeah, lucky you. Anyway, it would just be nice if we could do things besides sit around your house every single day." I said and started to walk away. He grabbed my arm and turned me to him.

"No one is stopping you." He said. But he knew exactly what was stopping me. Still, I took his words to my advantage.

"So you would be ok if I went out with people after work? You can come too, of course." I said.

"Not really my scene but yeah you can. Would you have a ride?" I'm not sure if he meant it as a dig, but it felt like one.

"Yeah. I'll figure it out." I said confidently. It was becoming a pissing contest and I had work to do, so I smiled and ended the conversation by telling him to have a nice day and kissing him on the cheek.

I felt lighter that day, and when I left the restaurant and headed to the front desk for the second shift, Grant and some of the others had made plans to hang out after work. Grant said he would swing by the front desk at 10pm and grab me before they headed out. When they did, Edna gave me a questioning look, but I just said I would see her at home. I wasn't going to let anyone make me feel guilty about living.

That night, and several other nights over the next two weeks, I attended beach parties, concerts and acted like the kid I was. I had a blast. The other waitresses were so fun to hang out with and Grant was always making me laugh. I was able to blow off steam, and not think about work, bills and everything I lost. And still went home every night and climbed into bed next to Claude. But for those couple hours each night, I felt free.

And then one night after a couple weeks of happiness, Claude decided to let his real feelings be heard. I had just come home. It was well after 3am. I was crawling in next to him, but before I could lay down, he sat up and turned on me.

"How long is this going to go on for?" He snapped.

I was startled and at first I didn't even know what he meant. So I just looked at him blankly.

"No answer?" He snapped again.

"I don't know what you're even talking about." I said. I had had a few drinks and focusing was not high on the things I could do right then.

"Going out after work. I never even see you."

"Well you never saw me when I was here and you played video games all night either. Plus, I told you that you could go out with us. Or hell, you could just take me out yourself!"

"When? You go out with them practically every night."

"Did you ask to take me out?" I snapped back now.

"No, because apparently I am just the person you live with now."

"That is bullshit!"

"Is it? It doesn't seem like bullshit. It seems like you are just using me for a place to live." He spat out. And that stung. Maybe because part of it was true. We didn't act like a couple anymore. At least not a young couple who had been dating less than a year. And what if it was true that I stayed with him because I had nowhere else to go? Thanks again Mom.

"I don't know what you want from me Claude. I work doubles all week, I either come home here and I am alone, even with you right here. I have the chance to go out and act my age and that makes you mad. I can't win." And just like it always happened, I started to cry. Whenever I was mad, the tears fell. I hated that. It felt like a weakness to me. But I was in way over my head. I was having big grown up relationship issues when I should have been studying for some english exam or doing a history project.

"I just want to see you once in a while. I want to feel like you're not just using me for a roof over your head."

To me, that was a low blow. It's not like I didn't come home to him every night. Even had sex with him, if it was what he wanted after I came in late. I still made his lunches and cooked his dinners when I was home. I still cleaned the whole house and paid to live there. Using him was not what I was doing. And for him to suggest that made me so angry. But since I had nowhere else to go, I decided that I couldn't keep this fight going either. He was angry with me and didn't see things from my perspective. He was eighteen. He had gotten his whole childhood. I had not. So once again, I grabbed my pillow and went to sleep in our living room. The couch was uncomfortable but it was better than staying with him when he was being hurtful.

"Sure, run away. You do that best" He said to my back as I walked out of the room. I didn't look back. I wouldn't give him the satisfaction of seeing me cry harder.

I didn't know how to deal with these types of fights so the next day, I was gone again before he got up. I went to work and tried to pretend everything was ok. But Grant could see right through me. Before we even opened for breakfast I had spilled my guts to him and waited for advice. He was around Claude's age, maybe a bit older. I wanted to hear his take on it. His advice was just what I needed to hear.

"Babe, he is just jealous. He wants to keep you all to himself. He wants you to be his dutiful girlfriend. Wait on him hand and foot. If anyone is using anyone, he is using you." He told me. He told me everything I wanted to hear. He held my hand and made me feel like I wasn't crazy.

Looking back, I am sure there was more than a little bit of method to the way he treated me. But I was way too naive to see it. What I saw was someone who understood my need to still be young and not tied down. And he made me feel young, and pretty. Not like the old lady I was becoming at fifteen.

Still, I almost passed on going out that night, but Grant wouldn't hear of it. He told me if I skipped it, Claude would know he had won and could control me, so I stuck with my plans to go out! I didn't see Claude at work at all that day, but I heard he was there. Edna was off. She didn't work most weekends because those were busy at the bakery. Thankfully I didn't have to face her either. Each night, when I said I didn't need a ride home, I saw the look of disappointment and judgment. I was relieved not to see it today. And as a bonus, Claude didn't even stop by after work to see if I needed a ride home from him. That told me all I needed to know.

So off I went with the gang from work. Tonight was a house party in a townhouse on the beach. I don't even know whose house it was, I just know someone in our group was invited and they took the rest of us. We hung out on the beach where there was music, drinks, dancing and even a little volleyball in the dark. I had played in Middle School and I was pretty good, so I joined the first game I could.

Grant, seeing me out there, joined too. He was on my team and for two games we dominated. Before we could start a third, he asked me if I wanted to take a walk to the water. I was hot so we resigned and let others who were waiting take our place. The house had a spotlight that pointed out to the water and since the tide was in, you could just see the start of the water. We walked down and put our feet in, hoping to cool off after sweating for two games.

"That was fun. I haven't played Volleyball in so long"

"It was. You're pretty good" He complimented me.

"Hey you're not so bad yourself." I bent down and put my hands in the water. I think he thought I was going to splash him, because he quickly squatted and splashed me. Only I had no intention of splashing him—until he did it to me! Then I let him have it. We laughed and he chased me, catching me and then tripping and pulling us both into the water. We were soaked and laughing so hard.

"I wasn't even going to splash you," I said, struggling to breathe while laughing.

"Well you looked guilty and I couldn't take a chance!" He laughed.

"Now we're both soaked!" I pointed out.

"So we are," he said, moving on top of me. His voice had turned husky. My head was in the sand and he slid a hand under it, pulling me closer. The kiss happened before I even had a minute to think. It was a nice kiss. Soft and searching. He was gentle, his lips soft and warm. I didn't stop him. I didn't even try to. Instead I leaned up into the kiss, encouraging it to continue.

In the movies, we see people making love in the surf. I bet a lot of people think that doesn't really happen in real life. But for me it did. Right there in the surf. Grant undressed me slowly. He took his time, exploring my body. The moonlight and the soft glow of the spotlight beam, let me see him and he saw me. When he took my hard nipple in his mouth, I felt like someone was lighting fireworks inside my body.

He reached down between my legs and rubbed me gently. Everything was happening, but it was at a snail's pace and the more he made me wait, the more I wanted it. No one, not even Eric, or Adam had taken so much time with me. He was not in any hurry. When he slipped a finger inside me, I think I shocked both of us by coming instantly. One finger was all it took. And yet I wanted more.

I grabbed him and stroked him. He was rock hard and I wanted to put him in my mouth, but he wouldn't take any of my hints. Instead, he kissed the length of me and went down on me, right there in the sand. He spread my legs and his mouth was on me, warm and wet. The ripples of waves lapped at my body as he did things with his tongue, I didn't even know could be done. As my orgasm built, so did my moans. Part of me was certain they could hear me up at the house and the other part of me didn't care if they could.

I came again, and before I could even wrap my head around that, he was back on me and moving inside of me. He was pushing into me, slowly. He had a slow rhythm and I matched him easily. He was kissing me and touching me, as if he had extra arms I didn't know about. It was so hot and so unexpected. The water, the breeze, the moonlight. This time, only he came, but when he did, he let out a loud moan that there is no way everyone didn't hear up at the house. Even with the music, the partying and the laughter. It was the sound of pure pleasure.

The whole thing was almost perfect. Almost, because right after he came, he also yelped in pain. I was going to ask what happened when I felt my own stinging pain and yelped as well. And this is why people having sex in the surf in movies is unrealistic. Because in movies, no one gets stung by a jellyfish. And that is exactly what happened to both of us.

We both jumped up, the moment lost by the pain of the sting. Both of us grabbing a leg, both with red raised bumps and searing with pain. I wanted to be mad that the stupid jellyfish had ruined such a perfect moment, but then I felt something warm running down my leg and it immediately dawned on me that, not only had I just had sex with a guy who wasn't my boyfriend, but he had cum in me and had definitely not used protection. So now I was in pain, and mad that I had been so stupid. That we had both been so stupid.

The night ended nothing like it started. We rinsed the sting as best as we could, before ringing out and trying to shimmy back into our wet clothes. We barely spoke, the pain was almost unbearable. We snuck out through someone else's property and found his car on the street. The others would need to find a new ride home. He didn't seem concerned by that. Before he dropped me off, he told me I should take a baking soda bath when I got inside and take some ibuprofen. But he didn't mention what we had just done, and he didn't kiss me goodbye, or even say he had fun with me. I don't know what I expected but it wasn't that.

I took the hottest shower I could, then soaked into a cool baking soda bath. I took some ibuprofen and without even looking at the bedroom door, I snuck into our living room, for another night on the couch. There was no way I could face Claude after what I had done, and besides I was still in pain. I eventually fell into a fitful sleep, but it wasn't all bad because more than once I woke up from a dream replaying our lovemaking on the beach. What had I done, and what was I going to do about it now?

Chapter 12
1988
"Love Bites"- Def Leppard

It isn't like I didn't feel guilty about what I had done. I did. It was wrong and I knew it. But I felt very trapped. Claude was good to me. For the most part. But he just wasn't that into me. And I guess I wasn't that into him either. We had a friendship, and he didn't make my skin crawl when we had sex, but there was no thrill. It shouldn't have been like that after such a short time. And here I was sort of trapped. There was definitely some truth in what he had said to me. I didn't have anywhere else to go. But I also wasn't a freeloader who was using him. I pulled my weight. I worked, I kept the house clean, and I paid my share.

There were many times while living there that I did way more than my fair share. For instance, Claude and his family had a dog. His name was Rusty. He was a German Shepherd. He had been with them since Claude was a small boy and they brought him when they moved from New York. He wasn't my dog and I certainly hadn't bonded with him. To me, he was kind of a nuisance because no one seemed to particularly like him, he was often just in the way, and no one cleaned up after him. He left dog hair all over everything, which I cleaned. If he had an accident in the house, everyone pretended not to notice. Eventually, they knew I wouldn't be able to stand it. A clean house was drilled into me. My mom had us cleaning from the time we could hold a sponge. So it was always me that cleaned up after Rusty and his never ending accidents. He was old too, so the accidents came more and more frequently.

One time, not long after the first time I slept with Grant—yes it happened more than once—I came home from work, to find Edna crying. When I asked what happened, she said Rusty had died. I felt sad for her, but I wasn't sad for me. Until I got more of the details.

She said that he had been sick during the night so after we all left for work, she had locked him up in mine and Claude's bathroom. She said she hoped it would contain the mess to one area. And it had, but he had gotten so sick that he had vomited and pooped himself to death. Back in the eighties, people didn't rush their pets to the vet unless it was serious. To me this was serious, but I understood why they hadn't. He was old, his time was up. Still, I wondered if they might have been able to help him, even if it did result in a huge vet bill. I knew Edna couldn't afford that so I just listened as she told me the story.

I asked what they did with him. She started to tell me that Eddie had taken him outside and buried him in the backyard. Claude was coming into the room, and I looked to see if he was upset. He showed no emotions. I was sure he knew but it didn't look like he had been crying or anything.

"The problem," Edna was saying. "Is that I cannot bring myself to go in there now. It breaks my heart to think of his last moments like that. But that bathroom needs to be cleaned. It's everywhere." She said matter of factly. I looked at Claude again to see his reaction. Stone Faced he said nothing.

"So our bathroom?" I already knew the answer. Claude grabbed a drink and started leaving the room. He had barely talked to me in a couple weeks and I was still sleeping on the couch.

"Yeah. I am sorry, but one of you is going to have to clean it before you can use it." Edna said, adding a sob for effect.

"Claude, did you know about this?" I asked. And as if my body knew what was going on, I suddenly had to pee. It had been hours since I went at work. Isn't that always the way?

He just shrugged. I was furious.

"So I suppose you expect me to clean it?" I said glaring at him. Again he shrugged.

"I wouldn't even know where to begin." He said. "I'll just pee outside."

"Maybe pick a corner? And figure it out? This is crazy. He wasn't *my* dog." I said, and I didn't care if it sounded cold. This was insane. It was unbelievable. But it was my reality.

At first I wasn't going to do it. In fact, I stormed off to our living room and paced. I contemplated peeing my pants before I would clean that bathroom. An hour went by and I listened to see if anyone else would go and clean it. The only sound I heard was Claude going to the bedroom and the video games turning on. Then I heard Edna close herself in her room. She and Eddie had their own bathroom. Claude's aunt did too. Claude had already said he would pee outside so if it was going to get done, and it had to get done, I was going to have to be the one to do it.

That day I was so angry, so sad, and hysterical as I wrapped a handkerchief around my nose and mouth, tied my hair back and opened the door. What I saw was absolutely disgusting. Diarrhea and vomit on almost every surface and covering the lower half of the walls. Part of me thought I should feel bad that Rusty died such a horrible death, but I was too pissed off to even think about that. This was a new low for me, and I cried the entire time I cleaned. I spent hours in there, first using roll after roll of paper towel to clean up all the messes. There were two trash bags full of dirty paper towels by the time I moved on to other cleaning. I used a bottle of bleach first and with yellow rubber gloves, I bleached every surface from ceiling to floor.

When that was done, I felt so sick. My throat burned from the straight bleach and I still had to pee so bad. The final step, when I was sure I had killed every germ, was the pine sol. I used two full bottles. I filled the tub with the two bottles and hot water. Then I took a bunch of rags and went over every surface again. More than once. When I was sure the bathroom was sterile–finally being able to pee and shower–I was exhausted. I went into our living room and closed the door. I no sooner did that, when I heard Claude leave his room and close the bathroom door. There isn't a strong enough word for how mad that one action made me. I didn't think I had anymore tears to cry but they came. They came hard, and they didn't stop until I had cried myself to sleep.

That is why no one could ever accuse me of being a user. I pulled more than my weight. I made sure of it. And no one would ever be able to say I wasn't a hard worker. I showed them. Not that they cared. At this point it was expected.

In the days that followed, Edna did thank me for taking care of the bathroom. Like I'd had a choice in the matter. And Claude did too. But only after he started getting the feeling he might lose me. It was actually a good week after the incident. I continued to take the bus to work and I didn't talk to him. I hadn't gone out with my work friends since the night with Grant, but I also didn't hang out with Claude either. I cooked dinner, did my chores and came into our living room every night after work and went straight to bed.

Then my day off arrived and I didn't spend it with either Edna or Claude. I knew I was taking a chance that they would tell me I needed to move out, but I strongly doubted it. They had a paying tenant who cooked and cleaned. I felt I had the right to be angry with both of them and I think they knew it too.

So on my day off I went to the beach. Alone, I laid in the sun. I read, and swam and tried to think about my life and the choices I was making. I never had time to think of a future, I just lived one day at a time. No matter how much thinking I did, I couldn't see any way out of the situation I was in now.

After a day of swimming and relaxing, I used an empty room to shower and change. It was almost dark when I emerged on the pool deck and found Grant looking around.

"Hey!" he said when he saw me. He looked adorable, his blonde hair mussed and his blue eyes sparkling. We had barely talked since that night. We had to talk at work but that was the extent of it. Until tonight. "I heard you were here."

"Yeah. I had the day off and I don't want to be at home."

"Wanna hang out with me? We could go back to my place."

Now I did want to do that. Very much. But I was also tired of being used for sex. Even really good sex. So I shook my head.

"I was gonna grab some dinner, I haven't eaten much today." I said and I could tell that wasn't the answer he expected.

"Well, let's go grab some dinner and take it back to my house. I rented a couple movies." Then he paused. "I'm not trying to get you back in bed if that's what you're thinking."

I smiled. "You sure about that?"

"I'm not saying it wouldn't be fun. But that isn't why I came looking for you. I really just wanted to talk to you about the other night."

So I agreed to go with him. I climbed into his car and I didn't care who saw me. Most people knew I couldn't drive so me catching a ride with just about anyone at work was not really suspicious.

He took me to a local pizza place where we both ordered calzones before heading back to his apartment. I knew he had a roommate but I didn't see anyone when we got there. He invited me to sit on his lumpy sofa and poured me a coke. He put on *Fatal Attraction* and even though I hadn't seen it, I gave him a sarcastic look.

"It's just what I picked. Stop reading into things. Before the other night, we were friends."

"I know we were. But then I cheated on my boyfriend with you and here I am at your apartment, behind his back again. Just kind of a weird coincidence that you picked this movie."

"I didn't even know I was going to have you over. You want to watch something else?" he asked.

"No, but since you brought it up, can we talk about what happened on the beach?" I asked.

"Can we eat first? You said you were hungry and I am starving." I conceded and we started the movie. As it turned out, we didn't talk until the movie was over. We were both really into it. And I wondered if it was even going to happen, when he pulled me close to him, after we finished eating. But pulling me close was all he did. He put his arm around me and held me gently, while we watched the movie. And when it was over, he got up to clean up our trash and refill our drinks.

"Are you avoiding the conversation?" I asked when he handed me a fresh glass of coke. "You're the one who said you wanted to talk about it in the first place."

"I do. I just don't know what to say. I mean I wanted it to happen, and it seemed like you did too." He sat down. "I'm not sorry about it."

"I'm not sorry about it either." I said honestly. "Well, I wish we had used protection. But that's my only regret."

He blushed. "Sorry about that. I didn't do a whole lot of thinking at that moment."

"Neither did I."

"Does Claude know?"

"No! And I have no intention of telling him. I hope that isn't your plan" For a minute I was a little panicked.

"No. I mean. I wouldn't do that to you."

"Thank you. Because I have nowhere else to go if I am being honest."

"Pretty shitty reason to stay with someone, isn't it?"

"Yeah. But that's the road I chose I guess."

"It's not too late to change the road."

"I wish that were true. But not too many people want to take in a fifteen year old high school dropout."

"You're more than that." His words were nice. I wish I had believed them back then. But I didn't and I didn't want to hear pretty words.

My life was what it was, and there was, in my mind, no way to change that. So instead of finishing the conversation with him, I leaned in and kissed him.

That was all he needed for an invitation. He took my hand, and led me to his bedroom. And that was the first time I didn't go home to Claude's–my house. Grant was always a gentleman with me. He led me to his bed and let me sit. He stood in front of me and kissed me gently, holding my head in my hair.

He kissed me like that for a long time. I didn't want it to stop. It felt nice. I didn't need, or even want sex at this point. What I really wanted was intimacy. I wanted to be held, and touched. I wanted to be told that everything was going to be ok. But back then, sex always came with intimacy and I took what I could get.

Just like on the beach, he didn't rush things with me. He gently laid me back and we kissed and touched for the longest time. It seemed to go on and on and I didn't want it to end. The only reason we moved on was because the more we kissed, the more I wanted it to keep going. I started kissing him back, more forcefully. I kissed down his neck and across his chest. I unbuttoned his shirt and ran my nails across his skin and scratched his back hungrily.

Little did I know then, those things drove him wild. He could control himself until I did things like that and then he wanted more too. He pulled off my clothes, and I helped him out of his. He grabbed a condom from his drawer this time, and when he entered me it was as good as I remembered it on the beach. It felt amazing and I matched his thrusts with my own. He took his time and I knew he was waiting for me, but I couldn't bring myself to fake it with him. Internal orgasms didn't happen for me, not during intercourse, but everything he was doing felt incredible so when he came I grabbed him and helped him bury himself deep inside me.

For someone so young, I was learning what men liked and I used those things. With Grant I did it because I wanted him to feel as special as he made me feel. He made me feel wanted and that is exactly what I needed. But he was disappointed I didn't come with him. He didn't say anything, but when he was done, he slipped quietly under the covers and covered me with his mouth. He did amazing things with his tongue on me. And he didn't return to the pillow until I came and cried out loudly. When he rejoined me he pulled me into his arms again and we both fell asleep.

We made love three or four times that night. I lost track of how many times we started and stopped. Every time I thought we were done, he would wake me again a short time later and we would go at it again. In the morning, I surprised him by waking him, by giving him head. He seemed to enjoy being woken up like that, so much so that we ended up in various positions, giving and receiving oral to each other for a long time until we both came once more and only then we finally really slept.

 We slept so long that I was late for work and so was he. I was worried about the two of us showing up together, but he came up with a story that he had picked me up, his car got a flat and we were stranded until AAA got there. As it turned out, no one even asked. And Claude, it seemed as if he had no idea I had never come home. I guess he just thought I was in the living room where I had been for a couple weeks. And since he didn't check on me there, he wouldn't know if I came home or not. It was the perfect set up, until it wasn't.

Chapter 13
1988
"Forever Young"- Rod Stewart

As the days went by, I was happy again. I felt young again, even though I still had to do adult things. I looked forward to work because it got me out of the house and I met lots of people both in the restaurant and at the front desk. Plus, I knew I could go out with friends, and more importantly, Grant after work. Claude and I hadn't really made up, but he did try to go out of his way to be nice to me. Ever since I cleaned up after his dead dog. He made sure he was up to drive me to work and he didn't give me a hard time about the amount of nights I went out with people from work. I think he could see that I was distant, and he was sort of trying to bring me back in.

I don't think he had any clue that I had stayed at Grant's more than once since that first time. He also didn't ask me to come into the bedroom. I think he was trying to work his way back into my good graces before he did that. There was definitely a wedge between us, but I don't think he ever thought it was irreparable. In his mind, I was staying with him because I had nowhere else to go. And he was right, sadly. I couldn't be certain but I also think Edna told him to give me some space. She had gotten used to the extra money I brought in, as well as all the cleaning I took off her plate. She never commented about me going out either.

Around Halloween, everyone from work started talking about attending this big Costume Party, one of the local rich kids was throwing. Even though I didn't want Claude to go, which was awful of me, I thought it would be wrong not to invite him. After all, he was still my boyfriend. Grant and I did a good job keeping whatever it was we were doing a secret from most. We never labeled it, but we both knew how the other felt. Those that might suspect something was going on with us, wouldn't say anything because no one wanted to lose Grant's friendship. He was truly a good person and he was very well liked by just about everyone.

On the way to work one morning, I decided to ask Claude about the party. It was the right thing to do.

"Jaret and Mandy are throwing this big costume party on Halloween at their parents house." I said excitedly.

"Oh yeah," He said. He was barely awake. Maybe if he didn't stay up all night on his game, he could be more of a morning person. But he did get up and went to school the work every day, so I couldn't complain about that. Now that it was fall, he was back in the school with the school-work program. He only had to take two classes per semester and he would graduate in June. He was done each morning by 9:30 and then he went to work for my dad. My dad would sign off that he was there and if he did everything right, he could graduate in the spring and be free to enlist in the Air Force. Sometimes I found myself envious of this. But for me to do it I would be twenty before I graduated. It just made more sense to get the GED. I didn't need a diploma for the military. Still I resented the fact that he could stay in school and I couldn't. He didn't even like school. But I would calm myself by promising that as soon as I could, I would take college classes and get a degree, even if it wasn't a law degree.

"I was thinking it would be fun to go. Maybe even dress up as some famous couple?" Doing a couple theme costume had always sounded like fun to me. My parents had done it at the V.F.W. a few times. They always seemed to have a blast together on those nights.

"Eh. I don't know. Those things really aren't me." He said. I should have known that would be his answer. It was always his answer. And while I was disappointed because I really did want a boyfriend who wanted to do things with me, I was also secretly relieved. I didn't want to have to avoid Grant all night. So I let the subject go. I didn't complain, but I didn't say anything back either. Eventually the silence must have gotten to him because as we pulled up for him to drop me off, he brought it up again.

"You can go if you want to. It's just not something I want to do."

Now, I planned on going. I didn't need his permission. But I was glad we didn't need to fight about it.

"Awesome. Guess I better come up with a costume."

"What about *Princess Peach*?" He said as I was gathering up my bag and purse to get out of the car. Of course he would pick a video game character.

"The only way you would see me in a costume from *Mario Brothers,* is if you were gonna go as *Mario.* That's not *my* thing." I said, using his own excuse against him. "See you when you get back to work." I said getting out and closing the door so he couldn't say anything else.

In the end, I went alone and was not any stupid video game character, though I did see a few that night, including *Princess Peach.* I decided to go as *Cyndi Lauper.* It was fun spraying my hair with all the funky colors and teasing it up like crazy. I clipped it randomly and teased it more. I put thick blue eyeshadow on, and eyeliner that looked like I painted it on with a small paint brush. I loaded both arms up with colored rubber bracelets, and picked a ripped, black lace, off the shoulder top and black lace skirt with sheer black panty hose. I got the craziest black and silver heeled boots and put scrunchies on my ankles. Even Claude let out a low whistle when he saw me.

"I almost wish I was going. You look great." He said. It was the nicest thing he had said in a long time.

"It's not too late." I said knowing he wasn't going to all of a sudden say he was coming.

"Nah. Just go and have fun."

"I will. I may not come home. If everyone is too drunk to drive, I'll just crash there. I have tomorrow off." I said.

"Ok well if you need a ride, call me. I will sleep with the cordless next to me and hopefully I will wake up when you call." He said. He was a deep sleeper; it was unlikely he would. But it also occurred to me that would probably be his excuse anyway, because he would probably be up all night with his games all night. Still, the gesture was nice.

Grant and a few others picked me up and they all commented on how great I looked. Grant was dressed like *Brett Michaels* and he looked hot. Surfer boy turned rock star. I couldn't say it out loud, especially not in front of *Princess Leia* and *Han Solo*. See, now there was a couple who knew how to celebrate Halloween. We picked up another girl, dressed as *Barbara Eden's*, *I Dream of Jeannie*. I couldn't help but notice how all the guys took in her beauty. I would be jealous if I had any right to be. But I didn't. I was at a party, drooling over a guy who was not my boyfriend. Just someone I was sleeping with behind my sort of boyfriend's back. Because let's be real, Claude and I had stopped acting like a couple for a while now.

The worst part of that was that since we had been sleeping together, I hadn't had my period. There was time, at least I thought there was. I wasn't really sure. But I was starting to worry that when we had been careless on the beach, I was going to find myself in even more trouble. I hadn't mentioned it to Grant. There was no reason to, until I knew for sure.

At the party, there were so many people in costume. The house, the pool deck, and even the beach below, was packed with people, loads of alcohol and some of the best costumes the eighties had to offer. A few that I remember were, *John Travolta, The Pink Ladies, Elvis, The T Birds, Ronald Reagan*, a few princesses, a slutty nurse, a *Freddy, Jason, Michael Myers*, and even a plain old sheet ghost. The host of the party was in a *Garfield* costume and he strutted around eating a pan of lasagna.

I had the best time that night. I danced with a bunch of the girls, I drank-way too much–spiked orange punch and laughed until my sides hurt. When a slow song finally started, I went to sit and get some rest. Grant had other plans. Before I could sit, he grabbed my hand and pulled me back up, to dance with him.

I started to protest, but he pulled me close and we started swaying back and forth to the *Pop Princess* herself, Cyndi Lauper. *Time after Time* blasted from the speakers.

"Look, they're playing your song," he teased, smiling down at me. I should have been concerned that someone would see us being a little too friendly, but I wasn't. I was way past drunk and people looking at us was so far from my mind. Especially when Grant was holding me so tight. It felt amazing. Yet somehow, I knew it wouldn't last. Nothing with me ever lasted. At least not things that made me happy. So I took it all in, while also waiting for the floor to crash out from under me.

When the song ended, I took his hand and led him outside. We walked across the pool and down the stairs. I didn't stop until we were out on the beach. I knew we were both walking, in a way that would fail even the easiest sobriety test, but I didn't care. We weaved through people in costumes and when we got to an area, shrouded in darkness, I turned and kissed him. Something about him made me feel so good and brave. He made me feel so free, and I couldn't keep my hands off of him.

After a few minutes of kissing, I pulled a little bit away from him, and without even thinking I blurted out, "I think my periods' late."

I thought he was going to balk at what I said and I regretted the words as soon as I said them. It was true about word vomit being something that really happened when people drank too much. I had just proven it. But he didn't freak out. He didn't even look upset. He just kissed me again. And then he held me against him.

"Let's just wait and see what happens." He whispered in my ear before kissing me again and again. It was the reassurance I needed. I was no longer afraid.

That night, we stayed on the beach all night. At some point, he ran to his car and grabbed two blankets and brought them down to where I waited on the sand. He laid one out and covered us with the other. He didn't try to have sex with me. He just held me. He held me all night long, and didn't let go until a long time after the sun came up. We knew people saw us and we didn't care. It was one of the most special nights I'd had in my short life. I didn't want it to end, mostly because I knew I was falling in love with Grant. I never wanted that feeling to end. So I stayed in his arms as long as he would let me that night, and into that morning.

Sometimes during that perfect night, he would wake up and kiss my head gently. Other times he would pull me close and hold me tighter against him. I responded by kissing his chest, or running my hand up his side. The feel of his skin was warm and sandy. Everything was just as it should be. Just two eighties rockers, holding on for dear life. And that is still how I remember that night, to this day. Because by the next evening, he would be gone.

The way I heard it, he was crossing Atlantic Avenue. He had run into an *Ocean Pacific* surf shop and was crossing back over to his car, when some tourist, who wasn't paying attention, looked at his radio for a split second, and ran him over. He was dead on the scene. At least that's what I was told. I think.

That day was and still is one that was so dark, I don't know what I heard and what I made up in my mind. All I know is, the one person who made me happiest in life was gone. Dead. Life over at the young age of 19. I couldn't and still cant think of him as anything but *Forever Young*. That song guts me every time I hear it, even now. I blamed myself. And why shouldn't

I? Trauma and bad things followed me around at every turn. This was just one more devastation in the life I was leading.

Chapter 14
1988
"What are you Doing New Year's Eve?"- The Carpenters

The days that followed Grant's accident were the absolute worst for me. For one thing, I had to mourn like a friend, and not like someone who was head over heels in love with him. That meant a lot of crying done in private. And not that I wanted a different outcome, because I was way too young to have a baby, but I started my period on the morning of the funeral. Of all days. The one thing that would have connected me to him forever, gone. I no longer had to worry about what would happen if I was pregnant. Instead I now mourned the fact that no one would ever know what it was like to have Grant as a father. Grant's whole life and the one that could have been, was over. Just like that. That thought made me sad for a whole new set of reasons. Deluded yes, but I was young and broken.

The day of the funeral I was hoping Claude would stay home. As it turns out, so many people from work wanted time off of the funeral, that Claude and Edna both volunteered to work so others could attend. My mother didn't go either and I was glad, but also thought it was lousy that as the general manager of the hotel, she didn't attend. There was a wake, but because of the accident, the casket was closed. I would never see his sweet face again, except in my memories.

I never thought much about meeting his parents but I certainly never imagined it would be at his funeral. An attractive middle aged couple, both crippled with grief, accepted condolences from a sea of people. I offered mine, and then immediately felt sick. I spent the rest of the wake sitting on the back steps, until everyone was gone. Even my ride was gone when I came out but I didn't care. In fact, I didn't look for the nearest bus stop either. Instead I made the three mile walk home.

At the funeral, I sat near the back but I stayed with the group from the restaurant. I know I was sobbing but I couldn't help. My feelings for Grant were a secret to most and the fact that I was sure he loved me too, but no one else knew it, made me feel invisible in my grief. That is until one of our friends, *Princess Leia* as a matter of fact, grabbed my hand and squeezed as the casket was taken from the church. She didn't let go. Even after others were leaving the church, she stayed by my side, gripping my hand warmly. When we were mostly alone, she turned to me and hugged me tight. I needed that hug so much, and I hugged her back, letting myself sink in her arms as I cried like I had never cried before. Then, just before she started to release me, she whispered to me softly.

"He thought you were something special. Don't ever doubt that. Carry that with you wherever you go in life. You made him happy. Grieve him, but don't stop living, he wouldn't want that for you." Her voice was so soft, like a blanket covering me in my grief.

I wonder if she knows how much those words meant to me on that day. Or how many times I have played them over in my mind. How much they still mean to me all these years later. Those words gave me strength so many times. But in those early days they allowed me to really grieve. And boy did I grieve.

I took a week off, and no one questioned it. A lot of his friends took extra days off, so it didn't seem suspicious. Not even my mother questioned me about it. The first few weeks, if I wasn't at work, I was on the couch crying. I let my cleaning and cooking suffer but Claude never said anything. I honestly don't know what he thought about how hard I was taking the loss. I sometimes wondered if he even noticed. Even if my eyes were red and swollen every time he saw me.

It was almost thanksgiving before I agreed to do anything outside of the house and that was only because my sister, her husband and their kids were coming to visit from New Hampshire. Because of that, I agreed to have

Thanksgiving dinner at my parents house. I needed to see my sister. I could, hopefully confide in her what I was feeling, and I needed that. Desperately. They arrived the day before and I told Claude, who agreed to come for dinner too, that I just wanted to go visit with them before the big day. I said something to him about sister bonding and he dropped me off at my parents that afternoon.

As it turned out, she knew something was wrong the minute she saw my face. How Claude and others closest to me didn't see it, I would never know. Or maybe they did but they didn't know how to deal with it. My pain was raw and my heart was broken. That day, she left the kids with my brother in law and she walked the beach with me while I spilled everything. She was quiet and let me talk. She didn't judge me. But when I was done, she hugged me tight. She told me she was sorry and let me cry it out one more time. Then she hit me with some tough questions.

"So if you were in love with Grant, what does this mean for you and Claude?" She asked as we started the long walk back.

"I don't know. He's more a friend than a boyfriend at this point. It wasn't like that in the beginning but it feels that way now. It has for a long time."

"And you feel trapped? Like you have nowhere else to go?" She asked bluntly. Somehow she just got it. Maybe because she had been pregnant at 16, married the father immediately and divorced him after the birth of their third child. Or maybe because my mom had forced that marriage on her and she knew exactly what it felt like to be trapped. She was remarried now, and happy. But she had been there.

"Yeah. I mean I love Edna. And I thought I loved Claude. At one point I did. I think. But how could I love him and love Grant too?"

"Because you are way too young to be dealing with all these grown up emotions." She blurted out. "And our fucking mother sucks."

I laughed because she never mixed words.

"Yes she does."

"If you need to come home, we will make it happen. You can maybe live with us or Trisha."

"Really?" I asked even though I knew the last thing she probably wanted in her new marriage was her baby sister moving in.

"Yes. Of course. Think about it."

She had extended an olive branch. For the first time, I had hope for my future. Maybe I didn't need to stay with Claude. The only problem was what happened the very next day. It's funny how fast hope can be dashed.

Claude and I arrived early because my sister and I were planning on making the meal. As it turned out, my mother had taken a side job working on a river boat called *the Dixie Queen*. She was the food and beverage manager on the boat that took day and night trips out on the Halifax River. She said they needed more money but it seemed to me just an excuse not to be home.

For some reason she agreed to work on Thanksgiving even knowing my sister was coming for a visit. We all knew the real reason was so that she wouldn't have to cook the meal. Or at least we all thought that was the reason.

My sister Pearl and I got the turkey in the oven early and started on the rest of the side dishes, while we watched the *Macy's Day Parade* with the rest of the family. My dad was asleep in his recliner for most of it, but as it got close to dinner, he got up and started setting the table. He used our traditional turkey tablecloth and pulled out my parents' best dishes. These were dishes that were used maybe three or four times a year. Because of the warm weather, he set the table up on the lanai, a beautiful sea breeze making the room cool and inviting.

My mother was supposed to be home by 12:30pm so we had planned to serve after one.

As 2:30pm rolled around everyone was getting aggravated. Especially my sister. She was sure the turkey would be dried out if we waited much longer. But no one dared suggest we eat without her, because we all knew how that would end if she came in and we hadn't waited for her.

My dad was upset, we could all tell. He looked so much older this year and he also looked sad. He was pacing and he made the comment under his breath more than once, that we should just eat. Then he would walk away and pace some more. At 3:00pm, I think my brothers were getting worried and it occurred to me that we should be too. What if something had happened to her? But when the phone rang, I don't think any of us thought it would be bad news.

My dad answered and we heard him wish his friend Pete a Happy Thanksgiving. Pete worked at the hotel too and he had also taken a side job working on *The Dixie Queen.* We heard my dad ask Pete if he worked that day, but we couldn't hear the response. My dad said a few more things and then he ended the call. When he put the receiver down, he was calm. Almost too calm. He turned to us and said, "Let's eat."

As my sister and I served, Pearl asked him what Pete had said. My dad, eerily calm, said that the boat had docked at noon and he was watching football in a turkey coma, but he wanted to wish him a Happy Thanksgiving before the day was over. What surprised us, or maybe it didn't actually, was that my father was not worried about my mother's wellbeing. Most people who got the news that their spouse should have been home on time and wasn't, would have probably called the police. But my dad didn't. All he said was "let's eat." And that is what we were all doing, when my mom finally got home.

She walked in and we all thought she was going to be pissed. How dare we not wait for her to eat? That would have been her normal MO. But instead she came in practically floating. She was in a great mood, and it was clear she had been drinking.

"Oh! I am so glad you didn't wait on me." She said to everyone's surprise. Everyone except my dad, I think. "What a day! I was so worried about ruining the meal. The boat just docked thirty minutes ago! The bridge got stuck and we couldn't get through. We were stranded on the water for an extra two and a half hours! What a nightmare." She was rattling on without a care in the world.

When she finished speaking, she waited for a response. Unfortunately we were all speechless. From what Pete had told my dad, she was blatantly lying to us. I looked at my dad and could see how red his face was getting. If his grandkids hadn't been at the table, I think he would have let her have it, right then and there. Instead he remained silent too.

"What's going on? Ya'll too stuffed to speak. I just told you all what a hellish day I had. No one cares?" She was on the verge of being angry but she was also trying to play her cards just right.

In the end, it wasn't my dad that said anything. It was my sister Pearl. She never was one to keep her mouth shut about anything.

"You're fucking kidding us right?" She said, staring our mother down.

"Excuse me?" My mother's eyes instantly had fire in them but that didn't last after what Pearl said next.

"Your co-worker Pete called. He said the boat was back at normal time. Yet you stroll in hours later and lie to us? We came all the way here to spend Thanksgiving and whatever or whoever you were doing, was more important?"

That was it. The shit instantly hit the fan. There was yelling. My mother forgot she couldn't intimidate my sister anymore. She was an adult and no longer needed to fear her. So when Pearl called her out, try as she might, she wasn't going to win. My brother in law and Claude grabbed dessert and took the kids outside, while the adults went at it. My father admitted that he knew she was having an affair and this was just the proof he was waiting on.

"How dare you humiliate Dad like that?" Pearl screamed. "You are such a conniving bitch. Dad is leaving you and coming back to New Hampshire where he belongs. And boys, if you want to come too, you are more than welcome." She said to my brothers.

And that was the moment where my chance to leave Florida vanished. My sister had one extra room. If my dad and possibly my brothers were going with her, that left no more room for me. The knot in my gut was instant and yet I felt bad because I knew my Dad needed to get away from her. I couldn't be selfish.

"You will not take my boys!" My mother screeched. "You boys will stay with me!"

In the end, they went with my dad. My mother was so angry, but they were old enough to choose who they wanted to live with and they chose my Dad. That Thanksgiving went down in family history and has been talked about and recounted more times than I can count.

My mother, unable to pay for the house alone, moved her new boyfriend in while my dad filed for divorce. He was the Captain of the riverboat but time would prove he wasn't any more faithful to my mother, then my mother was to my father. Twenty years of marriage down the drain.

That night on the way back home, Claude brought up the dinner fight.

"So that was the most interesting Thanksgiving I've had in a long time." He tried humor.

"Yeah. Well my mother keeps us on our toes."

"Yeah, just like my Dad does at home." he said. It was true. I wasn't embarrassed. We both had messed up home lives, just in different ways. Claude had the goal to enlist, so he couldn't become anything like his dad and change the narrative. I had my own goals to never be anything like my mother. I wanted kids, there was no doubt about it, but not if I would treat them anything like she treated us.

"Well it's not something we wanted to have in common. But there it is, one fucked up parent each." I laughed.

He laughed too. It was the first light moment we'd had in a long time. It was nice.

"Hey, I wanted to tell you. I am really sorry about Grant. I know he was a good friend of yours and I know it hit you hard. I don't know how to deal with that kind of stuff but I am sorry. I just thought you should know."

The tears were in my eyes as soon as he said his name, but I couldn't let him see just how much pain it caused. I turned away and choked out a thank you. It was barely a whisper. Claude grabbed my hand and squeezed it gently before letting the subject go. After a few minutes, he spoke again.

"So, what are you doing, New Year's Eve?" He asked, a bit of lightness and laughter in his voice. The question surprised me. It was so unlike him.

I laughed nervously.

"I hadn't really given it any thought, why?"

"I was thinking I could take you out." He squeezed my hand again. "There is an ROTC military ball that night and I thought my beautiful girlfriend might want to go with me."

I almost asked where Claude was and what had been done to him. It had been a long time since he asked me to do anything. Had he ever? I suppose he had, but nothing came to mind.

"I think…No I know, I would love that." I said honestly. If I was staying in Florida and staying with Claude, it would be nice to have a real relationship. Maybe this was the start of it. So I went into the holiday season with renewed hope.

Christmas without my dad and brothers meant Christmas with Claude and his family. It would be a Christmas without family at fifteen. I heard at work that my mother took two weeks off to spend the holidays in New Hampshire with the boys, but she didn't bother to tell me herself. It would be weird having no family around for Christmas but I knew I was more fortunate than people who had no one around the holidays.

I was still mourning Grant, but my work friends started taking me out once a week. It helped to have people to talk to about it. It also helped to laugh and have a good time. I went back to spending time with Edna too. We decorated the house together. Her tree was old and fake, but we loaded it with tinsel, and ornaments. We strung cranberries and popcorn on it too. It looked like something straight from the cover of the *Sears Christmas Catalog.* We hung garland in all the doorways and sprayed canned snow in the corners of all the windows. We put plastic electric candles, the kind with the orange bulbs, in all the windows too. She had every popcorn plastic Christmas decoration ever made, plus a huge collection of Mickey and friends Christmas decor. We hung, and displayed and made the house look like our own winter wonderland.

We decided one night a week we would watch a Christmas movie together on TV and one night a week, we would get back to playing games. Claude joined in with the game night and made a point to come have dinner with me at work. At home, he ate dinner with me and not in front of his game. With my dad gone, he had a new boss, but he mostly left him alone since he was the only second shift maintenance guy. As long as he got his work done, he could come have dinner with me on his break.

When I had free time I filled it up by going Christmas shopping. Most of what I bought had to be sent home for my family. But I did pick out a few things for Eddie and Claude's Aunt Fran. I bought Edna her favorite perfume, a few nice shirts and a new board game called *Ea$y Money*. I also bought her a *Minnie Mouse* robe that was red with white polka dots. I knew she would love it. *Disney* was her favorite thing. I think it's where my love of it came from.

Claude was harder to buy for. I didn't want to buy video games because that just encouraged him to spend more time playing. But I caved and got him the new *Super Mario Bros 3*. I also got him some clothes, and I picked out a cologne I liked. He didn't really have one, so I figured I would help him find a good one that I would enjoy too.

Christmas came, and it was really hard for me. I loved the snow, and I loved being with family. It's always been my favorite holiday but this year, I had none of what I loved so much. Still, it was nice to see the joy on everyone's faces as they opened the gifts I had hand picked and wrapped for each of them. I got a pretty heart necklace with my birthstone in it from Claude, and a couple books I had been wanting to read. It proved he did pay attention when I talked. Edna gave mostly gift certificates to places like JC Penney and places we ordered take out from at work.

I called my Dad on Christmas Day and he passed the phone around to all of my family, so I could say hello and hear everyone's voice. I don't recall what that phone bill looked like, I just remember long distance calls were never cheap back then. It was a different kind of Christmas than I was used to, and I silently made a promise to myself that next year, I would spend it in New Hampshire, no matter what.

New Year's Eve came quickly and I found myself very excited about the Military Ball. Claude had to wear his *Dress Blues,* so I picked a dress that complimented that. It was a stunning red, silk off the shoulder, floor length gown. I had three inch red pumps dyed to match the dress and wore a barrette in my hair that had a beautiful red flower that rested against the one side of my hair, where I pulled it up.

When Claude saw me that night, he immediately started calling me his lady in red. At the ball, he requested *Eric Clapton*'s song by the same name and that was the one and only time we danced all night. It was a perfect evening. We had a wonderful dinner, listened to great music, and acted like a real couple.

He took my hand often and kissed me gently throughout the night. And it was from that night on, I went back to sleeping in the bedroom. Sex with Claude wasn't bad, it just wasn't something I longed to have. I did it when he initiated it, but I don't think I ever initiated it. He was very sweet to me, and he was really trying to bring us back together. I was happy about all of that.

He told me he loved me often and I was starting to believe we could be happy together. For once, things were starting to look up. Maybe, just maybe 1989 would be my year.

Chapter 15
1989
"When I'm With You"- Sheriff

When school was back in session after Christmas break, Claude got wonderful news. Between the classes he completed, and his work study credits my dad had signed off on, he was able to graduate early. He was still going to walk with his class in May, and officially receive his diploma, but he no longer had to go to school. He was so excited. I was happy for him too.

He met with the recruiter and they started making plans. He needed to start thinking about when he would leave for basic. It wouldn't be until after official graduation, but it did seem like things would happen fast once he signed all the paperwork. I had often wondered what that meant for me but there would be time to worry about that later. I was finally starting to feel better. I wasn't going to let anything get me down.

Claude and I were doing much better. He was more loving and affectionate. More like he was in the beginning. Now that school was officially done, he went back to working the same full time shifts as I did. We were saving money and then one day he suggested buying a new car. His old boat was in rough shape and like he said, I was getting my license in the next month, so having a new car would be good for both of us. He also pointed out that when he was off at Basic Training, I would have a vehicle to get to and from work. I wouldn't have to rely on his mom. It all sounded good to me.

Sometimes when I look back on this time in my life, I cannot believe how much life I lived before I even turned sixteen. It was insane. Not just all the adult situations, but all the sexual partners, close calls, love and loss. I think back and feel like I had to be so much older, but I wasn't. I was just a girl. And looking back, I am thankful I survived.

The day after he brought up buying a car we ended up at the local *Dodge* dealer. Claude knew what he wanted, all he had to do was pick the color. Before we left that day, we had purchased a white *Dodge Daytona* with T tops, black louvers and flip lights. Boy did we think we had arrived. It was a sweet car, but with it came an equally sweet car payment and increased insurance. It was not a sound financial move, but we did it anyway.

When we got home with the car, Claude took Edna and I out to celebrate. Dinner at our favorite place, *Bennigan's*. The food was always wonderful and even though I might have preferred it be a night for just us to celebrate our big night, I knew it was important for him to get his mom on board. He wasn't sure how she would take him buying a new car and taking on more bills. As it turned out, she was happy for him and didn't preach too much. She did, however, point out that adding me to the insurance might result in a sticker shock. Even as a female driver, she warned the premium would be double if not triple what we were already paying. We left the meal a little deflated. Still, it was one of the nicer memories.

That is until Claude said that maybe we would hold off on getting my license until he was leaving. Then we could save more and have a cushion for when the insurance went up. This irritated me because when we had talked about the payment, he was expecting that I would split it with him. If I wasn't going to be driving, I didn't feel I should have to pay for the new car. I already took care of the gas.

If he noticed I was upset he didn't say anything and when we got home, if I planned to bring it up, that changed when we walked in to find his Aunt Fran had passed away, sitting up in her chair. Her head was hunched over and it was clear she was gone. Everything that night became a blur and when we finally went to bed, after having the paramedics and coroner there, I had the hardest time sleeping. Claude thought sex would help. It was well after midnight when we finally went to sleep. Mine was fitful.

First I dreamt of Grant. That hadn't happened in awhile. Not since a couple weeks after the funeral. In my dream, I could see the car coming at him and I was screaming for him to move, but he couldn't hear me. The car in my dream, a white *Dodge Daytona*, hit him at full speed and I woke up screaming as his body flipped in the air. Claude, half asleep and having no idea why I was screaming, did his best to calm me down.

When I fell asleep again, I dreamt that we were behind on the car payment. The bill was coming and I had to go get it from the mailbox. In my dream it was imperative that I get it and pay it right then. I was walking outside to get it but the house had so many hallways in my dream and the more I tried, the more I couldn't find the mailbox. What woke me up this time was Eddie. He was yelling my name over and over. I couldn't see him, I could just hear him as I reached for the door knob. When I finally opened my eyes, I was standing at the front door, and he was behind me, still saying my name over and over. When I turned to face him, I was completely naked. But that isn't the worst part. The worst part is that I was no longer dreaming. I had actually slept walked out of our room and tried to go out the front door to the real mailbox. And since we had sex before going to bed, I was actually naked. Not just dream naked.

Mortified doesn't even begin to explain it. All the commotion woke Claude, and then

Edna. Claude, shocked at what he was seeing, ushered me back into our room. We passed Edna who covered her mouth with both hands as we passed. I truly thought I might die of embarrassment. For a long time, neither of us said anything. He just wrapped a blanket around me and held me, while I tried to piece together what had just happened. I had never walked in my sleep, but somehow whatever was going on with me tonight, I had. I read once that stress could cause it. It was a wonder I didn't do it every night.

"Well, I bet my dad has never seen anyone so sexy in his whole life." He said, trying to laugh it off. I just lowered my head even more humiliated. "Oh come on. It's not that bad." He tried again. "It's not like you're hideous. You're gorgeous. You have that going for you"

I shook my head and I honestly didn't know whether to laugh or cry. I never saw myself as anything but a chunky girl with too many flaws to list.

"How am I ever going to face your parents again?" I choked out. It was all I could manage.

"Well, just be glad Aunt Fran wasn't still here. That might have been what killed her, instead of old age." Now he was laughing. Not at me, but more trying to get me to relax.

"You're an asshole. You know that?" I said it with a slight chuckle.

He gave me a squeeze and then the laughter overtook him. I am sure he didn't mean to laugh so hard, but the more he did, I couldn't help it. I started laughing too. Then we both couldn't stop. It was another one of those nights, that even all these years later, can still make me turn red and feel as though I might die of embarrassment. But I have come a long way. Now when I tell it, it's from a place of calm. I can't change it so I might as well let people laugh about it!

But back then it was different. The next day, I didn't want to leave the room. Claude assured me it was fine. His mom was more worried about what might have happened if Eddie hadn't been up and stopped me from going outside. Until that moment, I hadn't even thought of that possibility. I still don't know what caused me to sleep walk that night, but it's only happened two other times in my whole life. Both times were nights after extra stressful days. Thankfully, the other two times it happened, I was fully clothed.

When I finally faced Edna, we got a good laugh about it. She even joked that next time Eddie got drunk and accused me of being her lover, he would know what her so-called lover *really* looked like. I was not amused, but her laughter and the lightness she made of it, made me laugh too. And in the face of so much embarrassment, the best medicine is laughter–trust me! I would know.

A few nights after the mailbox incident– as it was called, Claude picked me up from work and told me he wanted me to hear something. I thought he was going to make a joke at my expense or something but he didn't. In fact, what he did was the first of a series of truly romantic gestures made by him. He put a tape in the tape deck of our new car and immediately, a song started. I knew it right away. It was, *"When I'm With You," By Sheriff.* I had heard it before and had always really liked it. Rock Ballads were my favorite. But I wasn't sure why he was playing it now.

"I love this song, but I've heard it before. Why did you want me to hear it tonight?"

"Well because." He turned and took both my hands. "Because, when I heard it tonight, it made me think of you. And us. So I was wondering what you would think if this was *our song*?"

It really was a sweet gesture and I found myself so moved that he had chosen a song for us, and a beautiful rock ballad at that. I know I had tears in my eyes when I responded with a kiss.

"I love that idea. I'm usually the one to pick the perfect song for every occasion. I love that *you* did this for us. Thank you." I kissed him again.

And from then on, that was our song. The song he requested every time we went somewhere where people were dancing. The song that we would dance to at his prom. The song that would become our first dance on our wedding day–if we made it that far.

Chapter 16
1989
"Happy Birthday Sweet 16"- Neil Sedaka

Claude was never a romantic. He never really went out of his way to make me feel extra loved. So when he, on a rare occasion went above and beyond, it tended to be something that I never forgot. In fact, I cherished it more because it was so unlike him. My Sixteenth birthday was just such an occasion.

I will admit that leading up to it, I was feeling a little sorry for myself. I couldn't believe I was turning sixteen and I would have no family to celebrate. No sweet sixteen party. Nothing. So I tried to pretend it was just another day. Easier now, but when you're a sixteen year old, it sucks.

My friends from work made me take the day off and we went to the beach. Claude of course, not a beach person, didn't want to go. It was better that way because it meant we had a girls day. We laid out in the sun, swam in the hotel heated pool (it was too cool in February to be in the ocean), and had a birthday cake up on the pool deck. It was fun when some of the guests joined in and sang to me with my friends.

All in all, it was a good birthday. As I got dropped off at home, I had to admit it was better than I thought it was going to be. I was satisfied. So when I walked into our bedroom I was met with complete shock. Before I could take in everything around me, Claude hit play on his tape deck. Neil Sedaka began with his "tra la la la la la la la la, happy birthday sweet sixteen…" The whole room was lit up with candles and balloons. He had set a table with a sweet sixteen table cloth, plates, champagne glasses, and more candles. He didn't drink so there was sparking grape juice in the plastic stemmed glasses. There was a small cake on the table and what looked like a Chinese take out bag.   Claude was all dressed up. Shirt, tie, hair cut neatly and styled. He looked so handsome, but more than that, he looked adorable. He had put a lot of thought into all of this. Right down to the pink and purple streamers that I noticed last, hanging from the ceiling. My smile must have been huge because as the song played and I walked in, he smiled too. A big, bright smile that said he knew he had pulled off a genuine surprise.

I closed the door behind me and as I did, he came around the bed. Before I knew what was happening, he dropped to one knee, pulling a box from behind his back. Most of what happened next was a blur. *Neil* was still singing in the background, but when it ended, Sheriff started singing *our* song,

"I know this might seem crazy. But I have no doubt I want to spend my life with you.

Before we know it, I will be leaving for basic training and then I will be sent to some unknown base from there. I want you with me. I want you to be my wife." He opened the box. The ring inside was pretty, almost antique looking. "This was my great grandmother's diamond. It was cut by a miner in the late 1800's. I want you to have it, and wear it. I want you to say you will marry me."

Now I don't know what I expected for a sweet sixteen but it was not this. Not even close. It was romantic and sweet and absolutely crazy. And because I had no idea what to do next, I said yes.

He was so happy. I think at that moment I was too. I mean, someone wanted me for life. Why shouldn't I be happy? He loved me and I loved him. Marriage was that one expected thing most of us Gen Xers did right out of high school. I was just jumping the gun a little bit. I was going to be a military wife. The idea both thrilled and scared me. When I said yes, he slipped the ring on my hand and hugged me so tight.

That night, we celebrated with dinner. All my favorite Chinese food choices. We had cake. Yellow, which was his favorite, but it was topped with strawberries and whipped cream frosting, which made up for him picking yellow cake which I hated. Besides, I had chocolate cake at the beach. I learned later that Edna had made my cake at work and she was completely on board with his plan to ask me to marry him. That night we made love and made plans. He really wanted to be married before he left for Basic, so we planned a fall wedding. My only request was that we do it in New Hampshire so my family could attend.

By the end of the month, those plans had already been changed. That was because my mother, ever the buzz kill, wanted it her way or no way. And because I was a minor, I needed both my parents to sign consent for me to get married. Now they had done it for Pearl, so I didn't see it being a problem. But everything with my mom was always a problem. Why should this be any different? She needed more time to plan a proper wedding, and if I did in fact want it in New Hampshire, she needed it to be in June.

Of course I argued about it, but she was ready for me. She had received custody of my brother Kenny. She didn't even try for Tim. Kenny was always her favorite and she had easily guilted his young mind into coming back and living with her. When the judge asked him, he caved and said he wanted to live with mom. Therefore he was in the process of heading back to Florida. And if I wanted him to be at the wedding—and I in fact had already asked him to be *in* the wedding—I would have to wait until the following June. If I didn't, James would not be there. She would make sure of it.

For me, that wasn't an option. I wanted all my siblings there. So, once again she got her way. My wedding would be in June of 1990. Not because I wanted a hot, sticky summer wedding, but because that is what my mother wanted. She always found a way to get her way. She was the most manipulative person in the world. At least that is how her family saw her. Always have, and we probably always will. Claude was disappointed to wait too, but we decided to make the best of it. He would need to delay his enlistment a little bit, but he seemed ok with that. It would give us more time to plan and more time to pay for it–

because my parents weren't. My mother had the means, but she would never help financially. My dad didn't have the means. His health had gone downhill since they started the divorce and he was in Congestive Heart Failure. He had moved from working full time to being on disability and social security. The man who once had his life set up for an easy and early retirement, had made one mistake. He fell in love with and married my mom, and now the end of his life would be anything but easy.

One thing my dad was able to do for us was reserve the V.F.W. hall for our reception, at no cost. As a past Post Commander, they not only gave us the hall rental, but also a smaller hall for a bridal shower if we wanted it. We were very thankful for that help. My dad didn't necessarily want to marry me off, but as he told me later, he thought it would be a good life for me. Being a military wife would mean security and stability. Or so we thought.

The months that followed the engagement and leading up to Claude's graduation, seemed to go smoothly for the most part. Edna helped me with invitations, and we sent them away to have them printed. They had *The Precious Moments* on them, which had recently become all the rage. I wasn't sure what to do about Bridesmaids. I wanted to ask my friends from New Hampshire, but we barely talked at that point so it seemed weird. I asked my sisters and although they all thought I was too young, they agreed.

Claude asked my brothers, not having siblings or close friends of his own. And with that, the wedding party was set. We worked on lists of those we wanted to invite from both sides of the family. Coming from a large family, I found myself inviting people I barely knew. My mother insisted it was important and I didn't want to fight her on it. It just wasn't worth it. I never stopped to think that I was a girl making so many decisions that should be made by a woman. I see it now, but back then, so many of the people around me married young, like just out of high school, so I felt like I was just going with the flow.

We continued to work a lot, and as the days turned into weeks, I gave up thinking I was ever going to get my license. There was never time to teach me, and we didn't want to waste the money or the time on drivers ed. So I pushed it to the back burner. I continued to have Claude and Edna drive me where I needed to go. I took the bus when they couldn't. But each month when I mailed the check for the car payment that I was paying half of, I felt my resentment grow a little more. Still, I never spoke up.

It wasn't until another Spring Break came to an end, that I started to let it be known that it annoyed me that I still couldn't drive. There were nights I wanted to stay after work and hit up some of the *MTV* beach parties. However, buses didn't run that late and Claude hated doing anything like that. So if I stayed, I would have to pay for a cab to take me home. One night, as he was leaving work and I was staying I brought it up.

"Ya know it kind of sucks that I have to take a cab and pay money when we have a car that I also pay for. Do you think you could get around to giving me some driving lessons, so that I can keep the car and you can go home with your mom, on nights I want to stay out?"

He looked at me. He seemed surprised that I was asking. As if we had settled this all already and this is just how it was.

"I can try. But like my mom said, adding you to the insurance will be a lot more money. I thought we were saving for the wedding."

"We are, but come on. I'm stranded most of the time. I'm sixteen, I can drive. And it is our car, right?"

"Yeah, sure it is. But the money. It will be cheaper for you when we are married. That will make it cheaper for both of us."

"*When we're married*? So I can't get my license for another year?"

"It just makes sense. If we have to take more money for insurance, that's less for the wedding."

Immediately I was sorry I brought it up. Knowing he had no intention of helping me get my license for another year, pissed me off. And going out when I was pissed off wouldn't be any fun. So I changed my plans, and climbed in the front seat to go home.

"I thought you wanted to go out."

"I do, but I don't want to spend valuable wedding money on a cab. So now I just want to go home."

We rode home in silence. The rest of the week, I was extra quiet when we were together and he knew he had struck a nerve. A couple days later he came to have dinner with me. There was a big party on the beach that night that I had really wanted to go to. He knew that and this was his chance to get back on my good side.

"So I was thinking, what if we make time a couple nights a week and I will take you out driving so you can practice. Or maybe you can drive us into work in the mornings. That would give you hours too."

As planned, that did appease me.However, I couldn't help but feel like there was a catch. I wanted to ask what it was but instead, I thanked him and gave him a big kiss. If there was a catch, I didn't want to know what it was until after I had gotten a few driving lessons.

As it turned out Edna did most of my lessons. It wasn't often. Looking back it was just enough to keep me happy. But I was too naive to see that back then. What I saw was that I was learning to drive and even if it was a baby step, it was still a step in the right direction.

That night of the last big MTV beach party, I did go. But it wasn't as fun as I imagined. That's because I had to keep reminding myself I was engaged now. I was wearing the ring. Not that the guys who hit on me cared. If they saw it, they pretended not to. It was flattering and also tempting. But after seeing what cheating had done to my dad, and knowing I had been no better than my mother when I was with Grant, I decided to be faithful. It wasn't easy. I was still so young. And the guys were so attractive and attentive. Still, I made myself keep everything platonic that night. Guys back then, did not like the word no.

Eventually I just stopped going out after work. Most of the time the others I went with, would meet up with people and take off to hook up. I couldn't do that, so I spent the night dancing and drinking alone. It got boring and I finally just gave it up, all together.

Wedding planning went back to being my top priority and at some point the driving lessons stopped again. I didn't bring it up. It seemed pointless. I also had to start planning for prom. I was happy Claude was willing to go. I would never get a prom of my own, so going to his was the next best thing. One thing I became really good at over the years, was finding the silver lining in every situation. Sometimes I kept it positive to a fault. But if I am honest, it's what kept me going through all these hard years. I am thankful I was able to find that lining, even if sometimes it was just a tattered scrap. That silver scrap I often clung to was my lifeline. I wouldn't have made it this far without it.

Prom night, graduation, all of these rights of passage are supposed to be the start of adulthood. Unfortunately, I think that my adulthood all started way too early first with Gary. Then it became my full reality when I was only fifteen and my mom kicked me out of the house, thus forcing my need to drop out of school. This made everything Claude was going through both exciting and also depressing for me. In fact, he could have done without all of the pomp and circumstance. Not me. I looked forward to all of it. I took my time and picked out the most incredible royal blue ball gown for prom. It was satin and lace and the brightest royal blue. It fell off my shoulders and draped down out at the floor, like a proper Southern Belle's gown. I felt like a princess in it. I would twirl in front of the mirror and imagine what prom night would be like for me.

I pictured candles and balloons. I saw myself dancing the night away. And when I dreamt of it at night, it was Grant, not Claude, that twirled and dipped me. I know these should seem like warning signs, but I was so young and so very naive.

After prom would be Claude's long awaited graduation and I found myself having dreams, or more like nightmares. In them, I would be trying to get to the stage to get to my own diploma as they kept calling my name. But no matter how hard I tried, the path I took didn't bring me to the stage. When I finally found my way to where the stage should be, the crowds were gone and Claude was holding a diploma mocking me, saying *"are you looking for this?"*

I hated that I was missing out on all of it. I didn't resent Claude. It wasn't his fault. But I did blame my mother. I know some would say I didn't have to run away, but those that would say that, had no idea what my mother was truly capable of. I knew. Thankfully, I had Claude and Edna to help me, because if not I would have surely been homeless. And that is why I couldn't resent him. I was jealous of him, sure. But that wasn't his fault. That was simply a feeling I needed to work out myself. Unfortunately that wouldn't happen for a very long time. In the meantime, I was dealing with the end of my innocence. My childhood was over, like it or not.   I would be married before long, and any thoughts of going back to school and being a normal teenager were over.

I think that is why I wanted prom night to be absolutely perfect. I helped Claude pick out his tux. It was white with the matching royal blue bow tie and cummerbund. He had his mom help him pick out my corsage and I picked him the perfect boutonniere. Both of us wore white lilies wrapped in satin blue ribbon. I made a hair appointment and got a fresh spiral perm. But instead of wearing my hair down, I asked for the perfect Cinderella bun, wrapped in white lace ribbon that hung down delicately. I even paid extra and let the stylist do my make up.

The night of prom, Claude surprised me by telling me we were having dinner at *The Top of Daytona*. I didn't mention I had been there before. It was a nice gesture and he even made sure we had a window seat overlooking the ocean. We had an elegant dinner, and fancy Virgin Pina Coladas with fresh fruit and tropical umbrellas as garnish. We didn't get a limo because Claude said the Daytona was better than any old limo. He made a point to open my door, help me in and out of the car. At dinner he pulled out my chair. He was the perfect date. That is, until we got to prom.

We took the pictures at the entrance like all the other couples. But once we found a table inside that is where everything went wrong. Claude didn't want to dance. He hated dancing. So once he was in his seat, he only left it to get punch or to use the bathroom. A few times I asked if he would dance and it was always no. I asked if we could at least do one slow song and he finally agreed when they played, "Never Say Goodbye," because as he said, it was as close to heavy metal as he thought we would get at a prom. The one dance was nice, don't get me wrong, but it isn't what I ever pictured my prom night to be. Then again, this wasn't my prom, it was his.

And then, as if it was expected, he ended the night by asking if I wanted to climb in the back of our tiny car and "do it." He said something about it being a prom night right of passage to get laid. It wasn't the romantic night that it started out to be, but I agreed anyway. I thought maybe it could be fun and if Claude was willing to be spontaneous, I was all for it. Instead of fun, we had the quickest, most awkward sex ever.

For one thing the back seat was way too small, and by the time he lifted my giant gown, it ended up covering my face. That didn't stop him though. He slid my panties down, ripping my pantyhose trying to get those off, and the next thing I knew he was in me. A few minutes later, and that is being generous, he was done. His pants were zipped and he was making some awkward apology.

"Wow there really wasn't any room back there. Maybe it's only a right of passage, in the back of a limo with more room." He said, as he climbed out and fixed himself.

After he helped me out of the back I was ready to call it a night. What had started off with such great promise, just turned into another disappointment in my life. The positivity I took from that came much later in life, when I heard others say that their proms were not the romantic fairytale most of us envisioned as starry eyed teens. So I guess in that case, I got that right of passage correct.

Claude's graduation day wasn't a big deal to his family. It was to me. I was proud that he got his diploma and even though we didn't have a party, most of his family was still in New York. I took him and his parents out for a nice dinner to celebrate. I bought him a class ring as his gift, and made a really big deal about his accomplishment. Because to me, it was. I know Edna appreciated my efforts but it also felt like she thought I was going a bit overboard.

That night, I decided it was time for a talk with Claude about our future. After all, we would be married soon and moving wherever the Air Force sent us. He would be leaving for basic not long after we said "I do", and I didn't know how I would feel about living with his family, once he was gone. It was the perfect time for me to go back to New Hampshire. So, that night when he was still glowing about his special day, I told him I wanted to talk about our future.

"I was thinking that maybe we should look into moving to New Hampshire before you enlist." I started. When he looked at me thoughtfully, I took that as my sign to keep going. "I keep thinking that with the wedding being held up north, it would be easier and make more sense for us to plan from there. Then I could be established with a job and a home when you leave for basic."

"Well you know you can stay here when I enlist, right? You will be my wife." He said.

"I know and that's kind of why I don't want to stay here. I don't want to start our marriage living with others. We could get a small apartment up north and get jobs for the next year. It just makes more sense if we're going to be married."

I don't know why I thought he would argue the point because he didn't. In fact, he was so all for it, he asked my brother Tim to be on the lookout for apartments and job openings for us the very next day. I asked my sisters as well and within a month, we had a small studio apartment picked out in Milford, NH. I had gotten a job at a daycare, and he found a job at a screen printing company. All of a sudden, we were giving our notices to our jobs in Florida and to his parents. By the fall, we would no longer be living in Florida. I would be back with my family.

There was no doubt that Edna was upset to hear we were leaving. Our move meant so much change for her and I did feel bad, but I needed to be near my family again. Florida had been hard on me, and though I would still be making my own way, it would be in a place that I loved. For Edna, it meant working at the hotel alone. It meant no more rent from me, or cleaning and cooking or company. As soon as we told her, she started to put distance between us.

When I suggested game nights she was all of a sudden too tired. When I wanted to see a movie, she said she wasn't in the mood. Even at work, she was overly quiet. I know now it was because I was taking her baby away from her and I get it. But back then, I just thought she was mad at me. It hurt my feelings but I didn't know how to express that to her.

During that last summer in Daytona, I decided to spend as much time on the beach as I could. Soon I would be back to having four seasons. And I was so happy about that. For one thing, winter is my favorite. It always has been. There is nothing like a fresh snowfall. In addition, the Florida heat had always been so oppressive to me. I constantly said if I couldn't be in the water or in Air Conditioning, I could do without the heat. Don't get me wrong, I love the way my skin looks when it's tanned. That golden glow that takes me from porcelain to healthy looking in no time. Plus, I love to swim more than any other activity. But Florida was just hot, all the time. I could do all those things up north, and it would be far more pleasant.

Soon the disgustingly humid Florida summers would be a think of my past. But until then, I would take full advantage of living right at the beach. My days off became beach days. Even when it rained, I went. When I only had to work one shift a day, I spent the other shift at the beach. I read so many books on those last summer days. I had always loved to read, but right now my book of choice was historical romances. I could get through one every two days between work and my time at the beach. I devoured them, dreaming of romance and excitement.

Claude was busy that summer too, trying to get in shape. But he did make a point to take me out to a movie or a dinner every couple of weeks. We tried including his mom, but she was taking the fact that we were moving extra hard. I noticed, but Claude was mostly oblivious. I knew our leaving would make her sad, because then she would be stuck with just Eddie. But I had hoped she would at least spend time with us while we were still there. One thing she had agreed to was that she and Eddie would be coming to New Hampshire for the wedding. That made both Claude and I very happy.

So as we started packing and continuing the wedding planning, I couldn't help but think yet again, that this truly was the final chapter of my childhood. The complete and final end of

my innocence. Maybe it was that realization
that sent me reeling and led to what happened
next.

Chapter 18
1989
"Endless Summer Nights"- Richard Marx

As my last summer in Florida arrived, I was seeing the world very differently. I had lost so much and I was about to be married, tied down to one person for the rest of my life. That's scary for anyone, but for a girl at sixteen, it was a fear I tried burying deep down. I honestly didn't go looking for Joel, but somehow he found me. I have learned in my life that the powers that be, work in very mysterious ways.

It was early June, and I was on the beach at sunset. I had been there all day and I had my nose in a book, reading about romance since I had resigned myself to live without it. All of a sudden, I was aware that someone was setting their blanket up a little too close to mine. After all, the beach wasn't busy. There was plenty of room to spread out, so I glanced over, slightly annoyed at the intrusion.

Laying out next to me, I saw a very handsome guy with dirty blonde hair and matching goatee. He was short in stature, but had muscular arms and legs. He was wearing shorts and a tank top and was just settling in with a book of his own. He had a portable boom box that he flipped on, and old time country music started playing with just the smallest amount of static. Deciding he wasn't really bothering me—I welcomed the music—I went back to my book.

An hour later I started to get hungry so I looked in my little *Igloo Cooler* and pulled out my peanut butter and jelly sandwich. I grabbed my water too and started to eat. It was starting to get dark enough that pretty soon, I wouldn't be able to read anymore anyway. But it was still really warm and I wanted to get a swim in before darkness moved in. Swimming alone was one thing, but swimming alone in the dark was just stupid.

As I finished my sandwich, I could feel eyes on me, but I was doing my best to not look in his direction. I waited a few more minutes while I sipped on my water. When it was too dark for me to see the words well I got up, slid off my shorts and headed to the water. I couldn't see, but it sure felt like he watched me walk away.

The water always made me feel lighter. I swam and rode the waves for as long as I could. When I knew it was too dark for me to be swimming safely, I got up and headed back to my own blanket. The guy who I was certain had been watching me, was enjoying his own dinner now. The lights from the boardwalk made it too hard to read but gave enough light to see faces. When he looked my way, he caught me watching him.

"Hello." He said.

"Hey." I said back, grabbing my towel and drying off.

"How was the water?" He asked. I knew I shouldn't be looking but I would have to be blind not to see how handsome he was. He was older, maybe mid twenties. He was what I liked to describe as a short *Tim McGraw*. There was no doubt now he was definitely checking me out.

"It was beautiful. I love to swim." Gosh, I must have sounded cringy. Just like in *Girls Just Wanna Have Fun*, when *Sarah Jessica Parker* tells the class, "*I love to dance.*"

"Me too. Maybe we could go sometime?" This was my chance to be a grown up and tell the truth. I wanted to say yes, but it was clear he was asking me out.

"That would be nice. But I have to be honest, I am engaged."

"Ahh." He said looking at the ring I held up. "Then as friends? I'm Joel by the way."

I smiled. There was nothing wrong with that. So I nodded.

"I'm Martina, And sure. I would love having a swim buddy. It's safer that way too. "

"For sure. Your fiancé isn't a swimmer?" He asked.

"I wish. He isn't much of a swimmer or a beach person." I admitted. "But I love it."

"It's good you still do things you like. Most girls are so clingy, if their guy doesn't do it, they don't do it."

"Ha! If I did that with Claude, I would never leave my room. Either that or I would never do anything other than play video games."

"Oh boy." He said. "Sounds like a fun guy."

"He's ok. He's going into the Air Force after we get married."

"Oh so maybe that will make him more social."

"Maybe, or we will just end up with more flight simulator games." I laughed at my own joke.

The next thing I knew two hours of easy chatting had flown by. We just started talking and there was never an awkward moment, or a pause. We went seamlessly from one topic to the next. He was just fun to talk to and we seemed to have so much in common. One thing that stood out pretty early on, was that he had a tongue ring. I don't think at that point in my life I had ever met someone with one, so I found it very interesting, and sexy even.

The first time either of us stopped to check the time, it was almost ten-thirty. We were both shocked at how long we talked and how we simply lost track of how late it was. Still, neither of us wanted to end the conversation. Unfortunately, I had work in the morning and I still needed to get home. The buses were long gone which meant spending money on a cab, again.

"I can't believe how late it is." I finally said, knowing if I didn't head home soon, tomorrow was going to suck.

"Time flies when you're having fun." He said smiling. He was right. It was so nice just chatting with him. "Hey, you want a swim buddy tomorrow night?"

"I would, but I'm working a double."

"Bummer." He seemed genuinely disappointed.

"I can do it the day after at night." I offered. "Only working here on the first shift." I pointed towards the hotel.

"Oh you work here? Cool. Ok. What time can you meet?"

We planned late afternoon. He worked in construction but most of his free time was spent in the water or learning to surf. It made sense as to why he was so muscular. As we both packed up, he put his cowboy hat on, which I hadn't seen yet. Somehow, that made him even more sexy and even more *Tim McGraw* like. I started thinking meeting him again might be a very bad idea.

We started to walk the beach and he asked me where I was parked. I felt the same old embarrassment and anger bubbling up. I explained that Claude had our car and I would be calling a cab. The look he gave me only solidified how unfair it was for me to never have the car I paid for. It was a sore subject and it wasn't going away.

"Let me give you a ride," He offered. Once again, I can see how crazy it was now that I am an adult. If one of my kids hopped in as many strangers' cars as I did, I would be furious. Back then, it never occurred to me how dangerous it could be. And I know now how lucky I am that the cars I got in were mostly safe.

He drove me home and I made it safe. He seemed like a really good guy and I looked forward to having someone to swim with and hang out with on the beach.

Over the next three weeks that is exactly what we did. We hung out, we swam in the ocean and sometimes when it got too dark we would go swim in the hotel pool. He bought me take out once and I bought his dinner another night. If I wasn't at work, I was with him. We even laid out and just read for hours. He was always the perfect gentleman. He never once made an inappropriate move on me, even when sometimes he was so close I found myself wondering what it would be like to kiss him. He knew I was engaged and for a while we never crossed that line.

One night as June was coming to a close, I remember he asked me if I wanted to walk the boardwalk. I hardly ever did that, so I happily agreed. We walked the entire length, stopping occasionally to peek in a store or play a game. I bought some salt water taffy and he talked me into doing the horse race game where you roll a ball into a number to make your mechanical horse run. He won a cute unicorn stuffed animal and handed it right to me. It was always fun with him and we were always laughing about something. That night, after he gave me the unicorn, I took his hand. I tried to act like it was no big deal. I took it and started walking. We spent the rest of the time on the boardwalk holding hands. It just felt good.

Eventually it was time to go home and the magic of the night was over. He drove me home, but just before he turned onto my street, he pulled over and shifted the car into park.

"Everything ok?" I asked.

He turned in the seat to face me and took both of my hands in his. They were large, and rough from work and always being in salt water but they felt so good. His face had the look of both seriousness and concern.

"I don't know." He said. "You are sending me some pretty mixed signals." He said. Now this is where our age difference was evident. I was still at the age where I did what felt good. He was older, twenty five I had learned during our time together. More mature and knew there were consequences to every action. It didn't help that once again I wasn't exactly truthful about my age. I said I was 17. I don't know why I didn't just say 16 when he asked. But that one year seemed so much better somehow.

"I'm sorry." I started. "I didn't mean to. I got lost in the moment." I tried to pull my hands away, but he clasped them tighter.

"Don't." He said softly. "And don't be sorry. It felt nice. God. This is crazy. It felt really nice. But you are engaged! You have a fiancé that never wants to spend any time with you and I'm over her wishing I had *more* time with you." He pulled one hand away and ran it through his hair.

"I like spending time with you too." I said simply. It was true. "I don't know why Claude doesn't like to do stuff with me."

"Maybe you need to figure that out, before you marry him." He said.

I was quiet for a long time. I knew he was right. But I also had no idea how to fix any of it. Nor did I think I could.

"If you don't want to hang out anymore, I understand."

"That isn't what I am saying at all. I *just* said I wish I had more time with you."

"Listen, I have to marry Claude. He took care of me when my mother kicked me out. He isn't the best boyfriend but he will be a good husband and provider."

"So what are we doing then?" He asked.

"Having fun until I have to leave?"

"And you're really okay with that?"

"I have to be." I said. "Doesn't mean we have to stop what we're doing."

"What if I'm not okay with it? What if I want more?" He challenged me.

"How much more? Why can't we just be what we are."

"And what is that?"

"I don't know, I–" Before I could finish, he leaned in and kissed me. It was the kind of kiss that is meant to blow you away and it did. It was, if I am being truly honest, the best kiss I had ever had in my young life. I couldn't help myself, I kissed him back. It was everything I imagined it would be even if part of me pretended I would be happy if it never happened.

We kissed for a couple minutes and then he pulled away. He was still holding my face but he leaned back so he was looking into my eyes.

"This is what I want. I want you. If you can't see that...." his voice trailed off sadly.

"I see it. Just…." I looked down. I was more confused than ever. After another long minute of silence, he let me go. He put the car in drive and continued on down the street. I didn't know what to say. He didn't say anything either. Finally, I opened the car door and got out. The door closed between us, and still neither of us said anything else.

That night, I was so confused. I couldn't believe this was happening again. Only this time it was different. As I crawled into bed next to Claude, who was sound asleep, I felt both guilt that I was betraying him and sadness that I too wanted more with Joel. I was also pretty sure that I had just screwed everything up with him. Maybe I wouldn't have to worry about my latest predicament after all. When I finally slept it was fitful. I would doze but then wake up with more guilt and more anguish about what to do next.

The next day at work was long. In those days, we couldn't just shoot someone a text and apologize or try and work things out. In fact, we didn't even have each other's phone numbers. We made plans when we saw each other. We never left each other without making fresh plans, until that night. This left me with dread because what if he was done with me? What if I never saw him again? I obsessed over these thoughts all day. I worked a double and everytime the door opened at either the restaurant or the front desk, I imagined it would be Joel coming to talk. That didn't happen.

The next day I couldn't concentrate. I only had to work at the restaurant but I spent the entire shift getting people's orders wrong, forgetting refills and by the end of the day my tips reflected it. I left work and changed out by the pool. I needed to clear my head. I changed into my suit and dove into the hotel pool, swimming lap after lap. I lost count of how many laps I swam before my breathing demanded I take a break. Still, as exhausted as I was, my mind felt clearer as I dried off and laid down on a deck chair to rest. It was wrong that I enjoyed spending time with Joel. I knew that, but selfishly everything Joel was to me, were things I wished Claude was. I found myself once again wondering why I had agreed to marry him. Sure he took me in when I had nowhere else to go, but we had almost nothing in common. But he was my future and he meant a stable life.

Joel and I had so many things in common it was scary. And there was no doubt in my mind I wanted more with him. There was excitement and adventure. But there were also no guarantees with him. It was way too new for that. The what ifs were playing over and over in my mind. Eventually,I couldn't think anymore. I opened my eyes and saw Joel standing over me. At first I thought I was dreaming, but he smiled shyly and sat down.

"I just can't stay away from you." He said.

"Is it wrong that I'm glad about that? I was wondering if I would see you again."

"Here I am."

"Good." I sat up. "Wanna take a walk?" I knew that Claude was working a double and I didn't want to chance him seeing me talking to Joel on the pool deck.

As we walked down the beach, we fell right back into our familiar comfort. No words were needed but I still felt like I should clarify my position.

"Can't we just enjoy each other's company? No strings?"

"For now." He said. I wanted to ask him what he meant by that, but I was also too scared of the answer.

That night we ended up sharing a pizza on the beach. We had almost walked into Ormond and we were starving. I was still in my bathing suit so Joel went in and got it. We sat in the sand and ate, talking about anything and everything. It was like the other night hadn't happened. Except that after dinner, when we decided to take a swim, he pulled me into his arms and held me.

I didn't stop him. It felt too good. So, wrong or not, I let it happen. Whatever was about to be, I resigned myself to go along for the ride. Later in my life, when my own son would come to me for advice in a similar situation, I would tell him it was a bad idea. I would warn against the whole situation he was in. He had my guidance and experience. But he also had to learn for himself. Which is exactly what he did. Like his mama, he learned the hard way.

Back in the eighties, the 4th of July was a huge deal in Daytona. Fireworks on the beach, with cookouts at many of the hotels along the strip, was how we celebrated. This year, Joel and I made plans to spend it together. Claude didn't even notice. He was never one for fireworks or crowds, so his plan was already set to be home with Mario and Luigi.

I took the day off. Because I worked so many extra hours for her, my mom never complained when I requested a day off. She had her good points too. I was up early, said goodbye to Claude and took the bus to the beach. I could have asked him to drive me, but I was ready before the crowds and waiting for him meant getting stuck in traffic.

We set up near the hotel in case we wanted the pool, but bought tickets to eat at another hotel's pool deck BBQ. Since it was an all you can eat day, it made more sense to be closer to the food. Plus once you were set up, you didn't move. The entire beach would be packed by mid morning.   Joel brought a big blanket which we spread out and held down at the corners with each of our coolers. Mine was packed with snacks, his was packed with drinks. We had beach bags filled with towels, hoodies, extra blankets, our books, even a couple pillows for laying down and watching the firework display later on.

I remember that day with so much fondness. I laid out, Joel beside me, both slicked up with my Hawaiian Tropic Oil. We swam, read, and ate too many burgers and hot dogs. There was great live music all around us. As an added bonus, the waves were huge and I had the chance to watch Joel show his stuff on his surfboard. By the time the BBQ dinner was served, sausages and chicken with corn on the cob and watermelon, everyone was exhausted. The fun and the sun coupled with full bellies were the perfect combination to create mellow satisfaction.

After dinner we took one more swim before changing and plopping down on the blanket. We lay out and relaxed. After a while I pulled a sweatshirt on The breeze and my sun kissed skin was making me cool.   When the fireworks started, Joel pulled me in his arms again and we lay there together on his pillows watching the brilliant light display in the sky.

The fireworks eventually ended but we didn't move. It had been a long day and in his arms was as close to perfect as I had ever been. I vaguely recall him pulling a blanket over us, but it happened through the veil of groggy sleep. When I woke up again, my back was to Joel and he was pressed against me, in a perfect spoon. The blanket was on us both and it was no longer dark. In fact, the sunlight was so bright I jumped up. We stayed out all night!

Joel sat up immediately too and realized why I was in a panic. He tried to calm me down.

"Relax, come here. It's ok." He tried pulling me back down on the blanket but I was pacing.

"I never went home. Shit! What am I going to say? It's not like they haven't noticed!! It's almost ten."

"So what. We didn't do anything. Just tell them the truth. You fell asleep on the beach after the fireworks."

He was right of course. We hadn't done anything but fall asleep on the beach. My guilt still stemmed from the kiss. But I didn't do anything wrong. Nothing. Besides falling asleep in his arms and staying there all night.

"I better go either way. Claude is probably worried." Joel agreed and he helped me pack up. I told him I would take the bus home but he insisted on driving me. I was afraid Claude might jump to conclusions if he saw Joel, so I made him drop me off at the bus stop near home and I walked the rest of the way there.

At first when I came in, I thought I had worried for nothing. No one was pacing the house, in fact Edna was gone to work. Claude was in our room playing video games, clearly not worried for my safety. But he was annoyed that I hadn't come home.

"Where have you been?" He said not even taking his eyes off his game.

"On the beach. I fell asleep after the fireworks. Too much sun and swimming." I said honestly.

"So you just didn't come home?"

"Well when I finally woke up, there were no more buses anyway."

"You could have taken a cab." He said flatly. His whole attitude was turning me defensive. I wasn't a child and he was speaking to me like one.

"Yes and I also have a car I could have driven home if you would ever let me get my license." I snapped at him.

"I've explained this all before."

"I know. I can pay for the car payment and for your insurance, but I can't use it too." I said. Now I was livid.

"Oh God, here we go again!" He shouted. He jumped off the bed and threw his controller against the wall. I flinched as he rounded the bed and was suddenly face to face with me. "I have explained all of this a thousand times! Are you fucking stupid?"

I couldn't believe he had just spoken to me like that. I went to turn and leave the room but he grabbed my shoulder hard and spun me around.

"I'm talking to you! I asked you a question!" He ground out, his face red. His eyes bore into me.

"No, I am not stupid!" I yelled back. "But I am a sucker. I let you take my money for a car I can't use, while I beg for rides!"

This time he shocked me. He pushed me hard. My back slammed into the door behind me. I lost my balance and scrambled to get away.

"Oh shut up! When we move like *you* want to, you can get your fucking license and drive then!" He was yelling and in my face but I was barely registering what he was saying. I couldn't believe he had just pushed me. "Am I clear?" He snarled, grabbing my arm.

"Go fuck yourself!" I screamed back, as I pulled out of his grip as hard as I could. I left the room and went into our living room where my dresser was. He didn't follow me and I was glad.

I was shaking so badly as I threw some of my clothes into a bag. I had nowhere to go but I wasn't staying there. Not when he was being a crazy person. He never came out of the room to follow me, so I packed a second bag of bathroom items. When I left, I slammed the door so he would know I was gone.

I couldn't even believe any of this was happening. He had never treated me like this before. He was always kind. At the moment, he had flipped a switch. He was all of a sudden unlike the Claude I knew and had agreed to marry. As I walked down our street back towards the bus stop, the tears fell.

Part of me wondered if he would try and follow me. When he realized what he had just done would he feel bad? But the few times I looked over my shoulder, I didn't see him and for that I was thankful. For the first time, I was actually scared of him and I needed to put space between us.

I got on the bus but had no idea where I was even headed. When the bus stopped at the hotel, I got off. Even though I wasn't scheduled, I needed a shower and I needed some place to put my things down. I talked to the girl on the front desk and asked for a room for a couple nights. Thankfully we could get employee rates so I handed her one hundred dollars and I was set for four nights. I told her not to put the room in my name, as I didn't want my mother questioning why I was there. We came up with a fake one instead just to be safe. As an added bonus, the day after the fourth was my mother's birthday so she had taken the whole week off and I knew I wouldn't bump into her.

Once I was in my room alone, I dropped my stuff in the corner and took a shower. I cried as the water ran down my body, shaking. What the hell had just happened? It still seemed so unreal. After my shower I laid down on the bed, a towel wrapped around my hair and another around my body, and slept. I woke up feeling better but then I remembered what happened and I immediately felt sick.

That night, I got some soup from the restaurant and laid in bed watching TV. I wished I could talk to Joel, but I knew he wouldn't be around until the following afternoon. Those were the last plans we made. But I really wanted to talk to him. I also wondered if Claude figured I might come to the hotel, so I stayed in my room. He was scheduled to work that evening and I didn't want to bump into him. Not only was I still angry, but I was also scared of him. He had never acted that way before.

When I finally got to see Joel after work, I still had not seen Claude. He was either avoiding me, or had called out. I was ok with that. I was starving too. I really hadn't eaten anything except soup since the fourth of July, so when we met up on the beach, I asked if we could go out to eat and talk. He was in his bathing suit but gladly said yes. He changed up by the pool and we walked to a nearby seafood place on the beach.

I could tell he was concerned the minute I said I needed to talk. He listened intently while I explained what had happened. I could tell he was upset because I saw him ball his hands into fists, a few times as I spoke. He never lost his temper in front of me. In fact, he was so passive I thought he wasn't going to say anything. But when he spoke, it was soft and soothing.

"Babe, you know you don't deserve to be treated that way right? No one does." He said holding my hand. I just nodded trying hard not to start crying again. "Whatever you need, I am here for you."

That night, I asked him to stay with me. I just needed his reassurance and the comfort of not being alone. Like the true gentleman he was, he stayed with me and never tried anything. He held me, and whispered that I was worthy of love. I was worthy of someone who would take care of me and never hurt me. I just laid in his arms, willing myself to believe him.

The next night, he asked if he could stay again. I don't think he knew how much that meant to me. Being in his arms was everything. And that night, when he pulled me close, I kissed him for the second time. He didn't stop me. We kissed for a few minutes and finally he pulled back slightly and looked me in the eyes.

"Babe, you are beautiful. I wish you could see yourself through my eyes. I fall more in love every day."

I wanted so badly to respond but the confusion I was feeling was too much. I didn't even know where to begin with what I was feeling. So instead, I just kissed him again. My own way of saying thank you for trying so hard to make me feel special. Because he did. We spent a third night together—counting the night of the fourth. This time we kissed on and off all night. When one of us woke up, it started all over again. He was an amazing kisser. He knew exactly how to kiss me and when he stopped his lips were so soft, I just wanted more. But kissing is all we did. No one had ever been so slow with me. He treated me like I might break, every touch more tender than the last.

On our fourth night together, when I got to the room after a shift with Edna, he asked me what my plan was. He was holding me in bed, looking into my eyes. He knew I hadn't talked to Claude at all, and when I saw him at work, he just ignored me. Although he did look sad. I knew I couldn't stay at the hotel forever. For one thing, my mother was bound to find out when she came back to work. And even though it was cheap, I couldn't keep spending money on a room. Still I had no intention of going back to Claude. Not until we talked.

Edna had tried to talk to me about everything. She said she didn't really know what happened between us and I was pretty sure she didn't. If she did, what excuse would she have made for her son's actions. She just asked me if I would be willing to talk to him. She said he missed me and felt bad that we fought. This comment led me to believe she thought we had a little spat. I told her I needed some time and space, and that when I saw him, it didn't look too much like he wanted to talk. She assured me he did and all I said was 'we'll see.' I wasn't ready but I didn't need her going to my mother either.

"I'm not ready to go back." I finally answered Joel after a long pause.

"Why are you even thinking about going back? If he put his hands on you once, you better believe he will do it again." He said it softly, his eyes full of concern.

"I don't want to talk about him." I tried kissing him and he let me but then pulled away.

"Come stay with me for a couple days." Joel had an apartment he shared with three other guys. I could go stay with him, but then I would become his burden next. Nothing good had come from me running to Claude when my mothers abuse got too bad. Besides, I had to admit, I liked having him all to myself at the hotel.

"My mom isn't back for another three days. I'll extend my stay that long, and figure out something from there." I countered. "Besides, you and your roommates don't need me freeloading. I'll be okay here. Plus, I like being here. Just you and me. Is that wrong?"

We both knew that it was, since I was engaged to Claude—even if he was an asshole, I hadn't broken it off yet. But he wasn't about to say any of that. Instead of answering he kissed me. Tonight his kissing was different. It was as if he was pleading with me to be his. He didn't say that though. Instead he trailed kisses down my neck, across my chest. He stopped over my tank top taking one nipple then the other and playing with each through the material. I arched my back up to meet him. The tongue ring felt different, exciting.

When he got the desired whimpers out of me, he moved down further. His goatee tickled my bare belly. He moved slowly, and with precision. Lower still, he started to remove my panties and as they slid down my thighs, his mouth captured the wet softness he was looking for. He moved my legs apart and then he began doing things with his tongue, I had never even imagined. I wiggled and moaned, I couldn't stay still. He gave me so much pleasure, yet it seemed so effortless. When I came, I cried out clutching the bed and his head. It was the most incredible feeling. Exhilarating.

Afterward he just held me again. I could feel his erection in my back but when I reached down to touch him, telling him I wanted him, he just held my hand in place. He whispered in my ear.

"Not while you're still with him." He said softly. I hated those words. I still hate them when I think of them today. I know he didn't mean to, but it made me feel guilty. Like wanting him was wrong—and yes I know it was—but he made me feel loved. And at that moment, I didn't want to be right. I just wanted to be with him.

He stayed with me three more nights. In those three nights, he pleasured me three more incredible times. I knew he wouldn't make love to me, but on the final night I convinced him to let me go down on him. I was obviously nowhere near as good as he was, and I didn't have that magical tongue ring. But I wanted him to feel as good as he made me feel. I took my time, I teased him. I let him know just how incredible he was. I still don't know what he was thinking while I was doing it, but if his moaning and the way he grabbed my head was any indication, I think I did okay.

Afterward he held me so tight and that is how we slept. I never even thought about it being our last night together. I was too busy taking in every single second. It was one of those nights that you remember the rest of your life.

To this day, when I hear *Richard Marx* sing about *Endless Summer Nights*, I am instantly transported back to those first summer nights I spent with Joel. I remember every single moment and they truly did seem endless.

The next day when I saw Claude at work, I had no choice but to go to him. My mother would be back the next day. It was time to check out of the hotel. The only question was, what would happen when I finally talked to Claude. He hadn't come to me. Even as much as Edna told me he would. Nope, I had to go to him.

I found him in the workshop at the hotel. As I entered, I closed the door behind me. I regretted it as soon as I did. I hated that I was all of a sudden afraid of him. I had no idea what I was going to say. I had practiced so many things since leaving a week ago. I was going to ask him what made him think he could put his hands on me. I was going to ask him why he would do such a thing. I had so many scenarios planned out. But when the time came, it went something like this.

He turned and saw me. He took two steps towards me and then stopped. Tears welled up in his eyes and he could barely speak. He reached out and took one of my hands, and through ragged breaths he apologized to me.

"I am so sorry. I don't know what got into me. I should never have put my hands on you and I never will again. Please forgive me. I am so lost without you. Please, please come home. I need you. I'm begging you, let me prove to you how sorry I am."

I wish I could say that I didn't fall for his nonsense, but I did. He knew he was wrong but he also knew I really had nowhere else to go. The tears he shed did tug at my heart, I have always hated seeing anyone sad. Even when that person had done me wrong. So of course I forgave him and agreed to come home.

Chapter 19
1989
"Hard Habit to Break"- Chicago

     I wish things didn't change between Joel and I after that week, but they did. He wanted more, but he wanted it without Claude in the picture. I certainly couldn't fault him for that and I was too stupid to see such an amazing man staring me in the face. I was so afraid of being left homeless, that I clung to Claude for all the wrong reasons.

     After I moved back home, Joel and I still hung out, but it was nothing like that amazing week we spent together. He was still my friend, and we still went swimming almost every day. We would still hang out on the beach reading too, but the hand holding, the touching, the kissing, it all came to a complete stop. I hated it. But I said nothing because to voice it would surely make him force me to choose between my stability and the person I was actually in love with.

     One day, in early August I was really hating my choice. Claude had come onto me the night before. The first time since I came home weeks earlier. I was not at all interested, but I could only hold our fight over him for so long. So that night I gave in. I went through all the motions and afterward I rolled over and hated myself. It was wrong. All of it. The next day I decided I was going to talk to Joel. I had to tell him how I felt about him and just see what he thought. Should I try to end things with Claude? If I did, I would have to move to New Hampshire, but would Joel be willing to come with me? If not, maybe I could find a small apartment, or even one room, that I could rent. I needed to find out. With my two jobs I might be able to avoid homelessness.

As *my* luck would have it my mother was working when I came into the office that day. I hadn't even punched in yet when she called me into her office. I groaned inwardly. I usually managed to avoid her. In fact, I hadn't seen her much at all since she got back from vacation.

"Close the door," She said. This wasn't going to be good. I closed the door. She pointed to a chair indicating she expected me to sit. "So you wanna tell me why you stayed here for a week while I was away and why I had to find out from *Edna*?" She said the name with complete disgust.

I was totally taken aback. For one thing, I assumed after this much time, she wasn't going to find out. Plus knowing what my mother was like, and the fact that I had come home, why would Edna say anything at all? As if reading my mind she answered with her next sentence.

"Don't go getting mad at her. It came out when she was balancing the books. Dennis came across a room for an employee named *Patty Simcox*, which as you know was the name you used. She had no choice but to tell. And as usual you are being your sneaky, conniving self."

"I needed some space from Claude for a few days." I didn't owe her more than that. She always thought she could play mother when the mood struck her.

"You needed to get away from the man you are marrying in less than a year? So you're already trying to fuck up your wedding before it even happens."

"I'm back with him." I said. Most mothers would have wanted to know why I needed space, but not her. Her whole focus was on how I was the problem in this whole situation she knew nothing about.

"Yeah after you had your little fling with whatever guy you were out slutting with that week."

"Yeah, cause you know me so well."

"I know you're a little slut. Have been since you were what, twelve? Do not fuck this up with Claude! This is the one chance God is giving you to have a life after you whored yourself with half of Daytona Beach."

"Okay *Mom*. Thanks for all your help and guidance, as usual." I was being sarcastic and I was being brave because we were at work and there was a desk between us. I didn't think she would do anything that would ruin the reputation she pretended to have a work

"Don't be a smart mouth. You have these jobs because of me! Remember that! Without me, no job. So shut your mouth and keep your nose clean, before you lose the guy and the roof over your head." She snapped. I stood to walk out without another word, but she needed to have one more dig. "I'm serious you little bitch! Watch your step because you better believe I'll be watching!"

That night at work, I mostly ignored Edna. I know she didn't rat me out on purpose but I was still aggravated. She had to know that whatever Claude did was bad since I was gone for a week. She could have at least made an excuse to my mother. After work she asked if I needed a ride home and I told her no. I had plans with Joel, but I simply said I was going out and would be home later.

Before work I had been certain I was going to talk to Joel about us. I was willing to even explore the idea of leaving Claude and getting my own place. But my mother had threatened my jobs, and if I lost those, I would not be able to afford my own place. Suddenly talking to Joel seemed like a really bad idea.

He met me on the beach. He had been swimming because he was still in his suit, and his body was wet. He was so gorgeous. He took my breath away. Once I was settled on the beach with him, I let him tell me all about the waves. I still hadn't decided if I was even going to bring up what my mother had said. I wanted to. But it was easier to let him talk about his day.

"Sounds like you had a fun night." I said. "Mine was less fun than that."

"Oh no, how come?" He asked, concerned.

"Had a run in with *Mommy Dearest*," I said. This was my chance.

"I wish you didn't have to work for her. It would be better for you altogether if you didn't have to see her at all." He said.

"I know. But–"

"Well at least when you and Claude move to NH, she will be twelve hundred miles away."

"Yeah I guess. But then I'll be that far from you too." I said, trying to feel him out.

"You'll forget all about me." He said teasing.

"You know that's a lie. Somehow you have become my best friend over these last two months." I think calling him my friend was my first mistake, but who knows? Who knows if I hadn't used that term to describe him, if he wouldn't have said what he said next.

"So *best friend*," He smirked. "I have something to tell you." He said it turning to face me and sitting cross-legged in the sand. I looked at him and before he even spoke, I felt a pit form in my stomach. Something about the way he spoke and the look in his eyes, I just knew it wasn't something I wanted to hear.

"Okay? It sounds serious."

"Well I don't know if it's serious, yet. I um…I think I might have um…met someone." He said and immediately grabbed my hand like he expected me to run. I wanted to, but I had more respect for him than that. Now, if I could just keep my eyes from spilling any of the tears I could feel threatening. I had a million questions, but I did my best to act happy.

"Oh. Wow!" I needed to be happy for him. He had accepted me going back to Claude. I owed him that much. "So how did you meet her? Tell me everything." I really felt sick. I wasn't sure I wanted to hear everything.

"Well I met her on the beach actually. Yesterday. We started talking and just kind of hit it off." Just like we had. I thought I might puke. "She met me here again today. Her name is Ginny. She's a surfer too."

He had been with her earlier. Somehow that made me feel gross. Like had he told her to leave before I got out of work, so we didn't bump into each other. I had so many questions, none of which I had any right to ask.

"I'm happy for you." I said, but I think as hard as I tried, my face told a different story. He squeezed my hand.

"Are you? It doesn't sound like it. And that's ok. Trust me, I have never gotten used to you being with Claude. It hurts like hell. But if that's your choice, I respect it. Just know that I wish every single day you would pick me." He was giving me an out, but my mothers words kept echoing in my mind.

"I am so confused. Everything is a mess. And in one month, I'm supposed to move to New Hampshire." I said, hinting at what I wanted to say. "Would you…maybe…want to come with me?"

There was a long silence and I already knew the answer. Still I needed to hear him say it. I needed to know there was no way we could be together.

"God I would love to say yes. But my job is here. And surfing is here. And your jobs are here."

"Well if I don't marry Claude, I won't have these jobs." I pointed towards the hotel. "As of the end of summer, my jobs are gone."

"Ask to stay on." He said.

"I can't, my mother told me tonight that if I don't marry Claude I won't have any job here either."

"She said that?" He was shocked. I could tell. It almost seemed like he found it too crazy to believe. "What is wrong with her?" If I had a nickel for every time someone asked me that question about my mother.....

"Not in so many words but yes."

"Well she can't control you. You can get a new job." He tried.

"I can try. But where would I live? I would need these two jobs to afford anything. Even something tiny. And I still don't even have my license. Or a car."

"You're making excuses." He said, but I wasn't. He didn't know about my mother. He didn't know what she was like or what she was capable of. And even though I had told him things, most people found it hard to believe a mother could be so cruel and heartless. "If you don't want to be with me, just say it."

"Joel, I do. It just all seems so impossible."

"Listen, I am not going to beg you. I am in love with you, but I am so sick of driving you home to Claude every night. I sleep alone, and you're with him. Someone who doesn't even deserve you. You sneak to see me, and you think it's ok. It's not ok. I need all of you or I am moving on. The ball is in your court." His eyes were so soft. Even with all the passion in what he was saying, he never raised his voice. He was pleading with me to choose him.

Unfortunately, I just couldn't figure out how it would work.

"I need to think." I said, my eyes welling up.

"Then think. Figure it out. But don't take too long, because once you finally make a decision, I might have moved on. That's not a threat. It's really not. I just don't want to be your second choice anymore. And I don't want to say goodbye in a couple weeks either."

I nodded. I really didn't know what else to say. I wanted him to want me and I wished there was a way to make it work, but in everything he was saying, none of what he said translated to "lets move in together and make this work." Which would have been the easy way. Besides, I was too scared to ask him. Not only that, I didn't want him to have to take care of me. That is how I ended up in this mess with Claude. I needed to be independent. I knew it, I just didn't see how I could make it all work. It was way too much for someone barely sixteen.

"I will. I promise." And then, because I needed to, I leaned in and kissed him. Just a light peck on the lips. He let it happen, and kissed me back.

"I will be waiting. Now let me get you home."

I didn't want to go home. I wanted to stay right there with him. But we had said all there was to say, and hanging out now was just going to be awkward. We both needed to sleep on it.

"Can I see you tomorrow?" I asked as we were driving home.

He paused. When he spoke I felt so stupid for asking.

"I made plans to see Ginny." It sounded like he wished he hadn't. Maybe it was just wishful thinking. "Besides, you have some thinking to do."

This time I couldn't hold the tears from falling. It hurt that he was seeing someone else. And it was not lost on me that, if this is what he felt like when I went home to Claude, no wonder he needed me to choose. It sucked. It wasn't fair to him. I brushed the tears away as we pulled up to the house. I was going to make a quick exit, but he stopped me.

"Don't be mad at me. And don't run away from me."

"I'm not." I tried to sound normal but my voice cracked.

"Oh no?" He gave me a half smile. "You were gonna jump out without making plans with me. Were you gonna just skip giving me your decision and run off to New Hampshire too?"

"I wouldn't do that to you." It hurt that he thought I would.

"Then let's make plans. When is your next day off?" It was not for five days. But that is when he said we should talk. It would be the longest we had been apart since we met. He didn't suggest seeing me after work like he always did. He was truly giving me space to think and I hated it. Still it was better than nothing. I was going to meet him on my next day off. He asked that I make a decision by then. I promised I would.

Before he let me out he leaned over and gave me the tightest bear hug. He held me so close and caressed my hair.

"No matter what you choose, you will always be in my life."

I let the tears fall and when it was clear I wasn't going to let go of him, he slowly let go of me. Just like the day we met, he watched me walk all the way into the house. I could feel his eyes on me and when I got to the door, I turned and gave him a little wave. He smiled and I went inside.

That night I didn't sleep. I layed on the couch and thought about everything. I thought about Joel and how easy it would be to love him. I thought about my mother and all the hateful words she had spewed. Staying and being with Joel was risky for several reasons. For one thing, I would lose my jobs. I would be homeless, or I would need to have enough money for a first month's rent and security deposit. Most of my money was in an account I shared with Claude. The rest had already been sent to New Hampshire to pay wedding vendors. Because, I was supposed to be getting married to Claude. I also thought about Claude, who I did care for and in fact did love in a different way. I thought about the good times we had and tried not to focus on the one time he put his hands on me. But leaving Claude meant needing money, a place to live and basically for all the stars to align just right. My mother wouldn't help me. In fact she would be so angry, and spiteful, she probably wouldn't even give me a good reference for a future job. My dad was in no position to help either. If I was going to stay in Florida—and Joel was the only reason I wanted to stay—I would need to find two new jobs and an apartment, in less than one month. But I wouldn't know if it was possible until I tried.

  The next day as soon as my shift was over, I walked the strip and stopped in at any hotel that had a **HELP WANTED** sign in the window. I filled out several applications and I got lucky when the manager of *The Palm Plaza Hotel* asked if I had time for a quick interview. She liked me immediately and said if I could start in two weeks, I could have the second shift position. I was so excited, I thanked her repeatedly. Though it was an upscale hotel and the pay was slightly better than I was making at the Voyager, I would still need a second job. Still this first day had been promising. For the first time in a long time, I had hope.

I wanted to tell Joel, but I knew I couldn't. There were still four days before I would see him. But then I came up with an idea. As it turns out, it was a bad one. I took the bus back to *The Voyager*. I knew the odds that Joel was still out there were slim. But I had to check.

At first I didn't see him. I looked up and down the beach twice from the deck, but then I saw him walking. And he wasn't alone. He had a beautiful woman with long, jet black hair, and the longest tanned legs. She was actually taller than Joel but somehow it didn't matter. They were a gorgeous couple. My eyes went to their hands and seeing them holding each others', made my stomach do a little flip. I wanted to look away, but I didn't. I watched long enough to see them laughing and joking. Joel looked happy.

I left before they got any closer. Seeing them almost made me wish I hadn't gone looking. But it wasn't a secret. He had told me he was seeing her and I had no right to complain. The excitement of my potential new job was almost ruined by my spying. Before it could, I told myself it served me right. I put Joel through that kind of agony every time he brought me home to Claude. It was a situation we had put ourselves in. But now was my chance to fix my life.

The next day, I had to work a double. I didn't let that stop forward progress. I managed to make the time to call about a few apartments. I did not go out by the pool to look for Joel. Sometimes I could be smart.

That night, I went home and spent time with Claude. I needed to be fair to him too. I asked him if he was looking forward to moving to New Hampshire. He said he was, which surprised me. I asked him if he thought he would be happy there and he said yes. It wasn't so much a conversation as it was a question and answer session. The whole time I hung out with him in our room, he was on his game. Eventually, I took my book out and read until bedtime. It wasn't a bad time spent together, it just didn't feel like we were doing anything as a couple.

The next day, I spent the whole morning out looking for a first shift waitressing job. I knew the *IHOP* would probably take me back, but it was too far away from the Palm. I would lose an hour traveling between the two jobs if traffic was heavy on A1A. That would have to be a last resort.

On the fourth day, I went and looked at something advertised as a studio apartment on the mainland in Ormond. It looked more like an oversized walk-in closet with a bathroom and a small kitchenette that was way too close to the twin sized bed.   If the door to the oven was open, there was less than an inch to it touching the bed. I could fit one small dresser in the space and there was an actual closet that would double as a clothes and linen closet. Still, it was in my price range and if I was approved and I stayed in Florida, I would not be homeless.

As I was leaving the apartment I noticed there was a fish market across the street.. I had zero knowledge of fish, but when I saw the **HELP WANTED** sign on the marquee, I took it as another sign. Forty minutes later, I had a first shift job, as the store's new opener. As an added bonus, he offered me excellent pay.   I wouldn't smell great, but there would be enough time between my shift ending at the fish market and my start time at the *Palm.* I would be able to manage a quick shower, and a change of clothes before catching the bus to my second job.

How I had managed to pull all of this together, in such a short time, was beyond me. Now I just need to make it through the fifth day, and then I could tell Joel my great news. I was so excited to tell him that not only had I made a decision, but I had a plan to make it all work. And I had done it all on my own.

 After my last shift, I couldn't help myself. I wanted so badly to see Joel and tell him everything. I decided to take a chance and see if he was on the beach. This time I found him right away. He was over in front of the hotel next door, the one we had spent the fourth of July at, but again he wasn't alone. And the minute I saw him I wanted to run. He had Ginny in his arms and they weren't just kissing, they were totally into each other. Like they were the only two people on the beach. They wouldn't have seen me if I was standing right over them.

 I should have looked away, but instead I took the scene in. Again, he looked happy and it occurred to me that seeing him with her was nothing like what he endured when he left me with Claude. Claude and I never kissed like that. In fact, we only kissed when we had sex, which was almost never. We didn't have the connection he clearly had with Ginny. And as much as I loved Joel, I wanted him to be happy. If that happiness was with Ginny, then that is what he deserved.

 I knew what had to be done. Or at least I thought I did. At first, I felt I needed to set him free. It brought to mind a picture my mother had always had in our living room. *"If you love something, set it free. If it comes back to you, it's yours. If it doesn't, it never was.*" But what I needed to do and what I wanted to do, were two very different things. So when I went to meet Joel the next night, I went with what I wanted, because I was so tired of doing what I needed. Somehow, I had pulled off everything I needed to in order to stay in Florida. I took that as a sign that my staying was meant to be.

I was there first. It wasn't like him to be late. In fact, he was always waiting on me, never the other way around. When he finally got there a half hour late, he looked flushed and sweaty, like he had rushed all the way. I didn't even wait for him to sit down. I stood up and wrapped my arms around him. I kissed him without thinking and smiled.

"I choose you." I said. Saying it out loud before I could change my mind. Only his reaction wasn't what I expected. He smiled back, but it was a sad smile. There was no excitement. He looked almost disappointed in my choice.

"Babe, let's talk." He tried to pull me down into the sand, but even his tone was scaring me. I didn't budge. Whatever he was about to say, I needed to be able to bolt. I could just feel it.

"What is going on?" I didn't even recognize my own voice.

"Just let me explain. Please."

"Explain what Joel? You told me to make a choice and I did. You told me you were in love with me and you were waiting for me to choose you. I just did. What is there to explain?"

"Honey–" He started.

"No! Don't call me sweet names if you're about to break my heart! Just tell me what is going on!" My voice was unrecognizable in my panic.

"I don't want to break your heart. And I do love you. I am always going to love you." He paused and the silence was deafening.

"But?" I knew there was a but, I saw it in his eyes.

"This week, with Ginny. I think I might be falling for her too. Hard. It just happened. And it was just so easy. No baggage." He looked down.

"Joel, you knew I came with baggage! You knew that! I know it wasn't fair to you but I came here to tell you I choose you." Maybe I should have told him about the apartment and the two new jobs. Maybe I should have begged him. But in the end, I couldn't do any of that. I didn't have it in me. As hard as I worked over the last five days to make it all work, this was just another kick in the gut.

In the end I just gave up. Defeated once again. Joel apologized and promised we would keep in touch. He had even written his phone number down for me to have. We hugged and I walked away crying. When I was out of his sight–he watched me walk away one more time–I tossed his number in the pool trash can. I had just lost another person, and another thing that could have truly changed the course of my life.   The irony of how hard I tried to keep him that week, was like a slap from my mother, right across the face.

That night I went home and started to pack for New Hampshire. We were leaving in three weeks and it was time I got ready. It was time to get my head out of the clouds. The next day when I got to work, I planned to call the Palm Hotel and Hull's fish Market and decline their job offers. But before I could, my mother called me into her office yet again.

"Just so you know, the manager of *the Palm* called here for a reference. Needless to say, she had rescinded her job offer. You will be leaving for New Hampshire at the end of the month. Is that clear?" She snapped.

I just nodded and walked out. I didn't even have it in me to fight her. The only positivity I could take from the fact that she sabotaged me, was that I no longer had to try and get the job back at *the Palm*. The joke was on her, I had no intention of staying in Florida anymore, and it had nothing to do with her. I had lost my only reason for staying and I only had myself to blame.

Many years later, when *Facebook* became a thing, I looked Joel up. I would be lying if I said I wasn't happy to see that he hadn't married a woman named Ginny. In fact, he didn't appear to be married at all. Although he did have a son, who looked to be about four in the profile picture with Joel. He was still gorgeous. A little graying but still muscular and sun kissed. They were on the beach. It looked like he was teaching him to surf. I almost sent a friend request but by then, I had learned my lesson about playing with fire. I checked him out and then kept on scrolling.

Chapter 20
1990
"We've Only Just Begun" - The Carpenters

We were finally in New Hampshire. We had a tiny apartment but it suited us. I had my job at the Daycare Center where I taught arts and crafts to three and four year olds. I enjoyed it because I loved kids. In the afternoons, I was in the infant room. I looked forward every day to rocking those babies and I dreamt of having a baby of my own someday soon. I don't think even I knew how much I needed someone to love. The added bonus would be to show my own mother how to do motherhood right. I knew if I ever had kids of my own, I would not be anything like her. If she taught me anything, it was what kind of parent I didn't want to be.

As our wedding day approached, Claude and I did get closer. There were no distractions. I made a point to have a nice dinner cooked for us each night and I set it on the table, so he didn't even try to play his game and eat. It was a chance for us to talk about our day and it was really very nice. The more we shared that time, the closer we seemed to get.

One night in the late spring, I got a glimpse of what life would be like without him and it scared me so much that I knew I must really love him. It started with a slight fever but after dinner he was burning up. He was complaining of pain in his neck and jaw and his temperature spiked to 104. We didn't have insurance, we didn't even think about going to the emergency back then. I tried Tylenol. I tried cold compresses–like I had seen watching Little House on the Prairie.

When those things weren't working, I ran him a cool bath. I know now that this is extremely dangerous, but we were two kids just trying to figure it out on our own. As he lay in the tub shivering and moaning in pain, I tried soothing him any way I could. I promised him everything would be ok. But when he fell asleep in the tub and I had trouble waking him, I finally decided to call the hospital. They told me to bring him in right away. Unfortunately I still didn't have my license, but there was no way he could drive. So, I drove him illegally and prayed I didn't get caught.

It was a really scary time for us and being seventeen didn't help. Like everything else, I was learning as I went. By the time we made it to the hospital, he had begun to develop a giant cyst on his neck. The doctor told me that was also closing the back of his throat. They had an Ear Nose and Throat Specialist come in to drain it, and put him on some very strong IV antibiotics. The labs they ran on the cyst all turned out to be benign, but I remember the waiting to hear that news was torture. My response to the whole situation solidified to me that I truly loved him and did not want to see anything bad happen to him. It wasn't your typical head over heels infatuation. It was a love of friendship and respect.

When June arrived I was more than ready to marry him and start our lives. We didn't have a lot of money for a honeymoon but we booked a long weekend away in Vermont at a quaint little Bed and Breakfast. It was a place I found on a brochure, back in the times where you had to call and book a stay, sight unseen. It turned out to be a beautiful place but I booked it based on price and the tiny picture on the front of the brochure, which was taken at Christmas Time, when there was snow on the ground.

As promised Kenny was able to come to my wedding. My mother fluttered around all day like a doting mother. She made sure she got in as many pictures as possible and introduced us to all of her fake friends. Edna and Eddie came up for the week, and Eddie held it together until the reception. It was nice to have him sober for at least part of the day.

The ceremony was in a church, at my mothers insistence. It isn't that I didn't want a church wedding. I did. And it was held in my childhood church. The one I used to walk to alone on Wednesday nights in elementary school. The problem was that Claude and I hadn't made our Confirmation which was a required sacrament for the Catholic Church. So in a rush, we had to arrange to make it in the months leading up to the wedding. My brother Tim did it with us. It wasn't bad, it was just annoying to still have to do things my mother said. She was constantly holding my brother's attendance over my head. We made the best of it though. We even managed to have fun in the Confirmation classes, and just to get under her skin, we chose Confirmation names that would piss her off; Peter, Paul and Mary.

Finally the big day arrived. My sister Pearl made me a little late for the wedding. She locked our bouquets inside her house where the girls had all gotten ready. She has always loved telling this story, because she flirted and sweet talked our limo driver into climbing through one of her basement windows in his tuxedo. He was so enamored by her, he did it willingly. Too bad all he received in return was a monetary tip. I think he wanted more.

My wedding dress was very eighties with the puffy sleeves, layers of lace, satin and a long train. My hair, done by Pearl who was a hairdresser at the time, was a mile high, and pulled up in combs on one side, dotted with baby's breath. Claude wore a traditional black tuxedo with the white cummerbund and bow tie. My wedding colors were peach and light green. They were my two favorites at the time, and they looked pretty together. Plus they were light in color so my bridesmaids wouldn't melt in the ridiculously hot June sun.

I had escaped the heat of Florida to come back to the seasons of New Hampshire, only to have my mother insist I get married in my least favorite season of them all. Summer. She did it on purpose of course, but even more frustrating was the fact that it actually was ninety five the day of my wedding. Totally unseasonably warm for the northeast in June, but what else did I expect? This was par for my life's course so far.

The ceremony was a full Catholic Mass but I have to admit, I took something very profound from the sermon that day. Our Priest talked about how even the best laid plans could and likely would go ary. He was of course making light of us being late, but while also teaching a valuable life lesson. Just because you plan and expect things to go a a certain way, life has a way of doing what it wants. And we should embrace it, because perhaps that was God's plan all along. It certainly has been true in my experience and looking back, I often say to myself, "I wouldn't have 'this' if 'that' didn't happen first."

After the ceremony, we headed to the VFW for our reception. I was a married woman. Claude and I shared our first dance together to the *Sheriff* song he had picked for us, "*When I'm with You.*" He hated to dance but he did it for me, and I cherished that moment. Still, my favorite dance of the day was by far, when I danced with my Dad to "*Daddy's Little Girl.*" I will never forget how he sang the lyrics about being his "*star on the Christmas tree*", quietly in my ear. I couldn't help but wish I had been able to stay hisLittle Girl for a few years longer.

      The reception was fun. A typical wedding in the eighties and early nineties. The meal was a luncheon buffet because that was what we could afford. Finger sandwiches, chips, potato salad. Nothing fancy. Crepe Paper Bells and streamers for decoration. We did *the Chicken Dance*, and a *Dollar Dance*. We tossed the bouquet, and garter. We listened to *Celebrate Good Times* and *We've only just Begun.* My dad proposed a toast and wished Claude luck in basic training. For our final dance, the guests made a big circle around us and we danced to "*Faithfully" by* Journey. The DJ picked that all on his own. It was supposed to reflect the fact that Claude would be leaving for the Air Force. We didn't even know where we would be stationed. But I took it seriously and vowed to be faithful to my new husband.

      My mother, not wanting to be outdone by my father, pulled me aside before we left on our honeymoon. I thought for a split second she was going to say something nice but then she opened her mouth.

"Well at least you didn't screw this up. Now that you have that piece of paper, I can wash my hands of all the embarrassment you caused me. You're his problem now. I still can't believe you wore white." She shook her head before going on. "Now hold on to this one, cause Lord knows no one else will want an overweight ruined woman." She leaned in like she had just been kind, and kissed me on my cheek. "Have fun on your honeymoon"

Someone had decorated the Daytona while we were inside at the reception with streamers, ribbons and cans. They wrote Just Married on the back window. People threw rice as they sent us on our way. Our bags were already in the back, and in two short hours we would be at the *Inn at Thatcher Brook Falls*. I was married. Not even a legal adult and I was someone's wife. It was scary and exciting all at once.

We arrived at the inn just as it was getting dark. The whole place was lit up with soft white lights welcoming us. The place was much bigger than I imagined. It spread out across a beautiful piece of land, surrounded by big trees, a gazebo, and a small pond, all of which was lit up as well. On one side was the large building that housed the rooms and the front desk. On the other side was an attached building that looked to be a small restaurant. Even with the soft lighting, I could see that the old Victorian Mansion was painted white with a blue-green trim.

Inside we were met by a lovely couple who welcomed us and congratulated us before giving us the keys and directions to the Honeymoon Suite. They explained how the breakfast worked and told us a bit about the attached restaurant. When they
 sent us on our way, I felt special. We were the honeymooners. It was surreal.

Our room was gorgeous. It had a beautiful quilted king size four poster bed on one wall and gorgeous old wood furnishings. There were two high back cloth chairs that faced the fireplace. Since it was June, we wouldn't be using it, but it still brought charm and character to the room. On the other side of the room, tucked in a corner, was a beautiful whirlpool tub for two. It was decorated just for us, with rose petals and candles. They had placed a chilled bottle of champagne in a bucket on the edge. I guess they assumed since we were honeymooners, we were legal drinking age.

I was so excited and Claude seemed to be as well. It was our wedding night. We set our luggage down and he came to me. He held me for a few minutes and told me that he was so happy I married him. I was happy too. In that moment, everything was finally right in my world. When we made love it truly felt like life was beginning for the very first time. I hoped the whole honeymoon would be as wonderful as that first night and that our life would follow suit. He never mentioned the fact that he was no longer using a condom. It was almost as though he expected it was okay. Since we were married he no longer had to. I didn't complain.

I couldn't wait to be a mother. I craved having a little person to love and care for.

The next morning, I woke him up by running a bath in the whirlpool. I played the sexy wife by doing a little striptease, trying to coax him into the tub with me. Unfortunately, I was met with excuses. The tub was going to be too warm, he didn't like baths, sex never worked in water–how he knew this since he never tried, I will never know. For me, water was an aphrodisiac. So I took a long soak with scented bubbles alone. When I got out, he was more than willing to have sex then. I embraced it, not wanting to ruin the trip with my disappointment.

The first breakfast at the inn was wonderful. Have you ever had something that tasted so good, you wished you could recreate it? Well that was the oversized blueberry muffins at the *Thatcher Brook Inn.* To this day, I have never had another blueberry muffin that even comes close to their perfection. Yes, they were that good. Claude and I walked down to the falls after breakfast and then took a drive to check out the *Ben and Jerry's Factory* right up the street. We had lunch and ice cream and by then Claude was ready to call it a day.

We went back to the room and made love before dinner. After dinner I took another solo soak in the tub. I even tried enticing him again, rubbing bubbles all over my naked body. He didn't bite. But he did suggest I immerse myself in the tub under the bubbles and he would take a picture, so we could remember how much I loved that tub. So that's what we did.

The next day we explored a teddy bear factory, went and picked up some Vermont sharp cheddar at a dairy farm, and maple syrup from a roadside stand. We were two people in love and though he couldn't keep his hands off me, it always had to be on his terms. It was always on the bed, and there was no variety to it. Still, I was thankful. Things were going well.

The third day was our last day and we had run out of things to do around the inn, but I found a brochure in the lobby for a place called *Santa's Village Theme Park* that was only a short drive away. Everyone, including Claude, knew how much I loved Christmas, so when I excitedly asked if we could go, he said, "sure." There was only one problem. When we got there I learned that Claude really didn't like going on rides. He walked around the park with me, but I went on everything from the old fashioned cars to the flume ride all by myself. He sat outside the ride and took pictures of me riding alone, but he never got on a single ride with me. I willed myself to have a good time despite his unwillingness not to try anything new. We had a nice day anyway, and we even picked out a "Just Married" ornament for our tree from one of the gift shoppes..

On our last night at the Inn, I tried once more to get him to come in the whirlpool with me. The water was exhilarating to me. I wanted to share it with him. I even promised him extra fun including a blow job, if he would just give it a try. I guess my persistence annoyed him and he snapped at me instead. I guess I only had myself to blame when we went to bed angry. I should have just kept my mouth shut and enjoyed the tub alone.

Chapter 21
1990
"Life in a Northern Town"- The Dream Academy

Claude and I settled into married life after the honeymoon. We learned how to manage on a tighter budget than we had in Florida. He enlisted and we were awaiting the information that would tell us when he would be leaving for Basic Training. Until then, we just went about our daily life. Work, pay bills, and take care of our little apartment. We did cookouts and birthday parties with family or friends on the weekends. Well I did, it was rare that Claude would go with me.

I got to see a lot of my old friends and I reconnected with my niece Leeann who was a little older than me. We had always hung out as kids, and she was newly married too. Her husband was going into the Army so we had a lot in common. I even helped her get a place in our apartment complex. It was nice having her around, and since I still didn't have my license, it was nice to have someone else who could take me places. There was no bus system in Milford, so most of the places I had to go, I walked.

I had stopped asking about my license. Somehow it always ended in a fight. Claude said he would make sure I got it before he left for Basic, and that had to be good enough. I would be lying if I wasn't secretly hoping he had to leave sooner rather than later. I was ready to have my license and be able to drive our car instead of walking to and from work in all kinds of weather while he rode in style.

About two months after our honeymoon, I started to get really sick. I felt nauseous and achy. After work I would throw something together for dinner for Claude. Even the thought of food made me want to vomit, so I would prepare it, and go straight to bed while he ate it. After a week of this, I started to think I needed to call a doctor. I couldn't keep anything down, and while I went to work, I was less than productive. In fact, when the kids napped in the afternoon, I would sit on the floor with them. I would lean my back against a wall and doze off with them in the dimly lit classroom. One day my boss caught me napping with them and asked me if I was ok. When I told her no and what I really needed was to call a doctor because I thought I was dying, she laughed.

I didn't find it amusing. I was weak and tired. I felt like every bit of me was being drained. But when she asked me if my period was late, a big lightbulb clicked on. Not only that, but it made me realize that not only was it late, but I had not even had one since before we got married. Immediately, I was excited but I held it in. Secretly, I hoped she was right and I was pregnant but I didn't dare tell anyone. If I spoke it out loud it might not come to fruition. So instead, I asked Leeann to take me over to the drugstore for cold medicine.

She dropped me off out front and I came back out a few minutes later, with a brown bag. Inside was a pregnancy test and a bottle of Robitussin, just in case she asked me what kind I got. She didn't. She was oblivious despite the fact that I was a bundle of nerves. As soon as she brought me back home I thanked her and told her I was going to lay down. I said I needed to shake this flu I seemed to have. Later on, she dropped off some chicken noodle soup.

Back in the day, you couldn't take a pregnancy test at any time of the day. In fact, the instructions said specifically it should be the first morning's urine. So that meant I had to wait all night, keeping the test hidden from Claude. I had no idea how he would react if I was indeed pregnant, but since we never used protection anymore, he certainly couldn't claim to be surprised.

That night was brutal. I made Claude dinner. Hot dogs were his favorite and he could eat four in one sitting. Just the smell made me want to die, so as soon as I cooked them, I lit some scented candles and went to soak in a warm bath while he ate. If he was wondering why I hadn't been eating, he never asked. I guess he assumed it was from the flu I had been saying I had for over a week now. Still, it would have been nice if he had taken care of me the way I did him.

After my bath I went right to bed. But I couldn't sleep. I was exhausted but of course sleep wouldn't come. I was so nervous. To make matters worse, Claude's video games seemed to be on max volume. At one point after midnight, I stomped out to the living room and snapped at him.

"Can you either turn your game down or shut it off and go to bed? I have to be up in a few hours ya know?" I was up every day at 6:00am for work. He didn't have to be in until 9:00 am.

He rolled his eyes and shut off the game. No apology for being rude. When he crawled into bed beside me, he tried to cuddle but I turned away from him, clearly upset. I wish I could have told him why I wasn't able to sleep, but I just didn't feel comfortable. I needed to be sure before I even broached the subject of a baby with him. Looking back, I can see how messed up that is, but that's the way it was.

The next morning I was up way before my alarm having held my urine since about 2:00 am. I rushed in the bathroom, shut and locked the door and peed on the stick. I paced, trying not to look for ten minutes was going to be hard. I took a shower and willed myself not to peek out onto the counter at the test. When time was up, I had my answer. Two pink lines. As bright as can be. I was pregnant. I sat on the edge of the tub and cried. I was so happy. Of course I was scared, but the joy outweighed the fear. I was going to have a baby! A little person that would need me and that I could love, the way a mother should love a child.

As excited as I was, I still didn't tell Claude. I needed to see a doctor first and make sure it was accurate. That day at work, I asked my boss if she knew who I should call. Since I didn't have insurance, she suggested I call the town's planned parenthood office. Once I had an appointment scheduled I could barely contain myself. It felt weird that the first person I told was my boss, but she already kind of knew. The next person I told was Leeann that night when I got home from work. I had to tell someone and she was eight months pregnant herself, so I knew I could confide in her.

She was so excited for me as well. She was glad I had an appointment with planned parenthood. She explained that once I got confirmation from them, I could apply for state insurance and they would help me find a doctor. Of course, once Claude left for basic, and graduated, my insurance would start with the Air Force. But we didn't know how long that would be, so I was off to a good start.

I will never forget walking into that first appointment all by myself. It was an old brick building in downtown Nashua. I don't know why I didn't want anyone to see me going in. I wasn't ashamed. I think I was just scared. My insecurity was a direct result of my being so young. I felt like everyone was going to judge me and my teen pregnancy, even if I was married.

That day I was given another pregnancy test, which confirmed what I already knew. I was indeed pregnant with my first child. I was given prenatal vitamins, and paperwork to get bloodwork done. Before I left, they booked my first three appointments with the three doctors in the practice that would take state insurance. I was told it was important to meet them all because there was no way to know who would deliver my baby when the time came. Finally, they helped me apply for state health insurance. I felt so accomplished. I was already doing everything I could to care for my unborn child.

That night, I was over the moon as I prepared a special Italian dinner to celebrate. The smell of my sauce made me nauseous but I was told by the nurse it should get better after the first trimester. I powered through, wanting the night to be memorable.   I had so much to learn about being pregnant and I couldn't wait.

When Claude came home, he asked if I was feeling better? I think the fact that I had two plates set at the table gave him hope. Either way, I was just glad he finally acknowledged that I was sick.

"No but I will be." I said hopefully. "Come in and sit down, I have some news."

He looked worried as he sat down.

"So I am sick. But it's temporary." I said.

"Well I didn't think it was terminal." He joked.

"Nope. In fact, it's really good news." I took his hands. "I'm going to have a baby!" I exclaimed, excited. He stared at me for a long time and I was starting to wonder if he heard me. "Hello? Did you hear what I just said?"

Slowly a smile made its way to his face. As if he finally realized what I had said, and he determined it was in fact, really was good news.

"What? Wow!! How do you know?"

"Well I took a test and then I had my first appointment today! I am pregnant and I am due in April!" I could barely contain myself. The more I thought about having a baby the happier I became.

"Why didn't you tell me?" He asked, sounding hurt.

"Because I wanted to be sure."

"And it's definite?"

"Yes! We're going to have a baby!" Finally it sank in and he hugged me tight. He was happy and that made me happy.

After that night, we told everyone we saw. My dad was first. He said he was elated for me and he was sure I would make a wonderful mom. I knew in my heart he was right. As much as I had wanted to be a lawyer, from the minute I thought I might be pregnant, I felt that being a mom was my true calling. I might not have been able to go away to college and excel there, but I could excel at. I just knew it.

A few weeks after we found out, we got more news. This time from the Air Force. Claude would be leaving for Basic in March and he would not be home when the baby came. There was no way to change it. Everything was already in motion. That's just the way it was in the military, he told me when I complained. He was disappointed but not as much as I was. Even though I had only been imagining it for a short time, every time I thought about the day our child would be born, Claude was there. Now I needed a new plan. I didn't want to be alone. I needed a new birth coach. As always, and just like the priest said on our wedding day, even the best laid plans sometimes go ary. My new plan was that my sisters Faith and Trish would be my birth coaches. I was getting good at learning how to pivot.

Pregnancy for me was wonderful. I loved being pregnant and hearing my baby's heartbeat first, then feeling its little kicks, was the best thing in the world. I got to hear the heartbeat more than most because very early on, I was diagnosed with *Preeclampsia*; High Blood pressure induced by pregnancy. The doctors had me coming every two weeks, and eventually they moved me up to going every week.

When the doctor ordered an ultrasound– they only did them *back in the day,* for high risk pregnancies– I insisted I did not want to know the sex. I wanted it to be a complete surprise. Claude would have gladly found out but I refused. I wanted to hear it on the baby's birthday.

As my pregnancy progressed, and the days got closer that Claude was leaving, he finally taught me to drive. He didn't have a choice. I turned eighteen right before he left, and I didn't get my license until two weeks after my birthday. I could finally drive and while he was gone the car would be completely mine. I was so excited. And then more things changed.

At my last prenatal appointment right before Claude left, my blood pressure was dangerously high. The male doctor I had, a kind older man who always treated me like a daughter, told me he was putting me on bed rest until the baby came. I explained that Claude was leaving for Basic and he said I needed to have someone to take care of me. He didn't want me out of bed for more than one to two hours a day. Looking back I am so glad that happened after I already had my license or I might never have gotten it.

This latest development meant I would be out of work sooner than planned. And with both of us essentially out of work, we could no longer afford our apartment. Sure, he would start getting pay from the military, but in the meantime, we had no choice but to give up the apartment. I moved in with my sister Pearl because she also lived in Milford. This made the last minute move much easier and as a hairdresser, her schedule was more flexible. She had more free time to take care of me.

On the last night in our apartment, Claude and I stayed up all night. All we had left was a mattress on the floor. He was leaving the next day and we would be turning in the keys. I could tell he was nervous. He also admitted that he was really going to miss me. He wasn't much for words of love, but sometimes even he couldn't help himself. He wanted to make love once more before he left but the doctor had forbidden it and while I could have bent the rules, I wouldn't do anything that could potentially hurt the baby growing inside me. So I compromised so he would be happy and sent him off with a blow job and a promise that we would make up for lost time, once he returned. The next morning he was sworn in by the United States Air Force and then he was on his way.

While he was gone, my sisters threw me a big baby shower. It was wonderful and I was *showered* with so much love and so many wonderful gifts. I wasn't surprised that my mother didn't show up. She had been invited but she didn't even respond. I wish I could say it didn't hurt my feelings, because I didn't want it to, but somehow I never stopped wishing she would someday turn into a good mom.

After the shower, the days on bed rest were so long. I read all the time. I read books on newborns. I read romance novels. I read true crime. I made a weekly trip to the library on my hour out of bed.

Some days, I drove to *Bradlees* or *Ames* to look at baby items. I had gotten a lot at my shower but I really didn't know what I was actually going to need. So each time I went, I bought a new bottle of *Baby Magic* lotion or baby bath. When I had about ten bottles of each, my sister declared I had enough to last me until my child went off to college. We had a great laugh about that at my expense and we still laugh about it today. I switched to buying diapers and wipes and as it turned out, you can never have enough of those..

After two weeks at Basic Training, Claude was able to start writing and could receive letters too. I had written to him every day since he left and when I got the address, I mailed them all in bulk. After that I sent a new letter daily and there was always one from him when my brother in law would bring in the mail.

Finally, it was April. The month my child would finally arrive. I could hardly wait. I started to become quite uncomfortable in bed so I would switch to the recliner whenever I could. When I was two weeks away from my due date, the doctor put me on full bed rest. No more outings. My blood pressure was still too high. I followed his instructions and although it was boring, I stayed in bed. It never occurred to me I could lose the baby, but I knew something bad would happen if I didn't listen.

My sister brought me more books, and I devoured them one after another. Claude was moving on to tech school, and he would be there until mid May. He finally had phone privileges and when he called, it was to tell me he found out where we would be stationed first. I had been hoping for something exotic or at least some place I had never been. Actually I didn't have high expectations, but I do admit I was less than thrilled when he told me we would be stationed in Georgia. Of all the places we could go, they were sending us back to the south. Right above Florida, all the heat, but none of the beaches. In fact, we were going to be inland, at Robbins Air Force Base.

I honestly could not think of one place I wanted to go to less than Georgia. It was, without a doubt, the last place on my list. In fact, it never even made any list. But like it or not, in May that would become our new home for at least the next four years. No more life in my favorite little Northern Town. Life was, once again, throwing me a curve ball. Thankfully, I was getting good at catching them.

Chapter 22
1991
"Masterpiece"- Atlantic Starr

The day finally came. I was a couple days overdue and I was sick of being in bed. Plus I had been cramping all day and achy. My sister Pearl said she was going to take me to Kentucky Fried Chicken for lunch. It was just up the street, so we could grab lunch, give me a short walk into the restaurant and stretch my aching muscles. It sounded like a great idea to me. Except when we were walking in, I suddenly felt the most incredible cramp I had ever felt in my life. It was so bad that I had to stop and grip the brick wall of the building. When it was over, my sister asked me if I was ok all the while laughing at how funny I looked holding on to the building for dear life.

"I think I just had my first contraction." I said calmly.

"Oh! Oh wow! Ok well, let me know if you have any more."

I didn't. We made it through lunch successfully. After we ate, she took me back home so I could get back into bed. I actually felt better having been able to get out for just a short time. The fresh air and change of scenery was exactly what I needed. Faith had to work that night so she started to get ready and I headed back to my room. Instead of getting in bed, I went to the rocking chair. I had just gotten comfortable when pain shot through me. I knew immediately I was having another contraction. When it ended I tried relaxing. I pulled my book out and tried reading. I got two pages read before I had another contraction. After the third one, I decided I probably should start timing them.

An hour later, Pearl came in to say goodbye before heading out. When she came in she caught me in the middle of another contraction.

"How long have these been going on?" She asked, exasperated that I hadn't mentioned anything since lunch.

"Since we got back. They're coming every four to five minutes."

"Jesus!" She said, "When were you gonna tell me?"

"I don't know? I thought maybe they were going to stop." I was breathless from that last one.

She made me call the doctor's office and just like she suspected, they told me to head to the hospital. I couldn't believe my baby was actually coming. Before we left the house we called Claude at the base. It was a process to get him on the phone because it was a payphone, and there was no telling where he would be on the base at any given time. When he finally came on the line, Pearl spoke to him because I was having another bad contraction. She told him we had a calling card and would call him when we were settled in at the hospital and give him the room number. My sisters' planned to videotape the birth for him on VHS, but I also hoped he would be able to be on the phone when the time came.

A few hours later I was settled into Labor and Delivery at the same hospital I was born in. My least favorite of the three doctors was on call. She came in and declared that my contractions had stalled, like this was a huge inconvenience for her. She wanted me to try a warm bath to get them moving again. When that failed to work, she started a pitocin drip. Sometime after midnight, she went home and the third doctor in the practice came in and broke my water. What a crazy feeling that was! One minute I was dry and the next I felt a warm water bath wash over my lower half.

I took in every moment as it happened. I was getting to experience all of this with my sisters, and I was grateful, but it was still hard for me not to feel alone. I didn't want to need Claude there, but the bottom line was, I was tired of nothing in my life ever going the way I imagined it. It didn't help that Claude hadn't even tried calling the hospital back at all. Pearl had called the base and left a message when she had my room number and I expected I would hear from him by now. But I didn't. I wanted to be his priority. He was my husband and this was his baby.

When I started getting emotional in the wee hours of the morning, coupled with some incredibly strong contractions, the doctor gave me an epidural. She said I needed to rest. Maybe it was because I was snapping at my sisters, or maybe it was because I couldn't express myself without crying. Whatever the reason was, I was glad I got one. It helped me doze through the contractions and my sisters took turns closing their eyes too. By the time the new shift of nurses came on, I was almost eight centimeters dilated. I asked Trisha to try calling Claude again. It was after seven in the morning. He should be up and he wouldn't be going to class until eight. Unfortunately, he was at the mess hall having breakfast. We had missed him again. The fact that he knew I was in labor and hadn't called me, was a sore subject that no one brought up, but everyone was painfully aware of.

My labor progressed quickly after the call and when the doctor checked me again, she said it was time to push. She explained to me how I was supposed to push through each of my contractions. I listened intently, wanting to do a good job. My sister Pearl would hold one leg and the nurse would hold the other. Trisha was behind the tripod ready to film.

I ended up pushing for well over an hour, and when I thought I couldn't push anymore, the doctor encouraged me. She cheered me on to "push one more time." I bore down and gave it all I had. It was that last push that pushed my baby's head out. After that, the next push seemed like a breeze and out came the rest of the body. I will never forget seeing first, the full head of hair and hearing the doctor tell me what I had waited nine long months to hear.

"Congratulations! You have a baby boy!" She said as she cut his cord and put him on my belly. I only had him a quick minute before the nurse took him to be cleaned up. My sisters were crying and I was sobbing. I had a son.

They were still weighing him and washing him up, when the phone rang. We all knew immediately who it was. Pearl picked up the phone, as she was the closest and said, "Here's your wife." She didn't hide the annoyance laced with her joy.

"Hello," I said through the tears. He said hello back. "We have a son!" I exclaimed. All cleaned up and swaddled they handed me back my baby. It was then that I knew I would never be alone again.

We never talked much about why Claude hadn't called all night, and when I mentioned that we tried to make sure he was on the phone when the baby was born, he just said he thought it would take longer. He thought he had time for breakfast. As it turned out, this became his thing. Even as far off into the future as I have seen, he was and never is on time for anything. Eventually I just accepted it and viewed it as his loss.

I named my first born son Brian Matthew. He had dark hair like his dad, but the rest of him looked so much like my brothers. He had their smile, their noses and even their eye shape. When I held him, all I saw was a Masterpiece. My first work of art. I was instantly in love, and I knew being his mother was exactly what I was supposed to be.

The next few weeks were a blur. First, I spent two days in the hospital learning how to feed and care for this little person I created. I wanted to breastfeed because my mother would never have dreamt of that. In fact, it was my sister Trisha who had done all my infant feedings when I was born. She was only ten when my mother declared she wasn't getting up at night to feed me and made it Trisha's chore. Thankfully all that did was forge a bond between my sister and I that we still share to this day. She went on to breastfeed all her children and that was what I wanted to do too. It sure wasn't easy but I knew I could figure it out and be successful.

Once we got to go home, the real work began. I was still healing from the birth but

Brian needed my constant care. He was a colicky baby in the beginning and it took some trial and error to figure out what I could and couldn't eat to keep him from being gassy. My favorite times with him were in the middle of the night. At those feedings, it was just him and I. I spent the time rocking him and singing to him. Our song became *Masterpiece by Atlantic Starr* and I knew every word. I sang it to him every night. I would change the word *girl* to *boy* and the words *my love* to *my son.* I vowed to him before he could even remember that I would dance with him to that song, someday on his wedding day.

Brian was almost a month old by the time Claude came home and met him. There was little time to adjust because a week later, we had to make the trip to our new home in Georgia. We would live in a two bedroom duplex on base. I couldn't wait to see what it looked like. I had everything I needed to make the perfect home, and especially the perfect nursery. It would be scary, moving where I knew no one, but like everything else, I took on a positive attitude.

One of the first things we did once we were in Georgia was to have Brian baptized. My brother Kenny–who Brian looked most like and my sister Pearl for taking care of me during the end of my pregnancy, were to be his Godparents. My mother allowed Kenny to come, because it was a religious ceremony and all of a sudden she had become holy. Not in real life, but in her fake life. Edna stood in for Pearl because she couldn't take the time from work which was better than having my mother do it. Being so close to Florida meant that both grandmothers were able to come to the baptism and meet their grandson. Eddie stayed home.

Our duplex was an adorable one story brick house. It wasn't big but it was just right for us. We moved in rather quickly and settled right into life in the Peach State. Claude had to rotate the shifts he worked, and his rotation started with eight weeks on third shift. My mother commented how I must be angry that he was getting away with no night feedings. She loved to make little digs. I just let her make her comment because a few minutes later she was digging at me coddling Brian too much. It didn't bother me at all. I was thankful for all the time I got to spend with my boy.

After working eight weeks of the third shift, he went to eight weeks of working second shift. By the time he was done with that rotation and started his eight weeks on days, Brian was seven months old. Finally, Claude and I would have our evenings together and I had to admit, I missed him. I loved my time being a mom, but I longed to be with my husband too. To my delight, he seemed to have missed me too.

The first two weeks, he couldn't keep his hands off me. At night, we would snuggle on the couch, watching TV and it always led to sex. It was like we were making up for lost time. However, by the third week, I was becoming exhausted. It wasn't that I didn't enjoy it, I did. But not long after we would make love, Brian would wake up for a feeding and he was not easy to get back down. Claude got to sleep like a baby through it all and in the morning head off to work. I was up most of the night and then almost all day with the baby. Plus I had to keep the house clean, do laundry, iron Claude's uniforms, and make all the meals. I also had to do the food shopping and take Brian to all his doctors appointments. So when I said no one night to sex, I certainly didn't expect the response I got.

He got so angry and started yelling at me. He accused me just not wanting him. I tried to explain my side of it, but he didn't want to hear my excuses.

"Give me a break!" He screamed. "It's not like you have to work! You get to stay home with a baby. I've seen you nap when he naps!"

"Claude, I haven't said no for two and a half weeks. Tonight I'm tired. It was a long day." I tried countering his anger by speaking softly. I tried reaching out to touch him gently. He ripped his arm away.

"You have no fucking idea what a long day is!" He mocked me. "You couldn't last one day doing all I have been doing!" He screamed again. And he stormed off, slamming the bedroom door behind him. I waited a while before going to the bedroom. I was hoping he would be asleep and cooled off, but when I tried the door, it was locked. He had locked me out of our bedroom as part of his tantrum.

I was so angry with him That night, I slept in the rocker in Brian's room. And for three more nights after that too. Each night when I tried the door after putting Brian down, it was locked. When he finally let me back in our bedroom, I tried to be happy we were no longer fighting. I hated fighting. But little did I know, that first fight in Georgia was just the beginning. What came next was even worse.

Chapter 23
1991
"Luka"- Suzanne Vega

Fighting with Claude became a regular thing. When he got home each night he found something to pick a fight about. Sometimes he didn't like what I cooked. Sometimes he would get mad because I didn't get to all the ironing. It didn't matter that I had been doing other things, like taking care of our son or buying the groceries for the meals he expected when he got home. Sometimes after he was done being angry at me, he would flip a switch and expect sex from me. I hated it because the last thing I wanted after being yelled at was to cuddle up to him.

I developed a coping mechanism so I didn't have to turn him down and deal with more fighting. Instead when he initiated sex, I would immediately roll over and get on all fours. If we did it doggy style, I didn't have to see his face. Which was a good thing because after he belittled me for an hour, his face was the last thing I wanted to see. Then I could close my eyes and count to about two hundred. I usually never even made it that far and he was done.

I hated that it had to be that way, but he had become a mean spirited, nasty person since we got to Georgia. Sometimes our fights would get so loud that I knew our neighbors had to hear us. I wondered if that's why every time I saw either of them outside, they always gave me a sad smile. I got my answer one night when the fighting got worse.

He came in and I made spaghetti and meatballs. He took one look at the meal on the table and started yelling about the 'same old shit meals every single night'. He wasn't wrong, we were a young family on a tight budget so we did have a lot of pasta meals. But pasta could often be found at the commissary, four for one dollar. I couldn't pass that saving up so I tried to make different things with it. I guess he was sick of it, because he made some backhanded comment about how we could eat better if I was working, before throwing his plate against the wall.

The sight of my son jumping in his highchair with the sound of the breaking glass, was enough to send me over the edge. On top of that, there was now spaghetti and sauce all over our white walls that I was going to have to clean. It was more that I could take and I let him have it.

"What the fuck is wrong with you?? You just scared Brian!" As if to prove my point, Brian was crying. I know my yelling didn't help, but I was so angry. "And now I get to clean up after your tantrum!" I shouted at him. "And if I did get a job, who is going to take care of Brian, keep up the house, iron all your clothes and clean up from your nightly temper tantrums??"

I hated yelling in front of Brian, but Claude had crossed the line. I was tired of his outburst and I was hoping by standing up to him, I would make it stop. But to my dismay, he let me know he was not going to accept me talking back. He crossed the room in two long strides and had my face in his hand in an instant. He squeezed and I flinched as he pulled me close. I had no choice but to look at him.

"You have a problem with my tantrums?" He growled. "Tough shit! You have a pretty easy life while I take care of everything so you can just shut your mouth!" Now he was yelling.

I pulled away from his grip, which hurt more but he was not going to demean me anymore.

"Funny that you throw that in my face, but for years while I worked two jobs and paid the majority of our bills, including the car I never got to drive, all so you could play video games at all hours of the day and night, that never bothered you!" There I said it. All my resentment came out. He acted like I hadn't been a hard worker, working twice as much as he did. I had been such a hard worker, I didn't even get to finish high school, didn't get to buy my own car, but instead I got to keep his mothers house clean and help pay all her bills, while he did whatever he wanted, working the bare minimum. And I never complained. I never abused him or yelled at him about it. We were a partnership. But if he was going to throw all of this in my face now, I was going to speak up. That was my next mistake.

He grabbed me again, this time shoving me as hard as he could into the wall. To make matters worse, it was the wall already covered in spaghetti. When I hit it, I felt it crack under me. I also felt the glass from the plate cut into my back. Brian stopped crying and looked at me, scared. His little frightened eyes broke my heart. I started to cry, but more from anger.

"What is wrong with you?" I said softly but with as much venom as I could muster.

"Fuck you!" He screamed as he stormed off toward our bedroom and slammed the door.

I got up and started to pick up the glass. I checked on Brian and put some cheerios on his tray. I went to the bathroom mirror to check my back. I was just leaving the bathroom–I had a decent size gash on my back but I would deal with it later–when there was a knock on my front door.

I didn't want to answer it. I was covered in spaghetti. But when the second knock came, a voice behind the door announced who was there.

"Open up please. Security Police." They said firmly. Security Police is the Air Force equivalent to other branches Military Police. My stomach knotted and I immediately knew that my sad smiling neighbors had heard enough. I put my head down and opened the door.

"Good evening ma'am we got a report of some type of domestic disturbance over here and we need to check it out." The first guy in uniform said to me, I was in no position to argue, so I moved back and let them in. I know I looked defeated but it's how I felt so I wasn't going to hide it.

Once inside, they could see the wall, the spaghetti and sauce, and when I turned to let them walk in, I knew they saw it all over me. They looked at me sympathetically. More than anything, I was embarrassed.

"Are you okay?" Was the first question they asked.

"Yeah." I said softly wondering if Claude knew they were here. "Just a small cut on my back." I said. I didn't offer to show him so he asked if he could look. I said yes. I wasn't going to argue with the base police. When he lifted my shirt, I heard him call for EMTs on his radio.

"Where is your husband?" The one who looked at my back asked me.

"He's in our room." I pointed down the hall. It was the only room with the door closed.

"Does he have any weapons?" They asked. I was thankful to be able to say no. His job in the Air Force didn't require any and he wasn't a person who had interest in guns.

Brian wasn't a fan of strangers in the house and he started fussing. I went and picked him out of his highchair. I put him on my hip and gave him a reassuring snuggle.

The rest of what happened was a blur. They brought Claude out of the room and he looked shocked and pissed that he had been caught. I am sure he assumed I had called them but then the SPs made a point of saying the neighbors hear fighting all the time. They questioned him about the wall, which did have a hole in it where I hit it and was stained with red sauce. They also asked me what happened in a separate room. I am sure they were worried I wouldn't tell the truth with him there, but I did.

The end result was that was told he needed to report to his commanding officer first thing in the morning. He was also told he had one week to have the wall cleaned, repaired and painted. And they were very specific that I was not to be the one to do any of it.

The EMTs bandaged up my back and told me to follow up with the base doctor in a couple days. They checked me head to toe, they noted the fingerprint marks on my cheeks. They also checked Brian. They knew he saw the pediatrician on base, but they wanted me to follow up with her in a week as well.

I will say that things were done differently back then because he was allowed to stay in the house with me. That would not happen today. Maybe it was because he was basically property of the Air Force and he knew what happened was serious but thankfully he didn't take any of his anger out about being caught, on me. I think the fear of being court-martialed smartened him up for the moment.

In the weeks that followed, things were really tense between us. He got in trouble with his superiors, if you could call it trouble. He had to take anger management classes. Despite all of that we barely spoke. He had moved out onto the couch which the SPs had suggested that night. They told him he should not expect to go back into the bedroom unless I invited him. It amazed me that he followed all of this. I have no idea what happened at his anger management classes but after two weeks he was done.

In the weeks while this was going on, I joined a Mommy and Me group at the church where Brian was baptized. I needed to get out and feel like a normal person for a couple hours a day. It was there I met my first friend in Georgia. Janet was an older mom, about twelve years older than I was, but her son Mateo was Brian's age. In fact they were less than a month apart. We hit it off right away. We exchanged phone numbers. She wasn't from Georgia either. She wasn't military, but her husband had relocated to Georgia for an engineering job. We were both in the same boat as far as not knowing anyone. It made us fast friends. I didn't tell her what was going on in my personal life. In fact, I pretended all was well. Little did I know at the time, she was keeping her own struggles from me too. Eventually we opened up to one another, but for now it was just nice to have girl talk and compare parenting stories.

About three weeks later, Claude finally started talking to me. I could have kept up the silent treatment. After all, I was the one who had been the victim. But I wanted to see if the classes had helped him. He was still my husband, and while I didn't like him very much at that moment, I did still love him. I owed it to Brian to give him a chance to fix himself.

He asked if we could talk one evening after I had put Brian down for the night. It was unexpected, and I was really nervous but I agreed. We both got comfortable on the couch and he sat down on one end. I sat on the complete opposite end, as far from him as I could. If he noticed, he kept quiet about it.

"I need to start by apologizing to you." He said softly. "I was completely out of line and out of control. I am so sorry for all of it. For putting my hands on you, for the yelling and belittling. For all of it." He was being sincere and there were tears in his eyes.

I nodded. At first it was all I could muster. I could accept his apology but forgetting was going to be the hard part. When I didn't say anything right away, he continued.

"You have every right to be mad at me. And even afraid of me, but I promise you. I am getting better. I was dealing with a lot. The changes in schedules, the demands at work, all of it. It's been really hard on me. I didn't realize how much of myself I would have to give when I enlisted. And I took it out on you. I shouldn't have and I was wrong. I will make it up to you. I promise I will fix this. I love you and I love Brian and I will do whatever it takes to make you love me again."

I wanted so much to believe everything he was saying. I wanted my little family back. I didn't want to dread him coming home or hate having sex. He was being so sincere and he looked so sad. It became easy to believe he was telling me the truth.

"I never stopped loving you." I said. He smiled. "I didn't like you very much." I smiled back. "But I still love you. You're my husband. For better or worse right?" I said, and I meant it.

"Richer or Poorer?" He joked.

"As long as you understand that poorer means lots of pasta for dinner." I attempted an ill humored joke.

To my delight he smiled and took my hand.

"I really am sorry." He said squeezing it.

Enough time had passed for me to calm down and he seemed to really be hurting over everything. I squeezed his hand back.

That night we talked for a long time. He vented about work. He told me about all the demands, and the stress of it all. He said the day shift was actually the worst because there was just so much going on and he never seemed to be able to do anything right. He was constantly being told to pick up the pace, or to redo things. Because it was Top Secret he couldn't give me specifics, just that it was taking a toll on him.

He said he couldn't wait to get back on the second shift. He still had to get through the third shift, which he started in two more days. But he said that was more boring than anything. And he was looking forward to seeing some of his friends once he made it through six weeks of third shift. Not everyone rotated shifts. Some stayed on the same shift they were assigned to and he had made friends on the second shift. When I asked about them he talked about a couple guys who liked video games and a girl named Amanda. She was a

Sergeant and he liked her because she was always busting his balls. He said she was really funny. I never pictured myself as a jealous person, but something about the way he got giddy when talking about Amanda, I had to admit, it made me see a little green.

That night I let him back into the bedroom and we had amazing makeup sex. He was loving, and caring. He took his time and was all about pleasing me. I felt special. Later, I scolded myself for thinking the extra attention had anything to do with all our talk about Amanda. I was just being silly. Or so I thought.

Chapter 24
1991
"I Want Your Sex"- George Michael

By the time Claude was back on second shift, things between us were so much better. His whole attitude was better. He was even helpful around the house, doing his own ironing when I couldn't get to it. He never complained about what I made for dinner, or any meal for that matter. He made a point to say he liked the lunches I packed and when we had meals together, he always asked for seconds.

It felt like a brand new relationship and I was so happy about that. We made sure to spend even a small time together each day, even when he was on overnights. We shared at least one meal together each day too. It made Brian happy as well.

However, once he started second shift again, he was happier than I had ever seen him and I caught myself thinking once again that it had to do with Amanda. He always had a funny Amanda story. And he would get so giddy while telling it. I would have been blind not to notice. He also started waking me up when he came in after eleven. It was always to initiate sex. He was fun and playful. It was so nice to be a normal couple for a change. But there was a nagging that this had something to do with who he was with at work.

Normal never lasted with Claude and after the first week he woke me up saying he wanted to talk. I was immediately concerned. However it was nothing bad, he just wanted to talk about sex. He started asking me about my deepest sexual fantasies. Back then, if I even had any, they were pretty inexperienced basic fantasies. I had barely begun to explore real sexuality. I was not mature enough. I guess this is how we all learn though. No one is born knowing it all. I told him I really didn't have any fantasies because I was pretty new to all of this. I told him that I loved oral, and that sixty-nine was always fun. He seemed to be trying to pull more out of me, but I didn't know what he wanted me to say.

Finally, he grew impatient. "Have you ever thought about having a threesome?" he asked.

It took me completely aback because up until then, that kind of thing never crossed my mind. I knew vaguely about it, from chatter during spring break. That was the extent of my knowledge at eighteen. I enjoyed sex with men, but I never thought about being with two men at one time. Ironically, that wasn't what he was talking about at all.

When I was too quiet for too long, he tried again. He clearly thought my silence meant something it didn't.

"Have you already had a threesome?" He seemed jealous by this thought.

"No, NO!" I said, a bit too offended.

"Oh. Well, would you ever want to try?" Apparently he wasn't too jealous. Maybe he was only jealous if he wasn't a part of it.

"I don't know." I said. "The idea of being with two men is intimidating."

"No. I mean with another woman?" He asked a bit too quickly. The idea of adding another man was not even on his radar. I guess this surprised me more than his initial question.

"Well I have never thought of that."

"But you have with two guys?" He asked.

"I never thought of it either way. But I don't think I am attracted to women so I thought you meant another man." I said honestly.

"Well, think about it. It could be fun." He said. I tried to think about it, but at first I didn't even know what I was picturing. And then, as if he planted the thought in my head, I knew he was picturing Amanda. I had no idea what she even looked like, but in my mind she was super model gorgeous and all this talk was for one reason. He wanted to have a threesome with Amanda. I was immediately hurt, but I needed to get more out of him. See if I was right.

"Wouldn't it be weird. Like having a stranger in our bed?" I asked.

"Well what if we knew the person?"

"I don't know anyone here except Janet. And that's not happening. She's married and she is my friend.'

"Well I meant what if you got to know someone and it was all mutual?"

"Maybe. I honestly never gave it any thought."

An older me has since given this plenty of thought and I can honestly say I wouldn't be opposed. I don't want to kiss and tell about older me, but as for younger me, I never thought about it before that night. My goal back then was to get married and start a family because that is what was expected of me. Younger me was also pretty old fashioned, thinking that once you got married you stayed faithful.

"Cause I was thinking." he continues on "It could be fun. Maybe even put the spark back in our marriage." I guess I really was naive because I thought it was already back. Ever since he had gone to anger management and changed his whole attitude. If you asked me things were wonderful. I actually felt like we were a newlywed couple all over again. The last thing I wanted was for him to start getting angry again so I played along.

"Ok but like I said, we don't know anyone." I hoped this would be a good stalling technique.

"Well, I might know someone." He blurted out.

"Oh?" I asked like I was curious and didn't already know who was on his mind.

"Yeah. I told you about her. Amanda! We were talking the other night and she asked me if I ever had a threesome. Come to find out, she likes having threesomes with married couples."

"Really?" It seemed weird to me, but he made it seem like something everyone was doing. And maybe they were. "But isn't that like cheating?" I asked.

"Not if we both consent to it. And she even told me she wouldn't do anything that we weren't all comfortable with." It was amazing how once he brought it up, he got more excited and couldn't stop talking about it. He rubbed up against me, so I could feel how hard he was already. "I think it would be a lot of fun." And then before I could disagree, he started kissing me. He gave me all the information and then ended his sales pitch by making love to me. He told me how much he loved me and how he wanted to please me in new and exciting ways.

I wish I could say he didn't think I was stupid enough to fall for all that, but he did. And what was worse was that while I wasn't falling for any of what he was saying, I also wanted to please him. I did not want to go backwards. He was finally happy. I knew if I said I wasn't interested he would get angry with me again. I hated to admit it, but that fear was enough for me to agree to it.

Over the next week he brought it up every single night. I made excuses. I said we couldn't do it in the house. I didn't want to do something like that with Brian sleeping in the next room. He had an answer for that. He said that Amanda already told him we should do it at her place. That meant we would need a sitter. He told me to ask Janet, but I told him I didn't want to use our friendship like that. Plus, Brain would have to sleep over there and I was not ready for that.

Every time he came up with a new idea, I found a way to shoot it down. Finally, he told me he had asked his mom to come visit for a weekend. He told her that he wanted to take me away overnight and the only person I would trust with Brian was his Nana. That isn't at all what I said. I said even that made me uneasy because I was still nursing him. He fixed that by giving me extra time to pump, by spending extra time with Brian while I did.

If Claude was being honest with himself, he knew I didn't want to do it. But he obviously didn't care. He wanted to do it, and that was all that mattered to him. By the time his mom arrived on the following Friday, I was sick to my stomach. I was popping Imodium for diarrhea. The last thing I wanted to happen was that I would need to run to the bathroom while we were fooling around. I even told him I was too sick to go, a last ditch attempt. He told me it was perfectly normal to be nervous. He said he was too. It would be ok after a glass of wine.

We had agreed that there would be no penetration. Between him and her, and so that she didn't feel weird, between him and I either. This first time would be all exploration and oral. The fact that he often referred to it as the first time, let me know without a doubt he expected this would become a regular thing. I would worry about that later, I needed to get through this first time. I kept telling myself it would make my husband happy and a good wife would at least try her husband's fantasies.

The night we went to Amanda's he was in a great mood. He was teasing me and flirting with me all day. It was fun so I played along too. I still hadn't met Amanda yet, so when a beautiful brunette with gorgeous bright green eyes opened the door I was shocked at how pretty she actually was. She was dark tanned, like she laid out often. She had perfect size breasts that strained against the olive green tank top she was wearing. Her ass and toned legs were perfect too. It was obvious she worked out, and was in great shape. If ever I was going to choose to have a threesome with someone, she was definitely someone I would have considered. But none of this was my idea.

He had told me before she was older than us. She had just turned 28, and he said she had threesomes with other couples on base as well. He assured me she had experience and would guide us the whole way.

She welcomed me in with a warm hug and invited us to sit down on her sofa. Claude didn't drink but he accepted a bottle of beer from her. She poured us both a glass of chilled white wine and then sat on the sofa to talk.

"So, Claude said you are pretty nervous about this. Trust me, it's a lot of fun." She patted my knee, but I barely noticed because I turned to glare at Claude for telling her that. She squeezed my knee to get my attention back to her. "I was thinking we could start with a little kissing out here, just to loosen everyone up." She looked at Claude then back to me, "Maybe a shot would help you more than that wine. You look pretty tense."

I actually hated the way she was patronizing me. I wish I had been able to speak up for myself. I wish I had done it long before getting to her house. But I hadn't been strong enough and now it was too late. Everyone was expecting it to happen. So I accepted the shot– it was vodka–and chased it down with the whole glass of wine. Having not had anything to drink since I got pregnant with Brian, it hit me harder than I expected. My head was swimming and my stomach started to flip.

Amanda talked for another minute then moved closer to me on the couch. She ran her hand up my arm and leaned in to first kiss me, then she kissed Claude. Then she pushed us to kiss each other. This shared kissing went on for a few minutes. She was touching us both and Claude was easily touching her as well. He touched me too, but I could see he was giving her way more attention. Amanda took my hand and placed it on her breast, encouraging me to join in.

When the kissing and touching seemed to have everyone turned on, she slowly started to pull away. I didn't mind the kissing, it was nice. I wish it could have stayed just that but it was clear they both wanted more.

"Why don't we all go take a shower. I have a nice big shower." She smiled at me, and reached over grabbing Claude's hand. She had definitely done this before. "Don't worry." She said to me like I was a child. "Claude already told me, no penetration tonight. Unless of course you change your mind." She said, smiling and winking at Claude. Again I glared at

Claude. He looked at me like he had no idea why I would be mad. He tried the innocent, '*see I told her*' look.

In the bathroom they started to undress and I had no choice but to join in. Thankfully Claude's body was less than perfect because I was incredibly self conscious of my post pregnancy body. And next to Amanda it was even worse. Naked, she was even more beautiful. Her breasts were perfect. They barely moved, but mine were now what fed my child. I did not feel sexy next to her at all.

In the shower, she lathered all of us up and there was more kissing, and a lot more touching. After we rinsed off she knelt down in front of Claude and started giving him a blow job. She encouraged me to join her. He of course was all for that. Still, sharing my husband with another woman was really starting to make me feel sick. I hated that he wanted this so bad. The shower seemed to go on forever. My knees were killing me on the tile. I hated watching her put him in her mouth over and over, so I was strangely relieved when he finally came in her mouth. I was hoping that meant we would be done for the night. No such luck.

After we got out of the shower she took us into her room, all wrapped in big fluffy towels. She pulled us onto the bed together but then it was like they forgot there were three of us. They got into a sixty-nine position and immediately acted like it was just them. I didn't even know what to do with myself. I was angry and I could feel tears burning my eyes. She was on top of him so she tried pulling me in, but I couldn't take my eyes off him. I was glued to what he *was doing* to her. At one point, I felt so out of place, I angrily tapped Claude on the shoulder. He looked over at me like he had no idea what my problem was. When I glared for the third time, and there was no mistaking why I was upset–I was basically watching them, no longer part of this so-called threesome–he answered my glare, by burying his face deeper into her. Which of course made her come, followed by him for the second time. The whole thing was so demoralizing for me.

Their orgasms turned out to be the end of that threesome. I don't think either one of them cared that there was no pleasure in any of that for me. They were done and that was all that mattered. This turned out to be a good thing because I could no longer continue to watch them. Amanda made a comment about us staying overnight but since Claude knew I was unhappy, he said maybe we could get together another time. I wanted to tell him he was out of his mind. She tried again suggesting we spend the night and maybe have some fun in the morning. I spoke right up before he could say a word and told Claude I would feel better if we went home to Brian. He knew I was pissed at him for the way he showed off with her. He was dumb but he wasn't stupid. He knew better than to try and convince me to stay.

The ride home was mostly silent. He tried talking to me once. I think he thought he might be able to salvage the night and excuse his behavior but when I ignored him he didn't try to talk to me again. When we got home, his mother did not question why we hadn't stayed out overnight. Maybe it was because I stormed off to bed in Brian's room and locked the door behind me. I heard Claude close our door and then I heard him on the phone. I knew he was talking to Amanda. He was famous for adding insult to injury.

His mom left the next day after breakfast. There was too much tension in our house for her to stay. I am sure she blamed me. He thanked her for watching the baby so we could have 'a date night'. I didn't say much. I wished her safe travels, but I wasn't going to pretend everything was ok, because it definitely wasn't.

Chapter 25
1991
"Hard Candy Christmas" - Dolly Parton

After that night things were awful between Claude and I again–just in time for the holidays. I was fairly certain he was now having an affair with Amanda. We weren't sleeping together, and though I couldn't be certain what time he came home, it was usually two hours after his shift ended. I didn't call him out on it. I was so hurt by it all. He never even apologized for the way he acted that night. The image of him with her was burned in my memory and I couldn't get rid of it.

I guess by this time I had learned how to cope with sadness and disappointment because I made the decision not to let what he did, and what he was doing, ruin Brian's first Christmas. So when my niece Leeann called asking if they could come spend Christmas with us, I said yes. I didn't even ask Claude. The idea of Christmas with just him was so unpleasant of a thought that I welcomed the idea of visitors. As it turned out, Leeann's husband was to report to a base in Florida after the first of the year. So the plan was, they would pack up their things and stop in with us in Georgia the week of Christmas. We would celebrate and they would leave after the first of the year for their new base.

Her son was celebrating his second Christmas–the first being when he was barely a month old–and since we both shared hard childhoods and a love of Christmas, it meant a lot to us to be able to give our babies happy memories. Even if they wouldn't remember, we would. So we started planning and before long, the plan grew. This Christmas, with these two baby boys, would be one for the books. To this day, we still speak of it fondly and laugh at how overboard we went when we come across the pictures of the tree loaded down with presents. It felt good at the time and was just what I needed. It also set the foundation for when we each had 'only' daughters and went overboard for them with their every obsession, from One Direction merchandise and concerts to Hannah Montana toys and movies on opening night. If it made our girls happy, we spent that money and spoiled them rotten. Things that never happened for us. It's our lifetime bond. It was a dream when we were girls and became a reality that started Christmas 1991.

I waited a day or two and then told Claude as he was leaving for work, the news that Leeann and her family were coming for Christmas. I told him I would be making up the den with an air mattress for them and that he could move back into the bedroom so there were no questions about us. He just nodded in agreement. What he didn't know then, was that by the time he got home from work, I had bought and set up a futon in our room for him. I was not going to share a bed with him, while he was sleeping with Amanda.   That night he didn't even question it. He slept on the futon and in the morning made it up so that when our guests arrived they wouldn't be the wiser.

When Leeann arrived it hit me how much I longed to have family come visit with me. Having it be Leeann, someone who was my age and lived a similar life, made it even more special. As soon as she arrived we were inseparable. We would leave the boys with her husband Rake, or both Claude and Rake while we went Christmas Shopping. We would stop for lunch and then come home with bags of toys to wrap. Another day we went to the commissary and spent our entire food budgets on Christmas dinner, the Christmas Eve meal, and ingredients to bake Christmas goodies.

Each night we cooked together making fun meals and baking things like sugar cookies, peppermint bark, and my dad's fudge. We drank wine and hung out long after everyone was in bed. When the house was quiet we would put on Christmas albums and wrap all the presents. There were so many. And even though the boys would never know the difference, we hid them all so we could pull them out on Christmas Eve.

That Christmas Eve we made a big meal. I had a Family Circle cookbook I got at my wedding shower. I loved it and used it almost every day. We attempted to make our own Chinese Food from the book, and surprisingly it was really good. Back then, getting take out was rare, so we planned this instead. It was such a hit it became my Christmas Eve Tradition for many many years after.

After dinner we helped the boys leave cookies out for Santa and opened brand new pajamas. We all got new pajamas, even the guys. Brian's were *Sesame Street* and I can still see him with his *Big Bird* slippers and matching bathrobe. He was my first, and though some memories fade over time, some find a spot in our minds and stay as long as we do.

After bath, we tucked the boys into bed and became Santa. To this day, when we look at the pictures from that Christmas Eve or talk about that year, we laugh so hard. There were so many presents, we could barely all fit in the living room together. The gifts went up the tree halfway and we had gotten each of them a Sesame *Street Big Bird* rocking horse. Those were out front with a big red and green bow, ensuring it would be the first thing they would see, when they woke up.

As we sat around the living room before bed, sipping cider I noticed that Leeann and Rake were cuddly. Claude and I, in stark contrast, sat in separate chairs. We barely glanced at each other. I found myself thinking how much different my life would have been, if I had just taken the chance with Joel. But I had been too scared for too long and when I finally got strong, it was too late. I reminded myself this was my fault, but it didn't change the sadness when I looked over at who I had married. Then I scolded myself because if not for that lapse in judgment, I wouldn't have Brian. And I wouldn't trade him for anything in the world.

That night when we all went to bed, Claude had been drinking. He didn't do it often because of his father so when he did it, it hit him hard. The first thing he did when he closed the bedroom door, was turn on me. The guy who had been laughing and joking with our guests all night was gone.

"Do we even have any money left? That tree is ridiculous! He isn't even going to remember any of that!" He hissed at me.

"Yes we have money left. I used my base charge card."

"Which I will have to pay."

"Well you could pay for daycare for Brian if you would rather." I snapped back.

"Keep threatening me with that and I will." He said, grabbing my face.

"It's not a threat. It's the truth. If I get a job, the money will go to paying daycare. For someone else to raise our son. And then who would watch Brian while your fucking Amanda?" He squeezed tighter at my defiance. "Go ahead, leave marks on my face. I am sure Leeann would love to call the SPs for me." I was only being brave because they were in the next room. He knew it too and let me go and shoved my face back. He sauntered to the futon and was snoring in three minutes.

Merry Christmas to me.

The next morning Leeann and I were up before everyone. It's always been that way with her and I. When we were little girls and my mom would ship me off to my sisters anytime we were on school break, Leeann and I would get up early. Some days back then, we would set the alarm for four in the morning. Our intent was to cook breakfast for the whole family. But since we were too little to use appliances, we would try to accomplish this with my Holly Hobby oven and her Creepy Crawler maker. Her parents never got a kick out of being woken at five for runny eggs and raw toast.

As we sipped our Christmas morning coffee we reminisced about those days. We vowed that if our boys did the same, we would wake up smiling and do our best to choke down the food because we would know how hard they worked on it. But this year it was her and I making breakfast for our families. Cinnamon Rolls from the can, thick crispy bacon, Eggnog and coffee. Things we could eat while we opened presents.

Finally everyone was up and seeing the boys' faces light up made everything worth it– even the abuse at Claude's hands. It was all worth it. I would endure whatever he did, if it meant in the end I could see the smile on Brian's face that Christmas morning. He was crawling by now, and pulling himself up on things and the first thing he went to was the big bird rocker. All in all, the entire day was a perfect Christmas day. And then it wasn't. Just as we finished dinner, Claude announced that he had to go drop off a few Christmas gifts at work. I knew he was lying. The only gifts he planned to deliver was to Amanda. I just knew it.

I didn't react. I knew if I did, Leeann would see it. So I smiled and told him to hurry back. Leeann and I cleaned up from dinner while the boys played with Rake on the floor. I was doing good. I would not let him break me. And then *Dolly* came on the radio.

Maybe I'll move somewhere, maybe I'll get a car, maybe I'll drive so far I'll lose track. Me, I'll be just fine and dandy. Lord it's like a hard candy Christmas. I'm barely getting through til tomorrow still I won't let sorrow bring me way down.....

It hit me so hard and I found myself sobbing in the sink full of dishes. Leeann was by my side in an instant. She came behind me and hugged me tight.

"What is going on?" She asked softly. I wanted so badly to tell her. But somehow telling her things weren't ok meant I had failed. Still, I couldn't keep it in any longer. Once I started talking it was like a flood gate had opened. The words poured out and I told her everything. I told her about the abuse since getting to Georgia, the threesome I was pressured into and how now I suspected him of an affair.

I admitted to my own unfaithfulness before we got married but also how I hadn't been unfaithful since the day we got married. When I was done, I had cried out all my tears and there was a huge weight lifted off my shoulder. Somehow, by speaking it out loud, it made everything so much more clear.

"I can't tell you what to do. I am the last person to give advice," Leeann said, as she held me. We had moved the conversation to my room and were sitting on my bed. "But you need to report the abuse. What happens when we leave? When we're not in the next room? He won't stop then. And what about Brian? What if he really hurts you? What will happen to Brian?"

Her words made so much sense. Maybe because she was pointing out how all this would affect Brian. I loved him more than I ever loved myself. I had to put a stop to all of it before it was too late. Yet saying I had to do it, and actually doing it were two very different things. Brian, and his safety had to be more important than my own fear. I made her a promise. I would confront him. She wanted me to do it before she left. It would be safer for me that way. So I made the promise and set the plan in motion.

His next day off was New Year's Eve so I planned to talk to him when he got home the night before. This would give me a couple days to confront him, and have them there to keep me safe if he was angry. In the days following Christmas, I used the time with Leeann to get stronger and plan what I wanted to say. When the time finally came, I was ready.

I waited up for him. When he came in from work that night, two hours later than he should have, I was sitting up in bed, a soft lamp on. I wish I could say when he saw me, he smiled. He did not. In fact, he didn't even try not to scowl.

I know my bravery came from knowing Leeann was in the next room, but if that's what it took, I would take the help.

"With Amanda again?" I asked in a way that said I already knew the answer.

"Unlike you, I have to work."

"Yeah ok. Keep throwing that in my face. That doesn't excuse your behavior."

"What behavior? I was at work!" He started to raise his voice then remembered we had company.

"So, if I call your commanding officer, will he confirm that you stayed two hours late tonight?" I countered.

He turned a bit pale but was doing his best to retain his composure. He nodded with a sarcastic flair.

"It stops today Claude." I said flatly. "The affair, the abuse. It all stops today."

"Are you threatening me?" He asked.

"No, I am telling you. I can't live like this anymore. You're my husband, and Brian's father. We both deserve better."

"And you think you will get better? A single, uneducated and unemployed woman with a kid? Who would want you? Where would you go? I keep a roof over your head."

His words hurt so much and it was not going at all how I had hoped.

"I thought you wanted me." I said, less confident than I originally felt. But it was the truth. "You told me you wanted me for life."

"I do. And I want to be Brian's dad. But you come at me with accusations and threats."

"No I wasn't. It's a fact. You are having an affair and I need it to stop. What you did with her right in front of me was bad enough. Then you kept it going on your own."

In the end, he knew he couldn't keep up his lies or his responses to me. It was way too obvious that he was having an affair and all the late nights showed that he thought he could flaunt it. He didn't count on me confronting him and calling him out.

With Leeann at the house, he knew he needed to fix the mess he had started. He didn't need any witnesses either. So he turned on the charm. He shed some tears, he held me and told me he was sorry. He was weak. He made mistakes and he loved me. He made promises to break things off and get us some couples counseling. He convinced me it was a big mistake and he would never hurt me again.

The best part was that he was true to his word. No more fights, no more coming home late. He was, as far as I could see, committed to our marriage. And it wasn't just until Leeann and Rake headed off to Florida. It lasted so long that I really started to believe it. But the problem with living in a lie, most people can only keep it up so long and for Claude, his limit was 6 weeks.

After Leeann left, things were good
again. Claude was back on first shift again and
it seemed like he had really broken things off
with Amanda. Maybe he was afraid I would go
to his commanding officers. Maybe he really
did want to work things out. He was with us in
the evening and was back to sleeping in the
bed. I did my best to put the abuse and
betrayal behind me. As my birthday neared, I
had hope that it would be a good birthday, like
the one when he proposed. I tried to let the
happy memories cover over the sad ones.

I woke up the morning of my birthday to
breakfast in bed with Brian and Claude. But as
soon as I sat up, I felt sick. Like I was going to
throw up all over the English muffin and peanut
butter. I asked Claude to take it away, but it
was too late. The nausea washed over me, and
I barely made it to our bedroom trash before
losing the entire contents of my stomach.
Claude let me go back to bed and I tried my
best to sleep the bug off.

By early afternoon I felt a little better so I
got up and took a shower. And that is where it
hit me. I might not be sick at all. When was the
last time I had my period? When was the last

time we had sex? He was back in the bed, so it was happening pretty regularly. If I didn't want him sleeping with Amanda I had to make myself available to him. And I had. My period was definitely late. This time I didn't have the energy to hide it from him. I needed to know.

I came out of my shower and asked him immediately to run to the drug store and get me a pregnancy test. His face went to instant shock, and something else I couldn't put my finger on at the time.   But he went to the store, because it was obvious he wanted to know as bad as I did. He came back with two.

"I know it says first morning urine, but I figured it couldn't hurt to take one today." He reasoned. So I wasn't about to argue. I wanted to know as bad as he did, even if it was for different reasons.

I took one of the tests and in less than ten minutes, we had an answer. I was pregnant. I didn't know whether to laugh or cry. For one thing, I wasn't even sure if I was still in love with Claude but I wanted to be. I was working through things with him, because I had committed to him. Still, it was not easy to forget the abuse I suffered at his hands. I thought when I left my mom I had left the abuse.

Then there were his nasty comments, about who would want me, with one kid and no education. Now I would have two kids. It made me feel even more stuck to him.

So when I told him, I shouldn't have been surprised by his reaction. Anger.

"Fuck!" He spat out. "Fuck fuck fuck!" And then I am certain I heard him say something like "she's gonna be pissed" under his breath, though when I questioned what he said, he acted like I was hearing things.

But later when it seemed like he calmed down, he said he was going to go get some ice cream for my cake, and kissed me gently before he left. Maybe I misread his reaction. Then again, maybe not. It took way longer than it should have and the ice cream was extra soft by the time he got back. I hated to think he went to tell Amanda, but if his renewed foul attitude was any indication, that's exactly what he had done. He was trying to pretend everything was ok as he sang Happy Birthday and let me blow out the candles. He was not a good actor.

"Well, I guess I'll call the base tomorrow. See how they do prenatal care." I said, trying to feel him out.

"Yeah. They might want to do their own test." He said, not looking at me.

"Probably." I said. "So are you happy?"

"I'm shocked." He said.

"Well you shouldn't be. You know how babies are made." I chuckled and as soon as I said the words, I knew why he was freaking out. If he was still seeing Amanda, and was telling her we weren't sleeping together, she would now know he was lying to her as much as he lied to me.

"I know." He tried a half smile. "Just didn't think it would happen so fast I guess."

"Yeah." I said. "But here we are."

I know some women try to trap men by getting pregnant, but this was the furthest thing from my mind. I didn't even think I would get pregnant since I was still partially breastfeeding Brian. Still, I couldn't help but hope this would make us closer. We had been so happy when I was pregnant with Brain. Maybe we could get back to that. Maybe he would break things off with Amanda for real now.

Before bed, he gave me my birthday presents. He got me a copy of *Beauty and the Beast* on VHS and a *Little Mermaid* movie case puzzle, that I could make into a big poster size picture, when it was completed. Now when I got it, I had no idea it would be a collectors item someday, but when the news broke that part of the castle was drawn to look like a penis, I was so happy I had this original copy, even if it was in puzzle form. Once it was pointed out to me, I could never unsee that penis again.

He held me all night that night. He hadn't done that in–well I don't know if he ever did. It was like he needed me as much as I needed him, what I didn't know, was why. I soaked it in, maybe this baby actually could save us.

As the days followed, we got closer and closer. The base doctors confirmed my pregnancy and we learned my due date was Thanksgiving day. I was so excited but when I brought it up to Claude he would smile and get quiet. One day about a month later, I found out why. Claude was at work on day shift and I was watching *Barney* with Brian. We were just finishing the *"I love you"* song when there was a knock on the door.

When I peeked out and saw Amanda, my heart sank. I had an instant knot in my stomach as I slowly opened the door and tried to appear casual.

"Amanda. Hi. What are you doing here?" I said.

"Can I come in?" She asked.

"Is everything ok?" I answered her question with a question of my own. "I didn't even know you knew where we lived."

"Yeah, well here I am. Can I come in?" She repeated.

I didn't want to let her in. I didn't feel comfortable, and this was before I became addicted to true crime shows like *Snapped* and

Dateline. It was just a feeling I had. But I'm a people pleaser, so I stepped back and let her inside. I watched her look around as she entered. I pointed to the chair. Brian was sitting on the couch and I didn't want her sitting with him. To make sure she didn't, I went to sit with him and tucked him close to me.

"Have a seat." I said. "I would offer you coffee but the smell makes me sick right now." I said. I was certain she knew I was pregnant but I was almost daring her to ask me why.

"Yeah Claude told me you're pregnant. That's why I am here."

Her boldness made me really uneasy but I did my best not to let it show.

"You came to talk about my pregnancy?" I asked, looking confused.

"Sort of. I know you're not naive. You know what's been going on." She started.

I didn't answer her. Of course I knew, but I was going to make her say it. "Claude led me to believe you two would be separating" Now this was news to me.

"Oh?" I questioned.

"And then I find out you're pregnant. Which means you haven't been faithful either." What the hell was she talking about? She paused, waiting for something from me. I don't know what she wanted, I had no clue what she was implying so I waited for her to go on. "I heard you went to the base doctors. Claude's superiors will think this child is his. That will hold up any separation."

Now it was clicking. She was implying that while Claude was being unfaithful to me, I was being unfaithful to him and got myself knocked up. Was she serious? I wanted to laugh in her face but I needed to hear more of her insane theory.

"Ok…." I said, daring her to go on.

"And we need this separation to happen. Because with me being pregnant too, there will be consequences on him. But if you tell the truth, then you can be with whoever it is you're sleeping with and then Claude and I can be together." As she spoke I looked around to see if I was on Candid Camera. I mean, was all of this for real? And was she really pregnant with Claude's baby? Had she just admitted that to me like it was no big deal? So I took a minute before speaking and then I let her have it.

"Listen, I do not know what *my husband* has been telling you but you are totally sounding stupid right now." I don't know where this bravery was coming from but her look said I managed to shock her. "This baby" I touched my belly, "is my husband's baby, whom I have been faithful to all this time. If I am understanding you correctly, you are also carrying his bastard child." Ok so maybe that was a bit much. The flash of anger in her eyes made me think I should be very careful. I shrugged as if her look didn't phase me.

"Bullshit!" She snapped. "You're really going to lie? They can do a paternity test you know! Why not just get rid of it now, and save yourself the embarrassment."

"You are the only one embarrassing yourself." I said. "And I will not be getting rid of my baby. I welcome a paternity test so that the world can see the fool that Claude has made of you——and me for that matter."

Amanda looked like she wanted to kill me. I didn't doubt she could if she put her mind to it, so I did the first smart thing I had done since letting her in.

"I need you to leave my house." She made no move. "Now!" I practically yelled.

"You're going to regret this." She hissed.

"Do I need to call the Security Police? Because I will." Thank God for cordless phones and the fact that mine was always within arms reach. I picked it up to let her know I meant business.

"Fuck you!" She spat out at me. But she got up like she was leaving. "He's leaving you. I promise you this. So you should figure your shit out."

"Don't you worry about me. Worry about your own mess." And then I clicked the button on the phone to turn it on. My next step would be dialing.

As soon as she was out the door, I jumped up and locked it. And then the tears fell. She was pregnant too. Claude was cheating on me and it hit me that he probably had every intention of leaving me until I wound up pregnant too. I had so many questions, and so much confusion. I wanted to call him and demand answers but I also needed to calm down and think. I put Brian down for a nap and I lay in my own bed. First I cried. It felt good to let it all out. Then I lay there and my mind didn't stop. What was I going to do? I was going to have a second child with someone who clearly didn't love me and who didn't deserve my love. To make matters worse, his mistress was pregnant too. Not only had he been abusive and I had forgiven time and again, but he was also unfaithful. He was not the same person I was with in Florida. He wasn't even the same man I married barely two years ago. And now his mistress was threatening me. I was still going over all of it in my head when my phone rang.

"Hello." I said, picking up the line in the bedroom, hoping it wouldn't wake Brian.

"Hey Mrs. Dooley." It was my dad. Immediately I felt some sense of calm. "How are you?"

Boy was that a loaded question. I decided not to say anything just yet.

"I'm ok Dad. What's new?"

"Well I was wondering if my little girl would be up for a visit?" He asked.

"What? Here? How?" I didn't understand what he was asking. He was a thousand miles away.

"Yes there. It seems I have been subpoenaed to testify against Dennis. You know, the hotel owner. So I have to come down. I was thinking of driving down and visiting with you on the way home. I could stay a few days." Now I wanted to see my Dad more than anything, especially right now, but with everything going on with Amanda I didn't know how that was going to work. Plus my dad was in his sixties and the idea of him driving all that way alone, scared me. And as if that wasn't enough, I also had so many questions about why he was testifying against Dennis.

As it turns out, the police had been watching him for a while now and they had a decent amount of evidence connecting him to child pornography. Since my dad had witnessed a lot of the boys going in and out of his room, he had a lot to offer the police.

My dad insisted he could drive and would stop half way and get a hotel so he would be safe. His plan was to stay overnight one night in Georgia with me when he made it this far, stretching the trip out and getting plenty of rest. Then after he testified in Daytona, he would come back to my house and stay two weeks. My sister Trisha was also planning to come later at the end of my dads first week with her kids. She would fly down and stay for the second week and then they would drive back together. We would visit places like Stone Mountain and the beaches of Savannah. Hearing the plans and the thought of having family nearby both excited and scared me. What would they all say when they saw the giant mess I was in now?

In the end, of course I agreed. It was just what I needed. Now I just had to wait a week until my dad arrived. And what a week it turned out to be. In fact, by the time my dad arrived my nerves would be frayed and I would be wound so tight he would have to be blind not to notice.

That's because for a solid week I didn't let on to Claude that Amanda had stopped by. I was waiting to see if he knew, and if he did he was really good at hiding it. He came in each night and acted normal. He held me at night, and if she had never stopped by, I would have thought everything was fine between us.

But it wasn't. And she was starting to scare me. On Tuesday, I felt someone watching me in the commissary as I did our grocery shopping. I was constantly feeling eyes on me, and finally as I turned the corner at the meat department, I saw her. She was there and then she was gone so quickly, that I could have convinced myself I imagined it. But I didn't. On Wednesday, I went to play out back with Brian in his *Fisher Price Cozy Coupe*, and I swore there was a woman watching me from my back neighbors windows. I could have walked over to see if Amanda's car was parked there, but I didn't want to know. On Thursday, I had just gotten Brian down for a nap and was going to read a new book, when someone rang my doorbell. By the time I got to the door they were gone. But as soon as I laid back on the couch again, the doorbell rang again. This time I ignored it. I was not going to give her the satisfaction. She tried one more time and as much as I wanted to open the door and scream at whoever it was to leave me alone, I didn't because the third time woke Brian and I had to get him back down. I refused to react.

The last day before my dad came was the last straw for me. It was a beautiful morning so I had the screen open and I was watching my favorite morning show, *Bewitched* while Brian played on the floor in the stream of sunlight that was pouring in. It was an episode that took place in Salem, Massachusetts, so I was extra interested. Even being from New Hampshire, I had never been to Salem, but I wanted to someday. So when Amanda came to the screen, I didn't even see her until she knocked on the metal.

I looked over startled to see her there and cursed myself for not locking the screen, when I opened the big door. Either she was starting to show, or she was just sporting an over exaggerated baby blue maternity blouse. I think it was the latter and I also think it was purely for my benefit. I didn't get up. She could hear me from there and I wanted to be close to the cordless.

"What now Amanda?" I tried to act unimpressed by her boldness.

"Can I come in?" She asked.

"No." I don't think she expected that.

"So you want to have this conversation in front of your neighbors? Should I talk louder?"

"What do you want?" Part of me wished I had already confronted Claude about all this. But the truth was, I was waiting for my Dad to come. I wanted his advice. And his protection. I hoped I was brave enough to ask him for it. But if I had already confronted Claude, I could call him at work right now and tell him to come get his girlfriend off our front steps.

"Have you decided what you are doing with your baby?" Wow she was something.

"Carrying it to term, delivering him or her and raising them. You?" I was never good at playing games and this was just annoying. Did she forget that Claude was my husband and the military would be none too pleased to hear he was getting women other than his wife pregnant. And Amanda was also a party of adultery. The only person who had anything to lose was Amanda. Well Claude too. I hadn't done anything wrong so I don't know what she was trying to prove.

"You know, accidents happen. I would watch your back if I was you." She said and this time her words managed to scare me. I tried to hide it.

"Is that a threat?"

"I already told you, it's a promise. I bet you wouldn't even be missed."

That stung. Would anyone miss me? Brian would. That I was sure of. What scared me even more was thinking she didn't just mean to harm me and her eyes went to Brian and then back to me. And that snapped me out of my fear and my mama bear instincts kicked in. I got up, slammed the storm door in her face and bolted it. I could see her shadow on the other side for a good minute. I was hoping she was shocked that I would be so bold. Eventually she walked away but she wasn't done.

She rang my phone every fifteen minutes that afternoon. All from blocked numbers. After the third hang up, I just shut the ringer off. If she was trying to scare me, she had succeeded but I would never let her know. Instead, I packed myself a suitcase and one for Brian. When Claude came home that night with expectations of having a weekend with his family and his father in law who would arrive at any minute, I let him have it.

"Do something about your fucking pregnant girlfriend." I said. His eyes went from my face to the suitcases. "And don't play stupid, she's been coming by, stalking me, even suggesting I get rid of our baby." I touched my belly protectively. "You don't want this family? Fine, but I am done living like this. My dad will be here by dinnertime. I will let him get a good night's sleep and then I am going down to Daytona with him. When we get back, you need to have made a decision. If you want her, fine. I will go back home. But Brian is coming with me and I will have this baby there."

And then I walked away to start dinner. I would fill my dad in once he was there but I was all done playing games. All my life, I wanted someone to want me, someone to care for me about me. I craved that feeling so much and it had led me to this exact moment. A moment that could change my trajectory forever

Chapter 27
1992
"Against All Odds, Take a Look at me Now" - Phil Collins

When my dad got to my house I asked him if I could go to Daytona with him. I told him I wanted to visit Edna with Brian. He was happy to have me along for the trip. So I loaded up his trunk with our bags and a playpen for Brian to sleep in. Claude was very quiet the whole time. He knew he couldn't argue my leaving and he probably felt a little relieved that I would be gone while he figured out this mess he had gotten himself into.

The next day, we had barely driven off the base when my dad turned to me and told me to spill it. I would have acted like I didn't know what he was talking about, but I couldn't hold it in another second. I did just what he asked and I spilled everything. I started with the violence and ended with the affair. I told him almost everything. I didn't bring up the threesome because I didn't want to scar him for life.

When I was done I took a deep breath. It seemed like the more I talked about it, the better I felt. My dad was quiet for a few minutes and I started to worry. I don't know why. I just didn't want to disappoint him. I felt like since moving to Florida that is all I had done. Now that I was married, I shouldn't still be disappointing him.

"Oh Mrs Dooley." He finally said. "We really failed you didn't we?"

What did he mean? Was he taking the blame for my mistakes?

"Dad, I–"

"No. I should have stood up to you mother. I should have stopped all the madness before we ever got to this point. You deserved so much better."

"I made my choices." I said quietly.

"You were too young to be making all those choices. And I should have stopped her. But you know what she is like. It's no excuse. I should have stood up to her. I let the fact that she is crazy hold me back. But it was my job to protect you. And I didn't. I am so sorry honey." He had tears in his eyes. I could tell that the time away from my mother had led to a lot of reflection on his part. He had regrets, but I did understand why he did what he did. To an outsider, they may not. I lived with my mothers crazy, and I totally understood why he didn't feel like he could stand up to her. Even now, as she left her husband for a younger man, and stopped raising all her kids by the age of 15 and younger, she was still living her best bi polar life while we picked up all the pieces.

My dad, who had been financially set for life when he met my mother, was now living on state assistance and struggling having lost everything he worked so hard for, over the years. We couldn't blame everything on my mom, we all have free will. But there was no doubt that life would have been different had I had a normal mother, and my father had a normal wife.

As we drove, my dad asked me a lot of questions. The biggest one was if I wanted to come home. Of course I did. But I also didn't want to break up our family. What would that do for Brian and this new baby I was carrying? It ultimately hinged on what Claude decided because if he didn't want us, it really didn't matter what we wanted.

My dad wanted me to think more about myself. He wanted me to make the decision that was best for me. Screw Claude. He had lost my fathers support the minute he had put his hands on me. It was a good thing I hadn't told him before this little trip to Daytona. This trip would afford my dad the time he needed to cool off before he saw Claude again. I promised my dad that I would give it lots of thought and he promised me he would help me move back home if that's what I wanted to do. I also promised him—he made me—that if I did stay, and Claude ever put his hands on me again, I would leave him that day.

The trip to Daytona started off really well considering the conversation. It was ironic that my dad booked a room at *The Voyager*, since he was giving a deposition about the owner. As we checked in, my mother caught sight of us but she didn't come out to greet us. She waited until we were settled in our room to ambush us. Away from anyone she didn't want to see the real her.

"What do you plan to tell them David?" She asked my dad as soon as she pushed into the room..

"The truth. Hello to you too Joan." She closed the door to the room and didn't even look at me.

"You need to be careful. He stands to lose everything." She snapped. "He won't take kindly to that."

"I honestly don't care what he loses. If he is doing what they say he is doing, he should be in jail. And you know it. You're only worried about what you will lose as usual." He snapped back. "Because if this place goes down, you're going down with it." He meant she would likely lose her job.

"His father will bail him out. And in turn keep me on. He loves me." His father was a millionaire. My mother had a way of charming men with money.

"I'm sure he does." I mumbled under my breath. My dad cracked a smile.

"You shut up. What are you even doing here?" She turned on me.

"Spending quality time with my dad. Why do you care?" It was sad the amount of hate I held in my heart for the woman who gave me life.

"That husband of yours finally smarten up and kick your slut ass to the curb?"

"Ok Time to go Joan." He got in her face. "You don't know her at all and you no longer get to talk to her that way. We are here to do what was asked of me, and then we will be on our way. In the meantime, stay clear of my daughter. She has suffered enough at your hands." And with that he escorted her right out the door and slammed it shut. He hadn't been able to do it before, but he did it now and it felt amazing.

Our heart to heart talks continued the entire trip. We took walks on the beach and I confided in him things I had never been able to before. The hardest thing I confined was what happened with Gary. But he handled it the way a parent should. He held me while I cried and he shook with anger at himself for not knowing sooner or seeking justice for his little girl.

By the time the deposition was given and we headed home, I was closer with my dad than

I ever had been. And I was convinced that with him by my side, I could find the strength to leave Claude and go back home. I could have this baby alone, and raise my kids as a single mom. I might even go back to school and get some sort of degree. Maybe not law, but something.

So I was completely unprepared for what awaited me at home.

Dad and I walked into the house and found it completely spotless. Claude had rearranged the furniture and it looked like he cleaned behind everything too. There were fresh flowers on the table and a note that said I should check out the den. What I found there was a freshly painted room, and Brian's crib had been moved in there as well. He had set up a colorful area rug with crayola crayons on it. Seeing Brian's crib made me wonder immediately what he had done in Brian's room.

He had rearranged the whole room and apparently bought a brand new captain's bed. He put new airplane bedding on it and arranged all his stuffed animals all over the bed. I had to admit everything looked great. When I put my bags in our room, I found that he had also made our bed with new bedding and put fresh flowers on both bedside tables. He was definitely trying to impress me, but I needed to know what it all meant. And what was he going to do about Amanda and her baby?

My dad seemed really surprised as well. So when I asked him to watch Brian so I could go talk to Claude, he happily said he would. As soon as I pulled up to his work, I started to regret it. Was this the right time? Would I run into Amanda? I wasn't sure but I couldn't wait any longer. I needed to know if everything he had done was because he'd chosen us and our family.

I asked for him at the security desk and a few minutes later he met me outside. We walked to a nearby bench in silence but once we sat, he turned to me.

"I want you to stay. I love you so much and I love Brian and I am so sorry for everything I did. I am especially sorry for everything with Amanda. That was a huge mistake and you did not deserve any of that."

I didn't know what to say. I certainly didn't expect any of this. In fact, I had fully planned to come home and pack to move back home with my dad. This wasn't at all what I imagined. My silence must have scared him because he tried again.

"You were right about her. She was crazy. And they're sending her to another base." He said, hoping that last bit would be what I wanted to hear.

"Why her? Why not us?" I asked. "You are just as guilty as she is."

"But I didn't stalk anyone. She did. And I didn't lie about being pregnant."

I could feel myself start to shake.

"She was lying? She wasn't really pregnant?" I asked, tears filling my eyes. I don't think I knew until that moment how much the idea of her having his baby had hurt me.

He looked sad and shook his head no. But he wasn't sad that she had lied, he looked truly sad that she had hurt me. And that he had too.

"I am so sorry. I know you can't trust me right now. But I promise to earn it back. I fucked up. I fucked up so bad. And I want to make it up to you. Please. Please don't leave me. Let me fix this. I love you."

And that's all it took. He wanted me. He wanted us to be a family. I forgave him right then and there. I accepted he was human and told myself that what he did was no different than what I had done with Joel. We both had made mistakes and he deserved a second chance, even if it was really more like a fifth chance. I didn't want a divorce. I wanted a family and I wanted someone to want me. So we kissed and made up, right there on that bench in front of his work. And again, with a little more intimacy, when he got home from work.

By the time my sister arrived, we were all one big happy family again. Even my dad accepted my decision to stay. I could tell he was torn, but when Claude went to him, man to man and apologized for everything, promising things would be different from now on, my dad believed him. Or he said he did for me. Either way, the next two weeks were wonderful.

We spent days together exploring Stone Mountain and getting tan on the Savannah beaches. Our kids played in the sand and we all swam. It wasn't until the older kids started asking to go to Six Flags, that I found out I wasn't the only pregnant one. My sister Trisha was too and we were both due within a couple months of each other. That meant that Six Flags was out for the both of us. So my dad took the older kids and we spent that day with the babies, at the base pool. Claude was at work and I took the time alone to tell my sister everything.

Just like my dad, she was shocked then mad and finally sad for me. She said she wished she had known. She also expressed skepticism at Claude's complete change of behavior. She was my big sister, it was her job to protect me. So I didn't let it bother me when she said she would not be forgiving him anytime soon. She said she would wait and see. She also made me promise, just like my dad had, that if it went south again after they left, I would leave immediately.

It was so nice to have my sister visiting. We had been close before the move to Florida and I had missed that. Having that guidance and love in my life. She was always what I called my sister-mommy. Sometimes I truly think my mother moved us to Florida, to get us as far away from the kids from my dads first marriage. To erase any trace of that first marriage. I will never understand it. Why marry a man with kids if you were going to hate them? Why have kids of your own when you didn't have a maternal bone in your body?

Like why, when my parents first married, had she ordered all the pictures of his first wife be removed from the home. I wasn't born yet, but my siblings had just lost their mother. How cruel do you have to be to take away all they had left of her? And what does it say about my mother that she was so jealous of a dead woman, that she also needed the entirety of the home remodeled right down to the wall to wall purple shag carpet she had to have installed. It was as if she was marking her territory with her favorite color.

I am actually very fortunate that my siblings love me. My mother didn't want that either. She always made sure she treated me like a little princess when anyone was around. But behind closed doors, she made them care

for me. And I know that caused resentment.
How could it not? She used me to get to them.
But when my brothers came along and we all
got older, she didn't even pretend to like any of
us. Except Kenny. He was the baby and he
remained her baby for life. I get it, I have a
'baby' now myself and it's true. He does get
away with things Brian never got away with
growing up. But I love all my kids and I do my
best to show them all.

My mother didn't really like any of us.
We were there for status. She loved boating to
people that she had ten kids even though the
oldest two were her age and she certainly
hadn't raised them. But the real reason she had
kids was to have built-in servants. We got
chore lists from as young as five years old. And
these lists got done every Saturday before we
were allowed to leave the house. We also had
after school lists and nights that it was our
responsibility to cook dinner.

Our weekends started like everyone else
in the seventies and eighties. We got Saturday
morning cartoons until ten. This let her sleep
in. Then our lists with about fifteen chores each
started. Things like dusting the window frames,
door jambs and everything on every hutch and
shelf. Taking a toothbrush to the grout was a
fun one, changing all the bedding in the house
was another. All this was taken care of by her
kids while she slept in and went out dancing

and drinking in the evenings. But if we were noisy during those cartoons or while doing the chores, there would be hell to pay.

One time, Pearl and I were arguing about what to watch. I wanted Smurfs, she wanted something else. Well, we woke her up and we paid the price. We had our mouths duct taped shut until she was ready to get up for the day. Then we had to apologize for waking her. I did it, I was six. What did I care? I just wanted the duct tape off my mouth. Pearl was fourteen and was a pissed off teenager with anger and resentment towards her evil stepmother. She refused to apologize. Her punishment for that was the duct tape stayed on and my mother made her wear it until bedtime. And it only came off at bedtime because Pearl finally decided to apologize. In hindsight, I can't believe she got away with things like this. That duct tape messed up my sister's mouth for weeks.

The only good thing that happened when we moved to Florida was that while we still had our chore lists, she wasn't around to check them as often. So we rarely had to redo anything because she just didn't have the time to be overly picky or vindictive. Or maybe she just didn't have my siblings to torture anymore. As long as we did what was on our lists, we could go off and do what we wanted afterwards. The more we were out of her hair, the better. From that was born way too much freedom, but it was better than the things she had done to my older siblings.

All I know is that having Trisha back in my life and having my dad free of my mother's evil grasp, things would be different from now on. I had been alone in Florida and many times acted out of childish desperation. Now, I knew I had my family to lean on and I would never need to feel hopeless again. This helped as they headed back to New Hampshire and I navigated my new life of forgiveness with Claude. I knew it wouldn't be easy, but I was ready.

Chapter 28
1993
"Karma Chameleon" - Culture Club

By the time we rang in the New Year, we had a new baby boy. His name was Evan and he was the complete opposite of Brian. He was feisty, arriving five weeks early, being delivered by the nurse because he couldn't be bothered to wait for the doctor, but he was also a very easy newborn. No colic, he slept eight hours between nursing, and was always happy. It made me wonder what I had in store for me with him in the future. Surely he wouldn't always be this easy.

Things between Claude and I were still good too. True to his word, things were going smooth, and other than the fact that I came home from the hospital to a house that was a disaster area, he really had been an almost model husband. He still wanted to be on his video games when he wasn't at work, which is what I am certain he did the three days I was in the hospital having Evan, but he worked hard so I let it slide. Mostly. I am only human and I did curse him under my breath as I cleaned my filthy house, did three loads of laundry and washed all his caked-on dishes, four days after giving birth. I had learned a long time ago it was easier to do it myself rather than start a fight.

But as more time passed on, he did seem to be slipping back into his old habits. Barely spending any time with me or the boys. Only making an effort with me when he wanted sex. Leaving me to take care of both boys all the time. He almost never changed a diaper or spent time playing with them. One day I took Brian to the McDonald's play place and of course I took Evan in his carrier because even though Claude was home, he was playing some flight simulator game and couldn't even keep an eye on the baby, who really just hung out at this point.

As I sat with my boys alone eating my lunch and watching Brian play, I told myself to let it go. It was his loss. He was losing this bonding time with the boys and that was his own fault. I tried not to let it eat at me. In fact, being a good wife, I ordered him a Big Mac meal as we were leaving for home. But when I got home and saw he was still in the same position in front of his game, I will admit I probably slammed his bag of food down a little aggressively.

"Thanks?" He said cautiously.

"Yup" I started to turn and walk away, as he was unwrapping the burger.

"What is your problem?" He asked defensively. I spun back around to face him.

"Seriously? You haven't moved from that spot in two days!" There I said it.

"Yeah so! It's my two days off. I can do what I want."

"So do I ever get a day off?" I challenged him.

"Oh please! You have free time all the time!"

"Oh do I?"

"Yes! Every time they're napping or playing independently!" He was raising his voice by now but so was I.

"You're ridiculous? You know that right?"

"You wanna see ridiculous?" He snapped. "Here shove this sandwich up your ass!" And before I knew what was happening, he hurled the sandwich at my head, narrowly missing me and hitting the hallway wall instead.

I was so stunned, I just turned and walked away. This was exactly why I kept my mouth shut when things were bothering me. It never paid to speak up. It always ended in a fight and put me in some horrible situation. And as if having a burger hurled at your head wasn't crazy enough, as I got to the living room and started taking Evan out of his carrier, I saw him out of the corner of my eye, piecing the sandwich back together and even worse, taking a big bite. He wasn't one to ever let food go to waste, even if it had just been all over our floor. I shook my head in disbelief.

I guess I shouldn't have been surprised. If I was honest, food had become his vice. I never said anything because it didn't bother me. We were both changing and neither of us had the bodies we had when we got married. I'd had two babies and was definitely shopping a size up. But he had become addicted to food. So much so that he would eat several snacks in one sitting and was beginning to put on a great deal of weight. In fact, as much as he tried to hide it, he had needed to buy all new uniforms. I had also seen a notice on his night table, stating that since his last weigh in, he was now required to do aerobics on base, three times a week. I had not seen him go once nor had he mentioned it.

That night, he heard me on the phone with my dad. He didn't know why I had called him but I couldn't help but think he was worried I would tell my dad he had thrown a Big Mac at my head. I didn't, but still he lurked around, actually picking up Brian's toys and washing the sink full of dinner dishes to hear my conversation better. The best part about his sudden need to make up for earlier was that my call to my dad had nothing to do with him whatsoever. I called him because I heard from

Edna that Dennis had been indicted. The police had arrested him earlier that day at the hotel.

What I found out from the articles Edna read me, was that there was enough evidence to proceed with all the charges. It was all over the Daytona papers. The police had found an entire closet filled with various videos, allegedly taken by Dennis, of Dennis and many young boys, engaged in various sex acts. In fact, according to Edna, things were so bad that many people were calling and canceling their reservations at *The Voyager*. No one wanted to stay at a place where their money was used to pay minors for sex.

Edna had decided to resign before she could be let go. This was just a second job to her and she didn't need to be a part of such disgusting behavior now that she knew the rumors were true. But she also said that my mother was planning on going down with the ship. My dad got a kick out of that. She was going to stay and fight to work for a man who had physically, mentally and sexually abused children. If that didn't speak to her character, I don't know what would.

I promised to keep my dad up to date with all the news, as soon as Edna shared it with me and he promised to do the same. This is how we spread gossip and news before social media. It took a bit longer but had mostly the same outcome.

My dad said he was sure he would now have to testify and at some point would be back for another visit. That gave me something to look forward to.

After I got the boys to bed, Claude came out to talk to me. He was nice enough to wait until after my favorite show, *Dr Quinn, Medicine Woman* ended. I didn't ask for much, and I barely watched TV, but I loved that one hour on Saturday nights so much. It was like stepping back in time to a different world and I looked forward to it. So it was appreciated that he waited for the credits to roll and then came out to sit with me.

"I'm sorry. I was a jerk. I know you've heard it all before but I am under a lot of stress. My commander is all over me. He hasn't let all the shit with Amanda go, plus my records still show the times the Security Police were called here, and now they're on me about my weight."

It was news to me that his Commander was still mad about Amanda and the Domestic Violence. It made sense that he wouldn't just let it go, but Claude hadn't said a word about any of it. I couldn't help but think it was naive of Claude to think it would just be forgiven and forgotten by everyone. Still, I had forgiven it, so I guess it wasn't too far fetched he would think everyone would. He was struggling and I needed to be there for him.

"I didn't know that. I am sorry things have been hard on you. Things have been hard for me too, you know. But I don't take it out on you."

"What do you mean?" He looked confused.

"Claude, I was at the hospital giving birth and you let this house become a disaster area. Then you played your video games while I cleaned the mess, after just having a baby. I didn't throw dirty diapers, or dirty dishes at you!"

I needed him to see the comparison. It was always 'poor him'. What about everyone else? He got really quiet and put his head down. Maybe it had clicked. Finally.

"I am sorry."

"Accepted." I grabbed his hands and leaned in to kiss him. " Now let's talk about the weight issue. What happens if you don't go to aerobics? Or lose the weight they want you to lose?"

"I guess they will discharge me. I don't know. I mean I work with fat people. I feel like they're just picking on me."

"Well do the others that are overweight do the aerobics?" I ignored his insults and the fact that he didn't seem to care how serious this could become.

"I think so, I'm not sure."

"So just do what they ask of you. Make an effort. I mean what would we do if they discharged you? You have a family now, you need to take this seriously. We both do. And I will buy healthier food. I will get more fruit." He hated vegetables so I didn't even suggest that. "We can go on a diet together. It will help me lose the baby weight too." I suggested.

"That would be nice." I couldn't help but wonder if he meant that I wanted to help him, or if he just wanted me to lose the baby weight. It definitely came off as though my weight was bothering him. I didn't dwell on it. I just made a plan. Together we made a list of healthy meals we could both agree on, as well as a long list of healthy snacks he would eat. It didn't help that he was picky. But we made the list and I promised to do my part if he promised to start going to aerobics. He agreed and once again all was right in our world.

For the first few weeks of our diet, he tried really hard. He didn't miss a single aerobic class. I was so proud of him and I told him often. Even when he passed me on the race to lose weight, I kept the positivity going. It felt amazing.

And then the news of my mothers undoing arrived. And that felt like nothing I had ever experienced. It was about time the woman who treated her children and husband like the dirt under her shoes, finally wasn't landing on her feet. And it happened one thing after another.

First, the hotel folded. In order to give Dennis the best defense team to face the heinous charges, his father had to sell *The Voyager*. And in order to help the new owners thrive, they changed the name and let every one of Dennis' employees go, including my mother. They wiped the slate clean. In one quick move, my mother no longer had her high paying job. That would eventually force her to sell her house on Ormond Beach. A double whammy. But then I learned there was more. Dominoes.

My father had been contacted by the insurance company my parents had in New Hampshire. He learned they were still investigating the barn fire we had right before we had to sell the farmhouse in Hollis, New Hampshire. This was the first place my mom made my dad move after making him sell the house he had owned with his first wife. Even with all the remodeling he had done, she couldn't outrun the ghost of my sibling's saint of a mother.

The insurance company was curious why the horses had been sold so hastily right before the fire. So quick in fact, we all went to school one morning each owning our own horse and came home to learn that our mother had sold them, not even letting us say goodbye to our beloved pets. Those horses fetched top dollar for my mother. The next day, the barn caught fire. My father wasn't at home when the fire happened but my mother was. Even more unsettling, was the fact that almost all the animals we still had, were out in the pasture before dawn that day. My mother had made Trisha do it before catching her bus to school that day.

It had taken years of investigating and they may have let it go except my mother made one big mistake. She assumed she had gotten away with the first fire. And to be sure, my mother chose a different company in Florida, so that when that house fire happened just after moving to Florida, even though she wasn't home, she became their prime suspect. She foolishly thought no one would put the two incidents together with two different companies and in two different states. She was wrong. And they were closing in.

It would only be a matter of time, through new evidence they received, and they would be able to show how the explosion of a brand new double wide had happened. And when they did, she would finally begin paying for all the years of misery she caused everyone else.

She had hidden everything for so long, especially her true colors. But now, all of that evil had caught up to her. She had used her chameleon abilities for as long as she could. Now, she would be exposed. Maybe not for the abuse but for other evil things she had done. Karma is funny like that. My best friend has been telling me this for years, and even now I find it to be true.

She said, "Karma doesn't ever happen when you want it to. And it rarely happens in the way you want it to. But if you are patient, and you stay a good person even when someone isn't good to you, you might just get a front row to witness the Karma, when it finally happens to them." And she's always right.

Thank you my dear best friend, Stacy. That certainly has been something you have proven time and again, to me over the years. It is sad that my mothers Karma, though nothing like I imagined through all the years of abuse, actually brought me peace. And as much as I did enjoy it, I would have much rather had a normal mother. More than that I really wish I had been lucky enough to have a healthy and loving, mother-daughter relationship. Still, it wasn't all bad. As I said before, it taught me the kind of mother I never wanted to be. Because of that I have lived my life with my own children, in the way I wish mine had been. Filled with love, honesty and trust. Free of abuse and in such a way that they each got a childhood. They got to be kids, they got to experience a mostly carefree life. I made sure they graduated high school and always knew they could be anything they wanted to be when they grew up. And they have and always will have my love and support. Sometimes the worst things in our life, teach us how to be the best versions of ourselves. This was the case for me. And it wasn't over yet.

Chapter 29
1993
"Separate Ways" - Journey

It's so hard to understand, looking back, why I let my life get so messy. I guess that is the beauty of hindsight. We can say how we would have changed things if we had only known. But would we really? Because one little change would alter the entire outcome and if we are truly honest, we know we have to take the good with the bad. So as angry as I was with my mother for the choices she forced into my life, I had to thank her. For without them, I wouldn't have Brian and Evan.

As I reveled in my mothers undoing, I tried to remind myself that she must be really sick in order to do some of the things she has done in her life. But if a person is truly sick, and never seeks the help they need, or owns their own evil, they lose the chance to be forgiven. Especially if they never ask for forgiveness. So I rejoiced as she came undone because unlike me, when I came undone at twelve, she was an adult. *She* could handle it.

Back at home, Claude was still trying. But sometime around July, he stopped yet again. I caught him skipping aerobics more often than he went. And the obsession with food got worse. It was a given that he would make a snack after coming home from work late at night. I tried to have healthy snacks available but he began making hot dogs his go-to, midnight snack. And not just one, he would make four. Every single night. When I stopped buying them, he would just stop and pick up a package on his way home.

One night, he must have been exhausted after work. He started boiling his hot dogs on the stove, and sat down on the couch to wait for them to cook. I woke up to the sound of the smoke alarms blaring, and the entire house filled with smoke. Before either of us could realize what happened, the fire department was there. Thankfully the entire thing was contained to one pan on the stove where the water had simply boiled away, and the pile of hot dogs had burnt black. Still, no one was happy to be called to our house in the middle of the night, and now the place would need to be cleaned, perhaps professionally, to get the smell out. Surely this would be reported to his superiors and the fear of the repercussions made me angry. As soon as the house was clear and I got both boys back to sleep, I let him have it.

"Jesus Claude! You could have burnt down the house. And you clearly didn't need those hot dogs. You couldn't even stay awake to eat them!'

"Oh shut up! I was hungry!"

"Not that hungry! You fell asleep!"

"One time! I work hard! Unlike you!"

"I am so sick of this argument. I work as hard as you. I always have. This isn't about me. You're not even supposed to be eating that stuff. You're skipping aerobics and eating junk. You were making great progress! Don't give them a reason to kick you out." I pleaded.

"Oh you would hate that, wouldn't you?" he snapped. "Your free ride would be over then. You might actually have to get a real job! And by the way, I lost weight. Your fat ass is still hanging on!" He could be so nasty when we fought. But I wasn't going to let his words hurt me. I fought back.

"That's it! I am so sick of hearing about my *free ride.* I will get a job. I will find daycare. Then you will see how much I do around here and how much I save us on daycare! " Before I headed off to bed, I turned to say one more thing. "Get your own shit together, before my getting a job, is the least of your worries!"

The next day I was true to my word. I went to all the local hotels, my babies in tow and applied to work at the front desk. It was what I had the most experience in. I didn't want to wait tables. I was already exhausted, I didn't need to add to it. And as predicted, what happened to us next was even worse than I anticipated.

I got a job at a *Holiday Inn* in downtown Macon and started working the day shift. Because Claude was moving to the third shift, it meant I needed daycare while he slept all day. Luckily, I found it as quickly as I found the job, and from a state approved list of providers, no less. The woman's name was Qadeeja and she had three children of her own and she watched two others. She came highly recommended and her price was right. I could work and keep about a quarter of my pay after taxes and paying her. It seemed ridiculous to me but I needed Claude to see it in living color. It was the only way he would ever understand.

For two weeks, I worked my new job and brought my babies to daycare. I did my best to keep the house clean but the laundry, especially Claude's uniforms, suffered. He ended up having to pull them from the dryer more often than not, and iron them himself. Another thing that suffered was my healthy cooking. When I got home at 5:30 after picking the babies up, I would have to nurse Evan immediately. Even though I could pump at work, the older pumps never did a great job and I was always engorged by the time we finally got home. When dinner was eventually on the table, it was whatever I could throw together in a short time before the boys needed their baths and bedtime.

At the end of the second week I started to notice a change in both the boys. For one thing, Brian seemed really quiet and Evan seemed really tired. Sometimes, I would have to really rouse him, by stripping him down into his diaper, just to get him to nurse. And even then, it was a less than enthusiastic feeding. I started to worry that he was getting so used to the bottle that he wouldn't get a good feeding from me. So I stayed up that night and pumped extra. I decided I would try feeding him from the bottle. Maybe he just liked that better now.

The next day, I dropped the boys off and left the extra bottle for Evan. He hadn't wanted much of it that morning. I explained to her that he really didn't want to nurse, so I pumped that morning and asked if she could feed him first thing. I assumed he would wake up and be starving. Three hours later, I got a call no mother should ever have to get at work. It was Quadeeja. She told me that Evan seemed really sick and I should come get him right away.

When I got there, he was still strapped in his carrier and he was barely moving. I didn't even wait for more information. I grabbed the boys, their things and I raced to the base hospital. I will never forget how frantic I felt as I burst through the doors, begging someone to look at my baby.

"He is so lethargic." I kept saying. "Please see what's going on with him." I pleaded. The woman behind the desk answered me by handing me a clipboard.

"Fill this out." She told me. But I didn't have time to get upset with her because just as she handed me the clipboard, an older doctor appeared and shoved it back in her hands. His eyes were on Evan as he asked me what was wrong.

I explained that his sitter had called me to come get him and he was barely moving. The rest of what happened was a blur. That kind old man, I later learned he was a two star General, picked my baby boy up and whisked him into a room. Brian and I followed helplessly. What we learned was even more shocking than I had ever imagined when I said I would put my boys in daycare.

After lab tests, and exams, and almost immediate IV fluids, they determined he was severely dehydrated. A check inside Quadeeja's fridge revealed that every bottle I sent for the last two weeks was still there. After interviews with the neighbors, we learned that they had heard a baby crying almost all day, every day while he was there. And when a social worker talked to Brian, we learned what only a toddler could tell us. She asked him what he and Evan did all day at daycare. The disgusting answer was, "I played, Evan cried."

She was, of course, shut down immediately by the state. Too little too late if you asked me. And that General, well he saved my Evan's life. In a few days, he was nursing again. The doctor explained, it wasn't that Evan didn't want the breast, he just didn't have the energy to nurse. One more day in those circumstances, and we might have lost him.

That was it for me. I was so angry with Claude. I blamed him. We almost lost our son for a lousy fifty extra bucks a week. I quit my job the next day and I dared him to say something to me about it. Maybe I had never stood up for myself before, but I was certainly going to stand up for what was best for my babies. They were my responsibility and I took it very seriously.

A few weeks went by and we hadn't talked about any of it. To be fair, he was still on third shift and I was busy making sure the boys got back on their schedules. One day, while Claude was sleeping before work, there was a knock on the door. I answered it to find two military officers holding a piece of paper. They asked for Claude and when I said he was sleeping, they asked me to wake him up.

I invited them in and while they waited, I went to wake Claude. This wasn't going to be good. He hated being woken up. Being woken to deal with two officers in his living room, would surely make it even worse.

It took me a minute to rouse him, but once he was awake, he got dressed and joined me in the living room. As soon as the officers started talking, I knew I was right. This was going to be anything but good. They told him they had documented him missing more than ten aerobics classes without prior permission. His weight had gone back up and he was no longer making an effort. He was already on probation for domestic violence. Basically, he was on the thinnest ice with the Air Force. He had thirty days to get back on track or they would be dishonorably discharging him. I just couldn't believe someone who had wanted the Air Force so bad back in high school, was going to throw it all away like this.

When they left, things only got worse. He crumpled up the paper and threw it across the room. I wanted to get mad. He was blowing his career over something so stupid. He never had a weight problem and he could easily get it under control. He was choosing not to. Still, I decided to try a different approach. I went to him and tried to comfort him.

"Claude, let me help you. We were doing so good before. Let's get back on track." I reached out to wrap my arms around him but he shrugged me off. He walked away, slammed the bedroom door, and then I heard things being thrown against our bedroom walls. I let him do what he was going to do. It was better to stay out of his way when he acted like this.

Instead, I went to work on dinner. I made a big salad, grilled some chicken breast to put on the salad and sliced up some watermelon. I put his plate aside and the boys and I ate outside on our picnic table. When he got back up he wasn't dressed for work. Instead he went over to the phone and right in front of me, called in sick. Next, he went to the refrigerator to get his dinner. He must not have liked what he saw because I heard it slam, first into the trash and then the plate clunked into the sink. This was followed by a pot being filled with water. Hot dogs. He was just being an ass.

So I turned on the TV to make ignoring him easier. Brian was already in bed and Evan was asleep in his swing beside me. I was watching *Roseanne* when he came in and plopped down right next to me on the couch, with four boiled hot dogs on buns and loaded with ketchup. I continued to ignore him. I wanted to say something but I felt he just needed to get the tantrum out of his system. He would feel better after a good night's sleep. Or so I thought. But after his hot dogs, he proceeded to eat an entire box of *Cheez-its*. He washed it all down noisily, with a two liter bottle of *Mountain Dew.*

When the episode ended, I decided to head to bed. He needed to be alone. He was doing all of this to start a fight and I was refusing to bite. But he ran out of patience with me when he saw I was just going to go to bed without saying a word.

"Better start packing up because by the end of the month I will be out of the Air Force. I'm done with all this bullshit!" He said.

"You're done with what bullshit Claude? The free housing? The good job? How about the benefits? Are you done with those too?" I had tried to stay quiet but I wasn't going to let him throw his dream and his career away.

"I can get those anywhere and I won't have to live in this shithole of a state. We can go anywhere." 422

"We can't just go anywhere. We need to find a place to live, a job"–

"Well we both know it will all be my responsibility since you couldn't even hold a job for a month!" He snapped.

"Are you kidding me? That job almost cost us our son!!"

"Maybe you should have done a better job vetting the daycare you chose."

"You cannot be serious Claude! She was state certified and she was in our price range. She had excellent references. If I went with anyone else, we wouldn't have even taken home fifty bucks from me working! You know that! All for someone else to raise our boys? Does that make any kind of sense to you? And how is this my fault? You're the one who is gaining weight and not even trying to lose it! You threw out a perfectly good dinner!"

He was on his feet so fast, it took a minute for me to realize he was up and headed for the kitchen. When he came back he had the trash can with him.

"You want this perfectly good dinner." He started throwing the salad and chicken pieces at me, in handfuls.. "Here! You fucking have it! I am so sick of you and your shit food!" The food kept flying.

"Stop!!! Stop doing this Claude! For God's sake!" I was pleading, but inside I knew there was no coming back from this. He had crossed too many lines and I needed to put an end to all of it. Resigned, I looked at him sadly. "I'm done. I can't do this with you anymore!" I had finally reached my limit.

"Good! I'm glad! Leave!" He yelled.

"I am! You need to grow the fuck up!!" I yelled back. Just as quick as the words were out of my mouth, I regretted them because he was in my face. He grabbed my cheeks as hard as he could and looked me in the eyes, with more hatred than I had ever seen from him. Then just as quickly he pushed my face away. Too late, the damage was done. I needed to get away from him. I went to pick up the phone on the kitchen wall. I was going to call my dad, but as soon as it was in my hand, he came up behind me and ripped the whole thing off the wall.

I looked at him, stunned. Where had the guy who loved me and took me in when my mom kicked me out gone? This guy was nothing like him. Or maybe he had just never known stress back then and now that he did, he had no clue how to handle it. The Air Force had changed him and it had not been for the better. At least not in the ways he handled following their rules. It dawned on me that growing up, Eddie and Edna set very few rules, so maybe the whole thing had just been too life altering. He was so used to doing what he wanted, when he wanted and now he was expected to do what they asked of him.

I needed to call my dad, or my sister because my mind was set. I was leaving. There was no doubt anymore. He had put his hands on me again, and I had made them a promise. It stopped right here. But as I looked towards the bedroom where the other phone was, he was one step ahead of me. He bolted for our room and ripped that phone out of the wall too. Now I was scared. I needed to get out but the boys were down the hall, in the complete opposite direction of the front door.

"Claude, what are you doing?"

"You will leave when I say you can leave!" He yelled. "Who are you going to call anyway? Who would want you? Look at you!"

"Stop yelling." I tried being calm again. At this point I had no idea what he would do next. I tried reasoning with him. "You are going to have the Security Police here if you keep this up!" And as much as I wanted to be away from him, I really didn't want to see him get in more trouble. But he was too far gone to care.

"Let them come!" He screamed. "All of this is because our fucking nosey neighbors couldn't mind their own business in the first place!" He yelled that extra loud so they were sure to hear him. I couldn't believe how he was blaming everyone else for his mistakes and bad behavior.

In the end, he got exactly what he wanted. The Security Police showed up and when they saw the phones ripped off the walls, that was enough for them to take him in. He was arrested first and then admitted into a psychiatric hospital for an evaluation. All of it ended with a Dishonorable Discharge that could be changed to a General Discharge, if he managed to stay out of trouble for five years. Sadly, it was exactly what needed to happen. He would get the help he needed, and I filed for divorce. We might have been good friends, but we were not right for each other. Still, I wouldn't change any of what happened, because the marriage gave us both two beautiful boys and they alone were worth it all.

I too got the help I needed. The Air Force helped me get in touch with my family and we made arrangements for the boys and I to move back to New Hampshire. They helped me hire movers, and they moved all of us. Once Claude was discharged, he decided to go to New Hampshire too, so he could be near the boys.

I tried to be his friend so we could co-parent together, but he continued to blame everyone but himself for how things ended. I didn't let it hurt me and I didn't let it hold me back either. I moved in with my Dad, and he became my built-in babysitter for the boys. Now, I could go to work and know they would be safe. I drove a school bus during the day. The boys went with me on the bus so it became the perfect mothers job. And then I got a job as a waitress two nights a week. I even enrolled myself in community college. Maybe I would get that law degree after all.

It had taken me some time but I was going to be okay. And I didn't need a man to do it. I just needed to believe in myself. I needed to love myself. Somehow I lost all of that after we moved to Florida but I was finally finding it again. I was growing up and even if I had been a far too sexual, semi-feral, way too independent, self reliant Gen Xer, I had turned out alright. I was a twenty year old who had already lived so much adult life and still had my whole life in front of me. Since I was twelve, I had been put in a wide array of adult situations. Some of it was my fault and some of it wasn't. Blame didn't really matter. What mattered was that I experienced it and lived to tell about it, just like so many others, who grew up Gen X. Most of us grew up way too fast and way too free. But we would all be okay in the end. Because we may have grown up at the speed of light, but we had the best music, the best hair, and there is no question, we are the best generation there ever was! At least that's how I see it.

Made in United States
Orlando, FL
17 March 2025

59540830R00249